More Critical Praise for Nina Revoyr

for *Southland*

- A *Los Angeles Times* Best Seller
- Selected for the *Los Angeles Times'* Best Books of 2003 list
- Winner: Lambda Literary Award
- Winner: Ferro-Grumley Literary Award
- Winner: American Library Association's Stonewall Honor Award
- Finalist: Edgar Award
- A Book Sense 76 Pick
- Selected for the InsightOut Book Club

"The plot line of *Southland* is the stuff of a James Ellroy or a Walter Mosley novel . . . But the climax fairly glows with the good-heartedness that Revoyr displays from the very first page."   —*Los Angeles Times*

"Compelling . . . never lacking in vivid detail and authentic atmosphere, the novel cements Revoyr's reputation as one of the freshest young chroniclers of life in L.A."   —*Publishers Weekly*

"If Oprah still had her book club, this novel likely would be at the top of her list . . . With prose that is beautiful, precise, but never pretentious . . ."
—*Booklist* (starred review)

"[A]n ambitious and absorbing book that works on many levels: as a social and political history of Los Angeles, as the story of a young woman discovering and coming to terms with her cultural heritage, as a multigenerational and multiracial family saga, and as a solid detective story."   —*Denver Post*

"Nina Revoyr gives us her Los Angeles, a loved version of that often fabled landscape. Her people are as reticent and careful as any under siege, but she sifts their stories out of the dust of neighborhoods, police reports, and family legend. The stories—black, white, Asian, and multiracial—intertwine in unexpected and deeply satisfying ways. Read this book and tell me you don't want to read more. I know I do."
—Dorothy Allison, author of *Bastard Out of Carolina*

"Subtle, effective . . . [with] a satisfyingly unpredictable climax."
—*Washington Post*

"Fascinating and heartbreaking . . . an essential part of L.A. history."
—*LA Weekly*

"An engaging, thoughtful book that even East Coasters can enjoy."
—*New York Press*

"A remarkable feat . . . Revoyr's novel is honest in detailing Southern California's brutal history, and honorable in showing how families survived with love and tenacity and dignity."
—Susan Straight, author of *A Million Nightingales*

"Dead-on descriptions of California both gritty and golden."
—*East Bay Express*

"*Southland* gripped my attention and would not let go until I turned the last page."
—*International Examiner*

"*Southland* is a simmering stew of individual dreams, family struggles, cultural relations, social changes, and race relations. It is a compelling, challenging, and rewarding novel."
—*Chicago Free Press*

for *The Age of Dreaming*

• Finalist: *Los Angeles Times* Book Prize
* Top Five Books of 2008: *The Advocate*

"Rare indeed is a novel this deeply pleasurable and significant."
—*Booklist* (starred review)

"[Revoyr] is fast becoming one of the city's finest chroniclers and mythmakers."
—*Los Angeles Magazine*

"Reminiscent of Paul Auster's *The Book of Illusions* in its concoction of spurious Hollywood history and its star's filmography . . . Ingenious . . . hums with the excitement of Hollywood's pioneer era."
—*San Francisco Chronicle*

"Fast-moving, riveting, unpredictable, and profound; highly recommended."
—*Library Journal*

"Revoyr beautifully invokes Jun's self-deceptions and his growing self-awareness. It's an enormously satisfying novel."

—*Publishers Weekly*

"Revoyr conveys in a lucid, precise and period appropriate prose . . . a pulse-quickening, deliciously ironic serving of Hollywood noir."

—*Kirkus Reviews*

"[Nina Revoyr is] an empathetic chronicler of the dispossessed outsider in L.A."

—*Los Angeles Times*

"Quietly powerful . . . settles to a close as deftly and beautifully as a crane landing on quiet water."

—*LA Weekly*

"Revoyr resurrects the *old* old Hollywood, from the time before talkies, and dreams it into existence once again."

—*Bookforum*

"Five stars."

—*Time Out Chicago*

for *The Necessary Hunger*

"*The Necessary Hunger* is the kind of irresistible read you start on the subway at 6 p.m. on the way home from work and keep plowing through until you've turned the last page . . . It beats with the pulse of life . . ."

—*Time*

"Quietly intimate, vigorously honest, and uniquely American . . . Tough and tender without a single false note."

—*Kirkus Reviews*

"Revoyr triumphs in blending many complex issues, including urban poverty and violence, adolescent sexuality, and the vitality of basketball, without losing sight of her characters. She creates a family, in all senses of the word, of characters who are complex, admirable, and aggravating; readers will root for them on and off the court."

—*Detroit Free Press*

"Revoyr focuses on a number of issues, including competition, interracial relationships, and same-sex relationships . . . A thoughtful work . . ."

—*Library Journal*

"A wholesome coming-of-age novel about two high school basketball stars, Revoyr's debut is a meditation on consuming passion and a reflection on lost opportunities . . . The basketball action, which builds climactically, honors the split-second timing and excitement of the game. Revoyr also evokes the feel of contemporary L.A., capturing crackheads, gang-bangers, and car-jackings in sharp, street-smart dialogue."

—*Publishers Weekly*

"Revoyr has unerringly caught the angst of teenagers, as well as the rarified, self-involved world in which they live . . . A sympathetic, tender rendering of the frustration of unrequited love."

—*Cleveland Plain Dealer*

"This book may in fact contain the most loving prose we'll see on basketball until John Edgar Wideman writes about his daughter Jamila, the gifted point guard for Stanford." —*Chicago Tribune*

WINGSHOOTERS

WINGSHOOTERS

BY NINA REVOYR

Published by Akashic Books
©2011 by Nina Revoyr

Hardcover ISBN-13: 978-1-936070-86-2
Hardcover Library of Congress Control Number: 2010928792

Paperback ISBN-13: 978-1-936070-71-8
Paperback Library of Congress Control Number: 2010922723

First printing

Akashic Books
PO Box 1456
New York, NY 10009
info@akashicbooks.com
www.akashicbooks.com

For Johnny Temple and Johanna Ingalls

How we fall into grace. You can't work or earn your way into it.
You just fall. It lies below, it lies beyond. It comes to you, unbidden.
—Rick Bass, *Colter*

I would burn soles of my feet
Burn the palms of both my hands
If I could learn and be complete
If I could walk righteously again
—Lucinda Williams, "Get Right with God"

ONE

In my apartment in California there hangs a picture of my grandfather. He is one of twelve men dressed in off-white baseball uniforms and plain dark caps, all seated in front of a boy in a baggy black suit. The men sit cross-legged or rest on one knee; their bats lean together like logs on a camp fire, surrounded by their gloves. Behind them stand two large, boxy cars with a banner draped between them that reads, *Buick Ball Club, Deerhorn Wisconsin*. Although the picture is posed, there is something about the quality of the players' postures and smiles that makes it seem like they just collapsed there, giddy and tired, and someone happened to capture the moment. The uniforms have a softer look than what ballplayers wear today—the caps are rounder and more pliable, the pants and jerseys looser, the gloves amorphous and lumpy—but the men look more like men. My grandfather, sitting in the lower right-hand corner, smiles at the camera from out of his open, handsome face as if he knows he'll live forever. The license plate on one of the Buicks has tags from 1925, and if the date is accurate, then my grandfather, Charlie LeBeau, is nineteen. Because of the cap, the usual shock of slicked-back hair that falls over his eyes, making him look playful and roguish, is held still. But even so, he is beautiful, and knows it. Farther back in the picture, a young woman leans out the window of another car, resting her chin in her hand, and I imagine she is staring at Charlie. Everyone, for all of his life, always stared at Charlie.

My grandfather grew up in the country five miles outside of Deerhorn, and played ball in the evenings after long days out in the fields. His family grew corn and potatoes and barley, and raised cattle and pigs, until the Depression made it impossible to keep the farm running and they sold it and made the move into town. By that time, he was married to my grandmother, Helen Wilkes, whom he'd met at the one-room school just east of town. Charlie was never a student—he was two years behind his class when Helen sat down in front of him, and Helen a year ahead of hers, their respective talents and deficiencies erasing the gap of three years that divided them. He kept pulling on her pigtails as she tried to listen to the teacher, and she finally married him, she said, to make him stop. They married—eloped—when Charlie was twenty and Helen seventeen, so he already knew her when the picture of the baseball team was taken. It could be that the relaxed, self-satisfied grin on his face has something to do with her. It could also be that the girl in the car—whoever she is—knows this, and that's why she looks so sad.

My grandfather never fought in a war. He was too young for the first great conflict in Europe, which took his father's brother, and too old for World War II. And he never held a position—say, sheriff or lawyer—that placed him above other men. No, Charlie LeBeau worked the same unforgiving, muscular jobs—at the meat processing plant, the car parts shop, the Stevenson shoe factory—that the other men did, but he always seemed larger than them, heroic. He was the best ballplayer in the region, a third baseman pursued by the White Sox, as his father had been twenty years before. But also like his father, he turned down the chance to enter the White Sox's minor league system because he wouldn't leave Central Wisconsin—and because he refused to play for the team that had recently thrown the World Series. He won the state skeet-shooting championship a half dozen times; I still have a letter, dated 1935, from the Thomason Gunworks Company, congratulating him on his perfect score in that year's contest and offering him a lifetime supply of free ammunition. He was simply, consistently the best shot in the state of Wisconsin, as he proved every fall by bagging more ducks, grouse, pheasants, and deer than his family could ever possibly eat. The gun case in my grandparents' dining room was his centerpiece, his shrine, filled with weapons of every size and capacity—some functional, some collectors' pieces purely for display, like the Springfield Rifle his uncle had used in the Great War. He also had three bows, regal, primal-looking things, and another case for his collection of fishing rods. Sometimes I would take out one of these rifles or bows just to hold it and feel the power it contained.

But it wasn't his skill with weapons that set Charlie apart. It was the way that other people related to him. Men gathered around him at Jimmy's Coffee Shop or Earl's Gun Store or in his own house to hear him expound on everything from the proper training of hunting dogs to the town's new traffic light; women lowered their eyes and blushed when he was near. And he paid back and increased this devotion in a thousand small ways—by changing tires or plowing sidewalks for the widows in town; by welcoming unattached men into his house for Friday suppers; by taking young boys to the baseball fields to work on their games, or out into the deepest woods, to hunt.

My grandfather was a man, in a vital, fundamental way that grown men simply aren't today, at least not in the city. And maybe that was why he was so disappointed in my father. Stewart LeBeau was as different from Charlie as a boy could possibly be—studious, dreamy, and unathletic. He hated hunting, and didn't care much for fishing or dogs, and while it wouldn't be exactly true to say he disliked sports, playing catch did not enliven him as it did the other boys in town. Stewart read, and spent his time with a few other serious, awkward boys, and behaved well enough in school to generally avoid having his knuckles rapped by the nuns with their ever-ready rulers. He was closer to his mother, my grandmother, who was glad to have produced a child she could relate to (they talked of books together, and he helped her with shopping and chores). Stewart, like his father, was born between wars—he was too young for World War II and Korea, and past the age for Vietnam—yet, unlike his father, he had no desire or ability to make up for what Charlie considered unfortunate timing, striking the second generation in a row. But while he was never *of* the town—not in the blood-deep way my grandparents were—he never did anything to openly defy it until his final, huge act of rebellion, which was leaving. He had applied to the University of Wisconsin without telling anyone (the nuns, who believed that the world outside of Deerhorn was sinful and corrupting, would not have approved), and he was the only boy in town who went to college. In Madison—much to his parents' distress—he acquired new clothes, new concerns, and a strange new set of friends. My grandparents' dismay must have multiplied by a thousand when he decided to marry my mother.

If leaving Deerhorn was so distasteful that both my grandfather and great-grandfather passed up a chance to play in the majors; if the town was so insular that my father's departure was seen as defection; if it had never, in all the years of its existence, been home to a soul who wasn't German, Polish, Norwegian, or French Canadian, imagine the shock of having to contemplate a daughter-in-law from Japan. And my mother, Reiko Tanizaki, was not Japanese-American—she didn't eat hamburgers or say the Pledge of Allegiance or speak English much at all—but real, born-and-raised-there Japanese. My father had met her in Madison, where she was an exchange student at the university. Maybe despite their language and cultural differences, they had something in common because they'd both made their way out of small country towns to try their luck in the larger world. But more likely, her sheer difference from everything Stewart had known was exactly what drew him to her. For their enclosed and turbulent marriage became the central drama of my father's life. It was the one realm where he could be extreme and heroic and foolish, just like his father always wanted him to be.

Although my grandmother cried and pleaded with him, my father was set on marrying Reiko, so Helen, tight-lipped, took a Greyhound bus down to Madison for the wedding. My grandfather did not attend, and you could say—as my grandmother often did—that the trip itself, not the color of Stewart's bride, kept Charlie at home, but my father rightly took his absence as disapproval. There was no way Charlie LeBeau would ever accept a foreigner into his family, and although he did finally meet my mother when my parents visited Deerhorn, he didn't smile for her or turn on his charm; she never saw who he was. My parents never stayed in one place long enough to get comfortable, anyway. Theirs was a traveling road show of a marriage, starting out in Madison, and making stops over the next ten years in Milwaukee, St. Paul, Fresno, Sacramento, Seattle, and finally Japan. I was only present for the last part of this journey—I was born in Tokyo in '65—and something about my appearance must have tipped their already precarious union completely over the edge, because by the time I was two, my mother started leaving us for days and even weeks at a time. I remember her absence more clearly than what it was like to have her with us, and I remember my father spilling whiskey and holding his head in his hands, pleading with her parents in his broken Japanese to please tell him where their daughter had gone.

I lived in Japan until I was eight. And when I think back to that time, I always see myself—although of course it isn't true—as having lived alone. My parents were always busy—my father worked for an English-language radio station (I was conceived, he once told me, while he was doing broadcasts at the '64 Olympics), and then for an English-language newspaper, which was staffed by hard-drinking expatriate Americans who behaved as if it were still the Occupation. My mother

worked too, as a translator for a tourist agency, and occasionally teaching Japanese to American businessmen,
both jobs that she considered beneath her. And when
my parents weren't working or going to parties, they
were wholly engaged in each other. In some of my earli-
est memories I am lying in bed, listening to my parents
argue—my father's voice low and guttural, my mother's
high, cobbling together short fragments of English into
an angry, disjointed string of accusations. They always
fought in his language. I could see their shadows move
across my ceiling when she stormed out of their room, his
shadow grabbing hers by the arm, hers turning and striking closed-fisted against his chest and shoulders. When
my mother finally left for good just after my sixth birth-
day, I almost missed their fights, which had been the
only sounds of life in that rented house. I didn't miss my
mother, or at least it seems that way now; I suppose my
mind has closed up whatever wound her departure may
have caused. It was her parents I missed, my grandparents in Osaka, my gruff grandfather whose eyes softened
when he read me a story, my laughing grandmother who
spoiled me with red bean ice cream and laid soft, caring
hands on my shoulder. But my father felt as uneasy with
them as my mother must have felt with his parents. The
circle of language and food and laughter that enclosed
my grandparents, my mother, and me could never really
include him. Even as a child, I understood that they em-
braced me in a way they couldn't embrace my father. But
once my mother left and they wouldn't tell him where
she had gone, he refused to let them visit or talk to me. I
understand now this must have broken their hearts, for
after my mother left I never saw them again.

It would have been easier for me if they had stayed in my life—they or my mother, but at least someone Japanese. It might have helped me navigate my time in Japan, or at least provided me with some kind of comfort. While my everyday life as a young child wasn't really so hard (as long as I was with my mother, people treated me like a regular kid; they might not have known I was half-white, or it didn't matter), everything got more difficult when I started going to school, especially after my mother was gone. Out of some kind of compromise, or as a nod to my mixed heritage, I attended both a Japanese school and a school for foreign children. I don't know, now, how this arrangement was possible, and there's no one around to ask. But I remember walking with my father to the English-language school, where the children of foreign businessmen, reporters, and graduate students (though not of diplomats; their children went somewhere else) spent their days in large plain classrooms with pictures of Mount Rushmore and the Eiffel Tower on the walls. At lunchtime, a teacher's aide would walk me to the Japanese school, where the children were quieter and wore uniforms and the learning was serious.

Both of these places were uncomfortable to me. I was the only Japanese child at the English-language school, and while my teacher, Mrs. Jemerson, tried to make me feel comfortable, it was clear that the white children didn't welcome my presence; they were enrolled there, after all, to escape me. (A year after I left Japan this school was destroyed by an earthquake, and on the front page of the Deerhorn newspaper there was a picture of Mrs. Jemerson being pulled by rescue workers from the rubble.) And the Japanese school was no better. My Japanese was fluent—better than my English—and I'd been born right there in Tokyo, but everybody knew what my father was, and they never let me forget it. Two years after my mother left for good, I told my father that I wanted to go to America, which we had visited once when I was four. If both the Japanese and the Americans disliked me in Japan, I reasoned, then in America all sides would embrace me. America was where my one remaining parent was from; America was the land of the free. And my father agreed for his own reasons, which I wasn't aware of yet—he'd heard that my mother had returned to the States, to live with a man they both knew in Sacramento. In late summer of 1973 we packed our few belongings and made the trip to Wisconsin, where my father left me with his parents while he went out to California to try and bring my mother back.

So I stayed with my American grandparents, whom I had met only once before, in the town they'd both lived in or near for all of their lives. And I doubt that Deerhorn was much different then, in the early 1970s, than it had been in the '40s and '50s when my father was growing up, or in the '20s, when his parents came of age. While people in other parts of the country were growing their hair long and smoking pot and wearing polka dot ties and bell-bottoms, the people of Deerhorn dressed in overalls and drank cheap Wisconsin beer. And while there were stories on the nightly news about antiwar protests, women's rights, the school busing crisis in Boston, and Watergate, these events seemed so distant and strange that they might have been taking place in a different country. Deerhorn remained stubbornly itself through all the changes around it—a small, isolated town surrounded by farmland and forest, laced through with clear, fast rivers and still blue lakes. The biggest employers in town were the meat-processing plant, the cheese manufacturers, the dairy, the shoe factory, and a factory that made clothing for hunters. My father's high school classmates all worked those jobs. By the time they were twenty, most of them had families.

It was, to say the least, a world entirely different from Tokyo. And I was just as alien to the people of Deerhorn as they were to me. They'd been scandalized by my father's marriage—for many of them, my mother was the first non-Caucasian person they'd ever laid eyes on—and now, in their minds, by bringing me back, he was inflicting on them the terrible fruit of his sins. But since they couldn't punish him directly for his unacceptable behavior and wouldn't dare to punish Charlie, they focused their displeasure on me. People glared and sometimes swore at me when I passed them on the sidewalk. No one welcomed me at school or at church. Older boys used me for target practice when I rode around town on my bike, most often throwing apples, but sometimes rocks. And when the occasional child did venture to talk to me—out of sympathy or boredom or just plain curiosity—his parents would soon put a stop to it. Because of the war, I'd hear them say, and I wouldn't understand until much later what they meant. Many of the older men in town had fought in World War II, and to them I wasn't just a foreigner; I was the Enemy.

And how did my grandparents react to all of this? In retrospect, my arrival must have been just as big a shock to them as it was to the rest of the town. Not only did they suddenly have a child in their house; that child looked different from them, and came from a different world. Although my stay with them was supposed to be brief, the original two weeks extended into a month, and then another, and then over a year, as my father kept trying to track down my mother. They welcomed me without question—I was, after all, their grandchild— showing a warmth they'd never extended to their son's wife. But they were ill-prepared to deal with the town's response. My grandmother, as much as she cooked for me, cared for me, patiently helped me with my English, never directly addressed what was happening. She gave me vague advice about strength in the face of adversity, and said that none of our trials compared to what Jesus had suffered. But my grandfather wasn't so passive. Although I didn't tell him any of what happened in town or at school—I knew instinctively that he wouldn't approve of complaining—the physical proof was undeniable. When a dark blue bruise would appear on my arm, left there by a rock, it was my grandfather who'd touch it tenderly and shake his head. When my knees got scraped up from being knocked off my bike, it was he who knelt down and sprayed them with Bactine. When a group of teenage boys chased me home one day, my grandfather went out to the front yard in his work pants and undershirt and challenged them all to a fight.

Let me make this very clear—my grandfather was a bigot. He wasn't shy about using racial epithets, or blaming blacks or Jews or Democrats for all the country's problems. But it enraged him that the town did not embrace me. After I had lived there for almost a year, it was obvious that quiet endurance was getting me nowhere.

One day, while I was waiting to see a doctor at the clinic because a rock had opened a cut at my temple, I looked up at Charlie and saw that his face was red with anger. He told me then, voice shaking and low, not to run away anymore. The other kids would never leave me alone, he said, until I stood up to them. After he took me home, he gave me a crash course in how to defend myself. He taught me how to punch, how to block incoming blows, how to throw rocks back with accuracy and strength. These lessons made my life there easier, and the irony strikes me only now: it was my grandfather, the rural, prejudiced white man, the father who refused to embrace his son's wife, who taught me how to survive as a child of color in America.

My presence was only one of the things that upset the people in town that year. There also was one other. Through the late '60s and early '70s, the local clinic had been expanding, and what was once a modest building had grown and transformed into a ten-story, full-fledged medical facility that took up three entire blocks on the outskirts of town. Even in my short time there I had noticed the change. The clinic was right across the street from the Deerhorn cemetery—a fact that had spawned many jokes about the medical staff's incompetence—and we'd passed by it during the one time my parents had brought me to Deerhorn, when we'd gone out to visit family graves. Then, it had been a small operation with a few local doctors who served only the town and the area immediately around it. But over the years, because of its central location, it was becoming the primary teaching clinic for that part of the state, and patients and nursing students began to come in from all of the surrounding areas. Even though the expanded clinic meant more jobs for Deerhorn residents, no one—at least among my grandparents' friends—really approved of its presence. A big clinic meant outsiders coming through in order to get medical care. It also meant newcomers—clinic staff, technicians, tie-wearing administrators—who didn't fit with the town's blue-collar sensibilities. And it was the clinic that was responsible for what happened to the town and my family, that fall and winter of 1974. Had I been the only change the town had to adjust to, it would only have been me who paid the price. But there was also the clinic. Or maybe it was bigger than that—maybe it was the town, or the state, or the whole changing, unpredictable country. Maybe it was something diseased or off-kilter in human nature itself.

It began on a Friday evening in early September. My grandmother was making supper—steaks, mashed potatoes, and spinach from the garden—while my grandfather sat in the living room with his friend Jim Riesling, watching the Brewers game on TV. I say "sat" but he actually lay, on the couch that was his alone, which had one of my grandmother's crocheted blankets draped across the back. My grandfather had spent much of the afternoon working in the garden—he'd picked the spinach and potatoes my grandmother was cooking—and he still wore his olive work pants and loose white undershirt. I'd helped him—I'd taken in small baskets of the harvested vegetables, and in between, while he knelt and pulled and shook dirt from the plants, I'd caught the butterflies that left jagged holes in the cabbage. Now, he was tired—he was sixty-eight then—but not too tired to entertain his company.

Jim Riesling was a bachelor nearing forty. Charlie had been his boss at the shoe factory until he'd retired three years before, and Jim, who wasn't the sort who liked to frequent the bars in town, needed a place to go on Friday evenings. Among my grandfather's friends, I'd always liked Jim the best. He was a quiet, balding man, and the gentleness that made him so awkward with women was also part of what made him so easy to be around. He sat in the big armchair facing the screen; I was sitting on the floor with my back to the couch.

Pressed against me, with his head on my lap, was my grandfather's dog, an English springer spaniel named Brett. He was nine then, but in his younger years he had won every major field trial in Central Wisconsin, and could probably have done even better, Jim said, had my grandfather been willing to travel farther than fifty miles from Deerhorn. By the time I came to live with my grandparents Brett was retired from competition; he spent his days lounging around the house and patrolling the yard, saving up his energy for those few weeks in the fall when my grandfather took him hunting.

When I arrived, Brett took to me right away—not because I had any special manner with dogs, but because I gave him attention. My grandfather was an old-fashioned owner of hunting dogs who believed that they were useful tools to flush and retrieve game, but otherwise belonged in the yard. I needed a companion, though, and couldn't have asked for a better one than Brett. The day I first came to the house he sniffed me up and down, cropped tail wiggling madly. When I sat down to pet him, he gave me his paw and gazed up at me with those sad springer eyes, thus staking his permanent claim.

The two men were drinking Pabst Blue Ribbon from cans, and Charlie let me sneak sips of his when my grandmother wasn't looking. Just as she called for me to come set the table, there was a loud banging on the screen door in the kitchen. That was the back door, so we knew it was a friend; official business always came to the front. Brett sprang instantly to life and ran barking into the kitchen. I could hear my grandmother talking to someone through the screen, then: "Charlie, can you come here for a minute? Earl's here to see you."

My grandfather stood up grumbling and made his way to the kitchen. I followed. Through the screen door I saw three men, not one. "Boys," said my grandfather after quieting the dog, "what's so important that you want to keep me from my supper?"

The man in front, Earl Watson, stood with his feet firmly planted and his hands poised by his hips, as if ready to pull a weapon. He looked at my grandfather so intensely I thought his eyes might bore a hole through the screen. "We need to talk to you, Charlie. It can't wait."

My grandfather stood looking at him for a moment. "Well, all right," he said.

He moved toward the door but Earl said, "Best that we talk inside," so my grandfather pulled it open and let them in.

As the men passed by, I held the dog by his collar and tried to move out of the way. I didn't much like Earl Watson. He was a strong, ageless man who could have been anywhere from forty to sixty years old, and he owned the gun shop on the main strip of town. Earl had fought in the war in Korea, and it was rumored he had killed a man with his bare hands. With his barrel-like body, thick biceps, and large, tense hands, he looked like he still could. Right behind him was Ray Davis, captain of the Deerhorn police. He was in his forties, an unlikely police chief—only about 5'6" or so, and soft around the edges, with thick brown hair he wore down to his collar, long for a policeman even in the 1970s. Davis was now one of the most prominent men in town, but years before, when he was a teenager, my grandfather—who had worked for years with his father at the shoe factory—had taught him how to hunt, and Ray still deferred to Charlie on most matters that didn't have to do with the law.

Last was Pete Drexel, my great-uncle, who was married to my grandmother's sister Bertha. Pete was my grandfather's usual hunting and fishing partner, a tall, easy-going man five years Charlie's junior who managed one of the cheese operations in town. Every weekend in the summer, we'd drive out to Pete and Bertha's place in the country, the men cooking ribs or venison over the large open grill while the women cut greens and made their mother's potato salad. Now Pete ruffled my hair as he filed into the dining room, and the four men together made quite a formidable sight—five, once Jim Riesling stood and joined them. My grandfather was five years older than the oldest of his visitors, almost thirty years older than the youngest, and two of them—Jim and Pete—were taller than him. But of all these men, he was still the most impressive.

The newcomers exchanged greetings with Riesling and then sat down at the half-set table. I tried to stay with them, but Charlie shooed me away, so I took Brett into the kitchen and we sat with my grandmother at the table against the far wall. Through the window I could hear the Thomas children next door, playing tag and yelling loudly, "You're it!" My grandmother touched the round glass vase that held a single rose cut from the garden, and looked up at the steaks that were cooling on top of the stove. "They could have waited till after supper," she said. "They know we always eat at five o'clock."

For my grandmother, talking to me was like talking to herself; she never would have spoken up to Charlie. She was a devout, quiet woman, the older, plainer sister of Bertha Wilkes, who'd been crowned the county beauty queen in 1931. According to Aunt Bertha, the whole town had been shocked when Charlie LeBeau, the handsomest boy in school, had picked Helen Wilkes to be his bride. But he ignored them all and insisted, as he still did forty-eight years after they married, that she was the prettiest girl in town. My grandmother had once been healthy and robust, but by the time I lived with her she'd been reduced by worry into a wisp of a woman who looked like she'd blow over at the slightest wind. She'd seemed especially worn and tired in the last few days, since a letter had arrived from my father. It had come from Kansas City, where he'd been staying for the last two weeks. But he was about to move on, he'd said, and he would write again when he got where he was going next.

I wasn't thinking, though, about my grandmother or my father just then; I was more interested in what was happening in the other room. I struggled to hear what the men were saying, but I couldn't make out their words. I did hear the tone of their voices, though—low, serious, and alarmed. For a long time, it was mostly Earl Watson talking, with Ray Davis and Uncle Pete adding a comment here and there. Then there was a long silence, followed by something from Charlie. More discussion, and the voices rose so we could hear a few words. I couldn't stand being left out anymore, so while my grandmother went down to the cellar to get some more beer, I stood up and moved next to the doorway.

"There's no way I'd ever let one of them lay a hand on my boys," said Earl. "Doesn't matter what it says on the license."

"You don't have to worry about it," my grandfather replied. "If you have to go there, make sure the appointment's with somebody else."

"But think about the people who don't get warning," said Uncle Pete. His voice sounded different from the others, more like a young man's; it matched his muscled, slim physique and his full head of hair, which was gray but as thick as a teenager's. "They go in to get a checkup, and pow."

"Well, we just got to make sure that people are prepared," Earl said, his voice low and grim. "If they know what they could be getting into, they'll just have to figure out something else. We spread the word wide enough, and her business'll be so slow she's bound to get the message."

"You haven't heard the worst of it," said Ray Davis, the police chief. "The husband's a substitute teacher."

"What? In Deerhorn?"

"That's what I said. And Janie Hebig's going to be out for a while because of her baby, so it's probably her class. Far as I know, he could be showing up this week."

The exchange reminded me that two of the men had

children or grandchildren who were in school with me. Uncle Pete's were older. Although it was hard to imagine him as anybody's father, he and Bertha had a grown son, Pete Jr., and his granddaughter Becky was in high school. But Ray Davis's oldest boy, Dale, was in the third grade. And Earl Watson had two sons—Jake, who was sixteen and a sophomore in high school, and Kevin, who was in the fourth grade. The seven years between them made people wonder if Kevin had been an accident, and the few times I ever saw Earl with the boys, he behaved as if Jake were his true son and Kevin an afterthought. One night the previous summer, not long after I'd come to town, my grandfather and I went with Earl and his boys to watch the Deerhorn Bombers, the local minor league baseball team. And while Earl patiently explained to his older son what the pitchers were doing, describing fastballs and changeups and screwballs that moved away from the lefties, his younger son kept tugging at the sleeve of his work shirt, insisting that he was thirsty. I don't know if Jake even cared about this lesson; he spent most of his time drinking and smoking with his roughneck friends—but Earl didn't brook the interruption. After one last tug from his younger son, Earl whipped around and yelled in a voice so loud several players looked up from the field, "God*damn* it, Kevin! Can't you see I'm busy here? Go drink from the goddamn fountain!"

Now, Earl made a sound that was almost a hiss and said, "They're coming at us from every direction."

"Well, it sure as hell better not be *my* boy's class . . ." said Ray.

"Damn mayor and his goddamn clinic."

"It's Boston," Ray said. "That judge and his crazy busing plan have given people all kinds of stupid ideas. It's a good thing they're not trying to pull that kind of stunt in Wisconsin."

"Well, if you ask me, they'll never last the week." This was Uncle Pete, and after he spoke there was silence for a moment.

Then Earl spoke again, angry and deliberate. "What makes them think they can move here, just like that? What makes them think that people are going to stand for it?"

"We've got to do something," said Ray. "Charlie, what are we going to do?"

And the men went silent now, awaiting my grandfather's word. It was a measure of the respect that people had for him that Ray Davis, the police chief, was asking him what they should do. I imagined all the men leaning forward in their seats, looking anxiously at Charlie.

"Nothing," he said. "Nothing yet. Pete's probably right. They'll get the message that they're not welcome here, and it will probably take care of itself."

There were grunts, whether of agreement or disapproval I couldn't tell, but it was clear the discussion was over. He had spoken. And soon all the men but Jim stood up and made their goodbyes, Pete kissing my grandmother on the cheek and pinching my ear as he left.

Sitting at the table later, eating the now-dried steak and lukewarm vegetables, I wondered what they'd been discussing. They were upset about someone coming, that much I understood—I pictured an invader of some sort, riding into town on a horse, cutting people down with a sword. And someone connected to this troublesome presence might even be at my school. I wondered if I should be worried, and if someone would tell my father—maybe this news would even hasten my parents' return. I was filled with a vague but chilling fear, and I wondered what could possibly be so dangerous and threatening that it so upset the strongest men in town.

TWO

I found out the next Monday at school. Like every other child in town between the ages of five and ten, I attended Deerhorn Elementary, the old, one-story brick building on the other side of town. It had always been a trial for me to get there. Although I'd figured out the safest routes by now, I sometimes still encountered kids who jumped out from behind trees to scare me or who tried to keep me off their streets. The most persistent of these was a girl named Jeannie Allen. Her house was situated in the cradle of a Y whose right arm led to the school. If she was out in her yard, she'd try to turn me around or chase me down the left side of the Y, adding a half a mile to my trip.

Jeannie wasn't outside her house that morning, but arriving at school was no relief. As I entered the hallway, someone shoved me hard from behind, and I couldn't tell whether this contact was accidental, or a special Monday morning greeting just for me.

"Morning, niphead," a fifth grader offered as he passed, and the girls around him giggled. The week before, a group of fourth graders had pushed me against a wall and made me count to ten in Japanese, but today I made it to my locker without further incident. I saw that there were fresh ink marks on the front of my locker, black scrawlings that were supposed to be kanji. The janitor had painted over them several times before finally giving up, and now things just collected, layer upon layer of jagged black marks, spelling out my difference.

"Your daddy's a Jap-lover!" a girl hissed behind me.

"Yeah," said her friend, "I heard her mama's a geisha whore."

"That *can't* be," said the first girl. "'Cos geishas are pretty. And Michelle's butt-ugly—just look at her."

I didn't reply—I never replied—and fought the urge to turn and face them. After I got my books, I walked quickly to class and kept my eyes trained on the floor.

Although technically, as a nine-year-old, I should have been in fourth grade, the school officials had decided when I arrived the year before that my reading and writing in English were spotty enough to keep me back a grade. It hadn't helped that I'd lived in Deerhorn for more than a month before I'd gone to school; because my grandparents didn't think I was staying, it hadn't occurred to them to enroll me. By the time it was clear I wasn't going anywhere, I'd missed several weeks of the school year already and was way behind my class. So now I was assigned to Miss Anderson's third grade class, a year below the rest of my age group.

Penny Anderson was a tall, dark-haired woman in her late twenties. She was completely unlike the teachers I'd had in Japan—both the stern, daunting teachers in the Japanese school, and the friendly but firm teachers at the English-language school. Miss Anderson always seemed nervous, starting to venture one way in conversation or movement, and then pausing and changing direction. She had a way of half-laughing that made it hard to believe she was really amused; her anger, usually accompanied by an almost comically furrowed brow, was equally unconvincing. Miss Anderson's one distinguishing feature was her beautiful voice. She sang in the church choir, and even when she yelled at you, it sounded like a lullaby. Often, in the mornings, she lingered at her doorway on the chance that the principal, Mr. Baker, would pass by. Everyone knew that Mr. Baker and Miss Anderson were boyfriend and girlfriend, even though he had a wife.

That morning, though, when I entered the classroom, Miss Anderson was sitting at her desk looking troubled. I wondered if Mr. Baker was absent this morning, but as all the children settled into their seats for roll call, the usual morning jokes and light chatter that went on before the bell rang were replaced by a strange and different murmur.

"He's supposed to come tomorrow? But my mom said Mr. Baker wouldn't let him."

"My dad said he'd come over himself, if that's what it took to stop it."

"I've never seen one before, have you? What do they look like?"

"I'm glad *I'm* not in fifth grade," said Brady Grimson, whose parents ran a diner on Route 5.

"Yeah," said Tommy Fry, the pharmacist's son, "and you'll never get there, either."

Finally, the bell rang and Miss Anderson stood up. "All right, children. Settle down. Did you have a good weekend? What did you do?"

Everyone went silent and rapt with attention, and this, more than anything, made me realize that something was wrong.

"Well, what did you all do?" Miss Anderson asked again. "Did anyone go on a car trip?"

Slowly, tentatively, Missy Calloway raised her hand. She was the smartest girl in class, a no-nonsense, stocky, bespectacled child whose farm parents treated her with bewildered respect, as if she were a visiting alien. Missy didn't waste her time on the childish topics that occupied most of our classmates, and I always listened to what she had to say. "Miss Anderson," she said, after the teacher acknowledged her, "is it true we have a Negro teacher coming?"

Miss Anderson started to draw herself up straight, and then fell back into a tired slouch.

"Yes, Missy, it's true," she answered, and the room exploded into chaos, thirty voices speaking all at once. Miss Anderson put her hands up to call for silence and the noise subsided a little. "The teacher's name is Mr. Garrett, and he's going to be substituting in Mrs. Hebig's class until after she has her baby."

Now everyone was silent. Finally, Brady Grimson spoke without raising his hand. "But . . . why is he coming?"

"I just told you. Mrs. Hebig is out because she's having a baby, and—"

"No, I mean, why is he coming to Deerhorn?"

Everyone looked at Miss Anderson, waiting, more interested and attentive than they ever were when she was talking about biology or math.

"I'm not sure, Brady. But I hear that his wife is a nurse over at the clinic."

The room was quiet while we digested this information. The one other time the classroom felt this way— tense, strange, uncertain, unbelieving—was when we heard that Mr. Greene, our P.E. teacher, had been para-lyzed in a boating accident.

Miss Anderson tried to teach that morning, covering a lesson on plants and oxygen, but no one was paying attention. My classmates whispered to each other when her back was turned, and for once she didn't really seem to care. Finally, at ten-thirty, she let us out for recess, and while the other kids all shifted easily into their out-of-class selves—chasing each other and yelling, jumping on the monkey bars and swing sets—I was still thinking about what Miss Anderson had told us.

A Negro teacher was coming to teach at our school, and his wife was a nurse at the clinic. A black couple had moved to Deerhorn, a town that, before my own ar-rival the year before, had never been home to a soul who wasn't white. In that town, in 1974, this was as dramatic and inconceivable as deer starting to speak or a flock of ducks flying backwards. To my grandparents and their friends, black people lived elsewhere, in big-city slums or remote country settings, deep in the backwater South. Blacks, they believed, were lazy and ignorant, and if any one Negro had not run afoul of the law, it would only be a matter of time before he succumbed to his basic nature and robbed a house or assaulted a woman. To them, the voting and housing laws of the 1960s and '70s must have seemed like capitulations, the equivalent of handouts from a weak-willed government and directly counter to the natural order of things. Blacks could be useful, yes, in *other* parts of the country, to work as field hands or nannies or cooks. But they were certainly not meant to be employed there in Deerhorn. They were not meant to live among whites.

This unthinking racism was so accepted and prevalent that people didn't even bother to disguise it. One of the reasons why people were discouraged from visiting places like Chicago and New York was that those places were known to be "dark." If a teenager stole a car or committed a petty crime, he was said to be acting "colored." The only black men who were respected were athletes—Dave May of the Brewers, MacArthur Lane of the Packers. But even they were only acceptable in their prescribed public roles—as sports heroes removed from everyday life. And there were limits to the admiration. Many people, including Charlie, had been unhappy that spring when Hank Aaron had broken Babe Ruth's home run record.

That morning, several teachers gathered near the steps that led down to the playground. Miss Anderson was there, and Mr. Sealer, who taught fourth grade. Mrs. Hood, the first grade teacher, stood next to him, and one step above her was the kindergarten teacher, Miss Gandt. Because I usually stayed on a bench near the steps and didn't wander out to the playground, I could hear their conversation, although they made no real effort to keep their voices down.

". . . can't believe it," Mrs. Hood, the first grade teacher, was saying. She was a small woman in her forties who wore her blond hair in a bun and had a voice so high you thought she was pretending. "I know they've been telling us, but I never thought they'd actually go through with it."

"I'll tell you, if Janie had known that *this* would happen," said Miss Gandt, the teacher from kindergarten, who was dark-haired and gruff, "she never would have taken the time off. She would have stayed in her class till the second she went into labor."

"Fred says she's all in knots about it," said Mr. Sealer, the fourth grade teacher. He was in his fifties, with a paunch and very red cheeks, and he was known to keep a flask of whiskey in his desk. "This country's going to hell and it's happening fast. I *told* you that mess in Boston was going to affect us. It's crazy—white children being bused into the ghetto, and those ghetto children let loose in white schools. The way things are going these days, with busing and all, it's no surprise they're letting niggers teach our children."

Mrs. Hood nodded and leaned forward so that Mr. Sealer could light her cigarette. "Not to mention his wife's going to be working at the clinic."

"But at least we can avoid the clinic," Miss Anderson said, sounding almost mournful. "With school, the parents don't have a choice. What are we going to do about these poor children?"

"Well, couldn't *you* do something, Penny?" Miss Gandt asked intently. "I mean, couldn't you talk to Steven?"

There was a silence. Although Miss Anderson's romance with Mr. Baker was general knowledge, it was rare that anyone referred to it so openly.

"He can't do anything, really," Miss Anderson said after a pause. "He's been talking and talking about how we need a long-term sub, and then this teacher comes along out of the blue. He's qualified—*over*-qualified even—he has a master's degree besides his credential. There's no way Steven could deny him without it looking like discrimination. I mean, if worse came to worst, there could even be a lawsuit."

Mr. Sealer scoffed. "That degree's probably not worth the paper it's printed on, anyway. The female's either. The schools are just *giving* diplomas away now, whether or not those people deserve it. I mean, who would ever trust a black nurse?"

"Exactly," said Mrs. Hood, her voice more squeaky than usual. "And anyhow, it's not discrimination to want to protect our way of life. We should be able to have some say about who our children are exposed to. Besides—what if more of them come? What if they have children? Before you know it, it could get as bad here as Milwaukee or Chicago."

"You're right, Gracie," Miss Anderson said. "It's about our way of life. We're just thinking about what's best for our children."

I walked home from school that day without anyone bothering me, maybe because they were so distracted by the news of the teacher. As always, I felt a sense of ease and relief when I turned the corner and saw my grandparents' house. Like all the other houses on Dryden Road, their place had two stories, with a basement and an attic and a long yard stretched out behind it. There was a covered porch in front with a dozen shaded windows, a row of sleepy eyelids half-covering rectangular glass eyes. Between the garage and the back door stretched a small covered walkway, and that's where I headed now. After I ran up the back stairs and into the kitchen, letting the screen door slam shut behind me, I gave Brett a quick rub on the head and went straight to my grandmother's side.

"Grandma, Miss Anderson told us a Negro teacher is coming."

She was cutting the ends off the string beans that Charlie had picked from the garden, and listening to Paul Harvey on the radio. Every day she spent hours on some such task—cutting, picking, canning, cooking—almost never leaving the house except for errands. She was an introverted woman, married to an outgoing and popular man—in pictures I have of my grandparents from the early years of their marriage, he is handsome and loose-limbed; she is tense and too severe to be pretty. They were an odd match in ways beyond their disparity in looks, and now I wonder if this fundamental difference in temperament—his ease with the world, and her discomfort with it—ever caused a rift in their marriage. Now she stopped cutting, knife edge flush against the wooden board. "That's right, Michelle," she said. "A Negro teacher."

"And his wife is going to work at the clinic?"

"I think she's already there."

She returned to her task, taking single green beans out of a white plastic bowl, snipping off one end, flipping them, then cutting the other. I stared at this procedure as if I had never seen it before. And although I knew what the answer would be, I asked, "Why is everyone so upset?"

She sighed and put down her knife. "It's hard to explain. But people don't like to feel like they have no say over who lives amongst them. There's no place here for people so different from us."

I didn't point out the obvious, that she and Grandpa had someone different from them living right there in their house. But she picked up her knife and set her shoulders in a way that made it clear the conversation was over. I left the kitchen and went into the living room to drop off my backpack. My grandfather wasn't there—twice a day, in the morning and then again after lunch, he walked uptown to Jimmy's Coffee Shop. Earl's Gun Store was right across from the coffee shop, and Deerhorn, in 1974, was the kind of place where Earl could leave the store unlocked while he had coffee at Jimmy's, and walk back across the street if he saw a customer. Charlie had taken me to the coffee shop a couple of times in the summer, and although the men usually ignored me after nodding hello, I couldn't have felt more privileged to be sitting among them if I'd been invited for a meal at the governor's mansion. "You know," Uncle Pete had whispered to me once; he often stopped by in the afternoon, "your grandpa, he brags about you all the time." I couldn't imagine what he said—I hadn't done anything special—but I believed Uncle Pete, believed in my grandfather's love; it was evident in the way his eyes softened when they fell upon my face; in the rough, gentle hand he rested on my shoulder.

But during the school year, I rarely made it to Jimmy's, and the hour and a half between the time I got home from school and my grandfather's return from the coffee shop was the longest part of the day. That afternoon, I opened the door to the attic and went up to my father's old room. Brett came with me. He was always at my heels as I moved from room to room; he slept in my bed; he lay on my feet during meals. Whenever I stood, he'd jump up too, and give me a look of excitement and questioning—ears perked, tail moving hesitantly, inquiringly, not sure yet whether the situation warranted a full-out wag. If I headed to the door with a leash or a ball, he was beside himself with excitement, jumping in circles and barking until my grandmother yelled for quiet. But if I just went to another room and sat down again, he'd continue to look at me for a moment, still hopeful, still giving me a chance to redeem myself, before lying down with a long-suffering sigh.

This is what he did now, once he saw that no adventure was imminent. My mind was on something else that afternoon. My father had put some old photo albums into a closet before he left, and I took them out and flipped through them until I found what I was looking for. In a few pictures of my parents in California, and in others from Japan, there were black men and women, clearly friends. In one picture from Tokyo, my father and an older black man were leaning together and laughing. I remembered that I'd met this man and his wife; they'd come over to our apartment several times. A few pages later I found some pictures of my parents in Bakersfield with a black couple around their age. There was nothing strange or threatening about the people in the photos—but then again, I wouldn't have thought that I was threatening, either.

Seeing these photographs made me think about my father's letter from the week before. I now considered the fact that it hadn't come from California. Since he'd arrived on the West Coast ten months before, all of his letters had been from the Sacramento area. But this last one had come from Kansas City. Because he'd written from several places the previous fall as he'd made his way out west, it hadn't struck me at first that this most recent letter didn't fit the usual pattern. Now it did. And then I remembered that his postcard before that had been from Salt Lake City. He seemed to be moving in our direction. Did this mean he was on his way back to Wisconsin? Could it be that my parents had reconciled, and he was keeping it a surprise? My heart jumped at this possibility. Now I tried to think about what he had actually written. He'd gone to Missouri for a music festival in the summer, to cover it for a radio station in Berkeley, and he'd liked the area so much that he'd decided to stay on there with friends. *It was so great, kiddo,* he'd written in his careless hand. *People relaxing, getting along with each other, just feeling the music. This is what the whole <u>world</u> should be like! I've got a couple of things to figure out and then I'll come and get you. Sit tight—I'll be ready for you soon.*

This sounded promising, but I wasn't sure I could believe it. Two weeks had already turned into thirteen months. And besides, as much as I wanted to see him, I didn't know how I felt about leaving. There was plenty I liked about being there in Deerhorn.

At four-thirty sharp, I went downstairs and took my usual seat by the dining room window. As soon as I saw my grandfather turn the corner onto Dryden Road, Brett and I ran out of the house. We sprinted all the way up the street, running straight at Charlie, and when he saw us, his face broke into a crooked grin. I barely slowed down as I hit him and threw my arms around his waist, the dog circling us and barking. "Whoa, Mikey," he said laughing, as he stepped back from the force of my blow. He often called me Mikey, and sometimes Mike; he only addressed me as Michelle when I was in trouble. Now he rubbed my head hard with his knuckles and asked, "How was school today?"

"Fine," I said into his shirt. I knew I wouldn't ask him what I'd asked my grandmother; I didn't want to talk about the nurse and the teacher anymore. Besides, I felt peaceful—my arms around Charlie, my cheek against his shirt, which smelled like Old Spice and fresh-cut grass. He disentangled me and we walked down the street toward home, me holding on to his, rough callused hand.

We sat down for supper at five. My grandmother served us chicken, scalloped potatoes, and squash, getting up several times to refill our glasses of milk. Finally, after all of our plates were half-cleared, my grandfather looked up from his food.

"Those kids still giving you trouble, Mike?"

I stared down at my plate, remembering the girls at my locker, the boy who'd called me a name. "No, not really."

"Well, if they do, you know what I told you now. Just pop 'em one." He made a fist and punched his other hand.

My grandmother turned to him. "Charlie, you shouldn't encourage her to be violent."

He leaned back in his chair, arms spread and palms up, appealing to her, resisting. "I'm not talking about violence, Helen. This is self-defense. Mike's got to be able to take care of herself."

"Well, I don't like it." She got up and went into the kitchen. From the harsh way she opened and closed the refrigerator, I could tell she was upset.

I wondered if my grandfather was annoyed at her—but when I glanced over at him, he winked. Then he reached over and poked me—in the shoulder, in the side—until I giggled and tried to swat his hand away.

When my grandmother came back to the table, with more butter for the squash, she looked at us disapprovingly. Then Charlie fixed her with that grin of his and said, "Thank you, sweetheart," and her expression finally softened.

Our good spirits restored, my grandfather recounted what he'd heard that day. Earl Watson had gotten a new order of shotguns, just in time for duck hunting season. John Berger's construction company had received a contract to build a dozen new houses near the clinic. Uncle Pete's secretary was pregnant again, her third child with that good-for-nothing Jerry Kolinski who Pete had fired two years ago. I stole glances at Charlie while I ate. His skin was a glowing brown, so tanned from working in the garden that he might have been that color all the way through. His hair was the color of barley, while my grandmother's had been gray for as long as I could remember. Watching my grandfather, I could see what it was about him that made women blush at him even now. He sat there in his trousers and green short-sleeve shirt, elbows slung on the table, looking at home with himself and the world.

He'd been sitting in the same spot a little over a year before when I emerged from the bedroom one morning. I'd taken a few steps toward the table and then stopped, surprised—my grandfather was always out of the house by the time I woke up, and although my father and I had only recently arrived, I knew it wasn't normal for Charlie to be sitting there doing nothing, as late as eight o'clock in the morning. But what also gave me pause was the way that he looked. He sat slouched over the table, leaning on his forearms, loose fists touching in front of him.

I had been there with my father about a week and a half, and already my first thought when I woke up each day was Charlie—what he was doing, how fast I could wolf down my breakfast and join him in the weeding or mowing he did before he walked up to the coffee shop. My father, who went out in the evenings after I'd gone to bed, wouldn't wake up until after ten. During the days he was restless, moving from front porch to back steps to attic to kitchen, avoiding my grandmother and her remarks on his shoulder-length hair, his stubble, the wide-bottom pants, the shirt with the three buttons open. In the afternoons he'd sit on the back steps with a cigarette and beer, eyes red-rimmed and watery. He didn't fit with his own family much better than he fit with my mother's; when Uncle Pete had come over the day before and he and Charlie had talked about hunting, my father just stared at the television and hadn't said a word.

Conversation over supper that evening, after Pete left, was stilted and strange, even before the nightly news came on. I already knew that the news meant arguments, or a tense quiet that was almost worse. As Walter Cronkite went through the stories of the day—the continuing fallout from Watergate and the bombings in Cambodia, the robbing of a bank by an antigovernment group, the drug overdose of a famous activist in San Francisco—I could feel the pressure building.

"Things are out of control," my grandfather said finally. "This country needs some order."

"The old order is exactly what people are trying to

break *free* from, Dad," said my father. "Everything's getting shaken up now. Things are changing."

Charlie made a sound of disapproval. "Sometimes change is more trouble than it's worth. Sometimes things should just stay like they are."

"But when those things aren't working anymore, then it's time for a new way. It's not just about the war and the government, Dad. It's about freeing people's minds, expanding their lives."

My grandfather was about to cut into his food and now he stopped, fork and knife poised over his plate. "Expanding their lives? What does *that* mean?" he asked. "People have responsibilities. They have commitments, routines. They shouldn't just be able to do whatever the hell they want."

"Yes, they *should*. That's what freedom's all about."

"Freedom," Charlie repeated. "Is that what you call it?" He lifted his fork and pointed it at my father. "Seems to me like you ran off and just *avoided* everything. Now you're thirty-two years old and you don't have a job, and you look like you haven't shaved in a year."

"I just *got* here. I still need to—"

"You forget with all your freedom that you're supposed to be a *father*. You can't just go out drinking all night and leave your child at home. What kind of example is that? What kind of life are you trying to make for her?"

"I'm not *trying* to make her life. That's exactly the point. I want to show her that there are all different kinds of ways to live. I want her to know that she can make her own choices."

Charlie moved like he was about to stand up, and

then lowered himself again. "She's a *child*, Stewart. She doesn't need to make 'choices.' She needs you to be a parent."

"I *am* a parent. I may not do things the way *you* would do them, but I'm still her father, and I'm still an adult."

"Are you?" Charlie said. "Then why don't you act like one?"

There was a brief, tense silence. Then my father pushed back from the table and stood up so fast his chair fell over backwards. He walked out of the house and slammed the door. My grandfather clenched his fist and raised it like he was going to hit the table, but he just let it fall and shook his head and didn't say a word.

The next morning, when I found my grandfather sitting at the table, it took him a moment to notice me. When he did, he raised his head and smiled sadly.

"Hello, Mike," he said, and his voice was soft and hoarse. He looked like a different man from the night before.

"Is my dad up yet?" I asked. I glanced at the door that led to the attic where he always slept. Suddenly I knew that whatever was wrong must have had to do with him.

Charlie took a deep breath and said, "Your father is gone."

"He didn't come home last night?" It wouldn't have been the first time. There'd been times in Japan, after my parents had argued, that he hadn't come home until morning.

Charlie's gaze was steady and he spoke carefully, as if to make sure I understood. "He *did* come home. But he packed up and left again early this morning. He heard something about your mother, and he had to get out to California." My grandfather stopped and uncurled his fists, touched the table with the edges of his hands. "He told us to tell you he was sorry that he didn't have a chance to say goodbye. But he'll be back soon, he said. He's coming back to get you."

I just stood there, not knowing what to think. I was used to having one or the other of my parents disappear. But both of them? "When?" I asked. "When will he be back?"

"A couple of weeks, he said."

Just then my grandmother came into the doorway; she must have been in the kitchen. Her eyes were red and puffy and her face was drawn. She and my grandfather exchanged a look, and then he turned back to me and smiled. "You don't mind this now, do you? You don't mind staying here with us for a while?"

The day that I learned about the substitute teacher, there was nothing in Charlie's manner or words that suggested anything was amiss. We finished supper and quickly cleared the table. After we all did the dishes (as always, she washed, he dried, and I helped put everything back into the cupboards), Charlie changed into his work pants and undershirt and we went out to the garage to get our baseball gloves. His was an old glove from his playing days, mine was a kid's glove, the color of dried blood, with the stamped signature of Catfish Hunter. Charlie had a pail of baseballs in the corner of the garage but we used just one that day, playing catch in the yard while the dog ran between us, following the flight of the ball. We didn't talk—he only spoke to tell me to extend my arm further, or to pull my legs together so grounders wouldn't sneak through; we just slung the ball back and forth through the cooling air. This—playing catch with my grandfather at dusk—was my very favorite thing in the world. And it was especially good on a day like today, when I felt stirred up and confused. Charlie seemed to know I needed physical activity; maybe he needed it too. We threw and caught the old baseball, sent it whirling through the air, heard its leathery thunk as it lodged in our gloves, until the ball began to blend in with the night and it got too dark to see.

When we went inside, my grandmother made us my favorite dessert—strawberries she'd canned and frozen during the summer, poured over French vanilla ice cream. We ate in the dining room, where Brett—once he realized he wasn't getting any food—lay down, yawned, and shook his head a little, as if the yawn was so large his head couldn't quite contain it. He rolled onto his side for a belly rub, which I happily gave him, scratching the spot just below his rib cage until his eyes half closed with bliss. Then we all went into the living room—Grandma sat in her recliner, me in the corner chair, and Charlie stretched out on his sofa—and watched TV until my bedtime. I got up and kissed my grandmother on the cheek, then stood behind my grandfather at one end of the couch and kissed him on his forehead.

"'Night, Mike," he said, and I scrambled off to my room, ready to go to sleep.

I *didn't* mind staying with them. I was comfortable there. Although I missed my father and wanted to see him, my grandparents were predictable and safe. As hard a time as I sometimes had in town and in school, their place, their house, was different. Even with what was happening at the elementary school, I felt, at least for that evening, like I was sheltered and protected; like everything could be all right.

THREE

The next morning—the substitute teacher's first day—I got to school without a bit of interference. There were no new ink marks on the front of my locker, no older kids waiting to taunt me. It was as if I had suddenly vanished, and I might have enjoyed this new anonymity if the mood hadn't been so tense. When I went into Miss Anderson's class and sat down at my desk, the entire room was abuzz.

"Have you seen him yet?"

"No, have you?"

"I heard Jackie Sanderson's mother wouldn't let him come to school."

"Well, if that was my teacher, I wouldn't come either."

"All right, all right, children, come to order," said Miss Anderson, and she sounded frustrated—not a good sign so early in the day. There were bags under her eyes and her mouth looked pinched. The class quieted down quickly and we waited for whatever she was going to tell us. Our school was small—two classes per grade—so whenever a new teacher came, or even a long-term sub, our teachers usually told us so we'd know to be friendly, even though new people were always greeted more with giggles and pointed fingers than with smiles. But though we sat quietly and waited for Miss Anderson to give her assessment of the black teacher, she took attendance and asked us to open our reading books and didn't mention him at all. We obeyed her and followed along in our books, but as we read about Chester the caterpillar, we were all more aware of what we hadn't yet discussed; it hung there like a threatening cloud. Finally, at ten-thirty, after a spelling test and a math lesson, Miss Anderson released us for recess.

We spilled onto the playground slowly, my classmates suddenly unsure of how to do normal, everyday things like playing tetherball or working the swings. Mrs. Hebig's fifth grade class wasn't out yet, and it seemed that everyone on the playground, both teachers and children, was waiting for them to appear—waiting to see if they bore visible signs of having spent the morning in the company of a Negro. While I sat at the bottom of the stairs on my usual bench, I noticed a lone figure a bit farther down, standing with his back against the wall. It was Kevin Watson, Earl's younger son, who was in the fourth grade. Although Kevin was my age, I'd always thought of him as younger. He was short and stocky, unsteady as a wolf pup stumbling out of his cave. Now, he put both hands behind him against the brick wall and rocked back and forth, his thick black hair, which was a bit too long in front, falling over into his face. Kevin often seemed at odds with the few friends he had, crying easily and throwing tantrums if he was left out of a game or passed over when they were picking teams for kickball. Judging from the rocking and the look on his face, that must have been what was happening now. He was sensitive and quiet, with brown liquid eyes and lashes as long as a girl's. His older brother Jake was burly and tough, more like Earl; he was one of the boys who'd chased me on my bike.

Thoughts of the Watson family quickly left my head, though, when the fifth graders finally appeared. And as they ran outside—and that is exactly what they did, run—they were immediately surrounded by other students. The whole mass of children moved down the playground away from the door, each of Mrs. Hebig's fifth graders flanked by two or three kids, as if they had just survived a spectacular accident and were being interviewed by throngs of reporters. The teachers who were outside on recess duty tried to look indifferent, but soon they too were inching toward the fifth graders. And I, who never joined in any gathering of students, just watched this from my bench. Although it bothered me how everyone was reacting to the new teacher, there was also a part of me that felt relieved. He and his wife, by attracting so much of the town's attention, had drawn it away from me. I was ashamed to feel this way, to be enjoying this respite, but there was no question that I was being glared at less frequently now, shoved around a bit less often in the hallway. And it occurred to me that at that moment, I could have walked out of the school and down the street and left the town forever, and no one there would ever have known the difference. But I didn't. What I did was sigh and stand up and walk back inside so I could spend a few minutes alone.

He was standing in the hallway across from the row of third grade lockers, reading something that was posted on the wall. He seemed amazingly tall, although in retrospect he was probably no more than 6'1" or 6'2", and he was younger than I'd expected—maybe thirty. He was the brown of dark chocolate, a lush earth-brown, and the loose-shouldered way he carried himself suggested that he was friendly. What struck me most, besides his darkness, was that he was wearing a jacket and tie, which was more formal than what the rest of the teachers wore.

I must have stood there staring at him for ten whole seconds before he turned and saw me. From the front he looked slimmer but still solid and fit, like he might have been a track star in high school. And then I saw his face—the broad cheeks and strong jaw, the warm brown eyes, the hair cut almost military short. And I remember thinking, because I didn't understand white people yet, especially white men, that Mr. Garrett's good looks and physical impressiveness would make people like him better.

"Good morning," he said, and his voice was resonant and deep; his smile revealed a set of brilliant teeth. He gave a little wave and I saw his mammoth hands, the long fingers, the lighter flesh of his palms. He seemed more relaxed than a man in his situation should have been, almost amused with himself.

I wanted to say something—like, it doesn't pay to be friendly, Mr. Garrett, or, I hope you know what you're getting yourself into—but I was terrified. Not of him, exactly—there was nothing threatening about him—but of something his presence was bringing out in people. And so I turned without speaking and ran back to Miss Anderson's class, hearing him laugh gently behind me.

I don't know what Miss Anderson talked about between recess and lunch, but none of us paid attention. While she tried to give her lesson, my classmates whispered and passed each other notes. I heard someone say that no one in Mrs. Hebig's class had spoken all morning, that the colored teacher had just kept talking as if he didn't notice. No one had actually seen him yet except for me—he'd gone back to his room by the time they came in—and had I shared my encounter, I could have enjoyed my classmates' attention for a while. But I didn't. It didn't even occur to me.

At lunchtime, after I received my tray of pizza burger, French fries, and milk, I went to my regular seat. There was a corner table that the other students avoided, maybe because it was too far from the gossip and food fights that usually occurred during lunch. That was where I sat every day by myself, and from there I had a clear view of the rest of the cafeteria. But because I usually kept my eyes down and concentrated on my food, it took me several minutes to realize that Mr. Garrett had entered—and I noticed only because the room had grown so quiet. He sat in another corner, across from me, eating his pizza burger and reading the paper. I wondered why he wasn't eating in the teachers' lounge—was he on lunch duty? But there he sat, among three hundred students, who all whispered and stared, the whole mass of curiosity, energy, and attention directed completely at him. He must have felt it—it was like the electricity in the air before a thunderstorm—but maybe that was why he had placed himself there, to get the shock all over with at once. And he had that same ease about him I'd seen in the hallway—the inexplicable calm, the near-enjoyment of the stir he was causing. Again I wanted to warn him—I knew he was trying to act normal, but he had to be careful. After he finished eating, he carried his tray to the dishwashing lady and handed it to her, smiling. She received it as if he'd given her something dead. Then three hundred sets of eyes followed him as he brushed his hands on his pants and walked out of the cafeteria.

As soon as he was gone, there was an explosion of noise. I couldn't make out clearly what anyone said; their voices and sneers and laughter all blended together. In Miss Anderson's class that afternoon, the boys kept telling her they'd seen the Negro teacher—and she kept saying yes, I saw him too; yes, he eats the same food as us; now please pay attention and open your books.

That afternoon, our phone rang off the hook. Bob Grimson called to report that his son had seen the nigger, who'd actually had the nerve to eat with the students. Junie Scott, whose granddaughter was in Mrs. Hebig's class, called to tell Charlie that her little Melanie had sat in the room with the Negro for hours and that she seemed to be developing a fever. Ray Davis called to say that people were asking if there was anything he could do legally to keep the fellow from teaching.

"Well, is there?" Charlie asked. "How'd he get hired in the first place? Why couldn't they have brought in someone else?" He stood by the window with the phone to his ear, the furrow in his brow getting deeper. "Well, someone needs to talk some sense into that principal. For Christ's sake, he grew up here, he should *know* better."

I needed to get out—away from the talk of Mr. Garrett, and away from the tension. So as soon as I finished helping my grandmother with the dishes from supper, I took my bike and the dog and rode out into the country. It was a beautiful September evening, the sky still blue and endless, and the breeze felt good against my skin. I pedaled easily, taking the back roads behind the bank, the one-screen theater, the A&W drive-in, the trailer park, and the baseball diamond where the Deerhorn Bombers played. I rode to the state park just outside the town limits with the dog trotting steadily behind me, then took the road that looped for a mile around the middle of it. Here, in a large, protected pasture that was part of a wildlife preserve, dozens of bison grazed peacefully. Two white-tailed deer raised their heads, saw us, and darted off into the woods.

The park was where I always came when I wanted to be alone. Maybe because Deerhorn was surrounded by so much country, maybe because the townspeople saw animals as things to hunt and use, not observe and protect, it did not have many visitors, except for the swimmers and fishermen who went to Treman Lake in the summer. This was incredible to me. Having spent my first eight years in a dense, overcrowded city, all this space and quiet was a luxury. When I'd first come to Deerhorn the year before, there were things I'd had to adjust to, things that felt strange and disorienting—the heavy food; the way people gave full voice to their joy or anger; the sheer size of everything from houses to cars to residential streets, which were twice as wide as our little alley in Tokyo. But the landscape was an easy adjustment. I'd taken to the park immediately—to the whole countryside, really—and my love for it only grew the more time I spent there. Often I seemed to be the only human within its limits, and I didn't mind this, in fact preferred it, for I felt an ease and a companionship out here in the country that I never felt in town. My father had thought differently about the country, I knew. All the open space made him feel restless, uneasy; he craved sidewalks and street noise, the sounds of human interaction. But I belonged out here, where there were no other people, only the trees and lakes and rivers, and grazing animals.

Brett belonged here too, and out in the country in the fading light, I loved to watch him run. Charlie had said he was from a line of dogs bred for conformation as well as hunting, and that careful breeding showed. He ran with a beautiful economy of motion, legs reaching forward and swinging back just as far as they needed to, no more and no less, in perfect synchronicity. The black of his coat looked like a blanket thrown over his body, but the hair on his chest was white, as if he were wearing an apron with ties that reached over his shoulders and met at the back of his neck. His head was mostly black but his muzzle was white, and a strip of white shot up between his eyes. When he stopped to look at something, he posed as if for a picture—chest out proudly, head up, long ears rippling in the breeze like a lion's mane. His front legs were planted firmly and his back legs extended and set, like he would stand his ground in the face of an oncoming army.

But when we got out into the open fields, he'd break out of his perfect trot and bound like a puppy, bouncing from rear legs to front and back again in an uncontained expression of joy. Because his field trial career was over, Charlie let his hair grow out, and his long black-and-white feathers hung from his legs, rump, and chest nearly all the way down to the ground. Every two or three days, I would brush him out—standing him up at first while I ran the brush through the long hair, which attracted any number of branches and burrs; and then rolling him over to expose his stomach, where I separated mats while he watched me, sober and trusting, pressing one paw against my face when I pulled too hard.

There was another reason I liked to have Brett around, and that was for my own protection. While he was loving and gentle with my grandparents and me, and playful with the neighborhood's female dogs (he would prod them with his snout or stick his nose up their butts until they snapped at him or hit him with a body check, which made him break out into a huge, panting grin), he was also protective. If we were outside and someone suspicious approached, he would shift instantly into a posture of challenge, tail raised and circling, low rumble in his throat. He had a deep, loud bark which could make people or other animals back away in fear. No loose male dog could approach without Brett chasing him off, and he once followed a boy who'd been teasing me all the way back to his house, grabbing a mouthful of the boy's shirt for good measure. It was always startling to see the transformation of that goofy, affectionate spaniel into a dog that was capable of doing harm. But he never did—he never had to. The threat was enough.

I rode the loop twice, leaving the main path a couple of times to take side roads through the woods and fields. Brett ran back and forth in front of me, nose to the ground. Because of his hunting training, he never ventured more than about twenty yards in front of me or fifteen yards on either side, always staying within shooting range. That afternoon he startled a lone fat grouse; it made a sound like the click of a key starting the ignition, then the whirring of a motor as it flew away. He

looked back at me as if to ask, why didn't you shoot?—
and then turned around and moved on. From there we
went over to Six Mile Creek, which ran along the border of the park. When the water was high, Brett would
make spectacular leaps from the bank and then swim
back and forth happily, tail circling fast as a propeller.
But it was low that day—there hadn't been much rain
in the summer—so he just ran down to the edge and
took a quick drink. A bit further on there was a small
gorge with a log as thick as a wine barrel lying across
it. Brett ventured out onto the log, lost his footing, and
slipped halfway off. He held on with his front legs while
his back legs dangled free and circled the air like a car-
toon character's; then he fell rump-first to the ground.
He caused a sizable *thump* when he landed, scattering
leaves and small branches and a few irritated birds, and
I was scared for a moment that he'd hurt himself. But
he jumped right up, shook himself, and ran over to me,
grinning.

We'd been out there for over an hour, but whatever
it was that compelled me to ride was not yet spent that
day, so we left the park and continued down the two-
lane road that led farther out into the country. There
were farms on either side of us, with cornstalks as tall
as people that time of the year. I saw cows in the fields,
and the ones closest to the road looked up as we passed,
their big faces with expressions blank as dinner plates.
There were a few horses too, whinnying and shaking
their heads, and I thought, what a fine thing to be such a
beautiful creature, posing in the light of the fading sun.

I was too young to realize what hard times country
people were having then. Family farms that had exist-

ed for several generations were being squeezed out by the big industrial operations, or, more mundanely, losing their children to cities and towns and simply fading out. But the evidence was everywhere. Some of the old farmhouses were sagging and frayed, as if they were as tired as their people from the unrelenting effort it took to keep the farms running. Rusted tractors and other machinery sat unused near collapsing barns, and the silos, which must once have been filled with harvested corn or wheat, looked empty and forlorn. I biked past farm after farm, each one in worse condition than the last, turning down smaller unpaved roads to get deeper into the country, and kicking up dust and gravel in my wake.

And then, without warning, we arrived at a cluster of trailers. I knew from driving around with my grandfather that there were little groups of trailers tucked away in all manner of wood and field. In town there were actual trailer parks, and also single trailers on private land, where people were reluctant or unable to build houses. Neither of these arrangements was strange to the town—Uncle Pete and Aunt Bertha lived in a trailer on three acres just outside the town limits, and their son and his family lived in one of the trailer parks. And while the trailers were unsafe in volatile weather (once, a freak tornado hit while Pete and Bertha were at the store, and they came home to find their trailer upside down in the street), there was no particular stigma attached to the people who lived in them.

But the trailers in the country were another matter. If the trailers in town were discarded as people moved on to bigger trailers or houses, this seemed to be the place where the old ones ended up. The trailers I saw that evening were like taped-together scraps of metal, many of the panels not matching in color or even fitting together properly. Some of them didn't even have steps in front—a bucket or a pile of bricks had been placed where the stairs should have been—and many of the windows were covered with plastic or cardboard. And the children who played in front of them were dressed in torn, faded clothes, their faces and arms streaked with dirt. They were skinny—their knobby knees were broader than their thighs—and their faces seemed collapsed somehow, absent of light, as if they were miniature old people rather than children. I knew these children existed, because a few of them were bused to school in town, including Billy Coles, who was in the other third grade class. They received baths there once a week because some of their trailers lacked running water, and they were regularly deloused.

But it was one thing to see an occasional skinny, unkempt child at school or in town; it was another thing altogether to see them here. I kept riding, a bit embarrassed, as if we had caught them naked. Brett ran along beside me and glanced over at them, but then kept his head down. The children just stared as we went by, but left us alone—to them, we might have been a ghostly vision. But I saw them all clearly, and could not look away—the dullness of their eyes, the unhealthy yellow tinge of their skin. People in town rarely mentioned these cast-off people, and when they did, it was in hushed tones of disapproval, not compassion. Even though I now work with teenagers who live in the inner city, I have never seen anything close to such poverty. These set-aside people were isolated, ingrown, removed from the life of town. As far as everyone else was concerned, they might not have even existed.

The next day, ten students from Mrs. Hebig's class were absent. There seemed to be an illness circulating among them that bypassed the rest of the school. But from what I could tell from the proud postures and self-conscious gaits of the fifth graders at recess, those who remained with Mr. Garrett were enjoying the attention. Since no one would talk to him, and no one else except for me had heard him speak, Mrs. Hebig's fifth graders were subjected to all kinds of questions from both children and adults: What does he talk like? Does he have any smell? Does it make you feel scared when he looks at you? And the teachers, for their part, seemed strange and agitated. They saw him but wouldn't talk to their students about it, despite the persistent questions. Did anyone sit next to him at meetings or in the lounge? Would anyone touch the coffee pot after he had touched it first? There was excitement and curiosity in everyone's questions, as well as the edge of something else I couldn't quite define. And there was anticipation too, the awareness that sooner or later something had to change, had to give.

The next day, and the next, there were fewer and fewer students in Mrs. Hebig's class, until by Friday only eleven reported to school. What I wonder now is not why parents kept their children at home, but why other parents let their children continue to go. I'd like to believe it was a decision that came out of deliberate thought, the strength to do what was right in the face of the town's small-mindedness—that was the choice I know my father would have made. But more likely the children who remained in class had nowhere else to go, or had parents who somehow didn't know or care that the regular teacher was gone. Whatever the case, the other teachers spent more and more time talking to each other on the playground and after school, and Miss Anderson seemed more nervous every day. On Friday morning, as she was handing back a spelling test from the day before, she stopped at my desk and cleared her throat. And since she so rarely looked at me or talked to me directly, I knew I was in trouble.

"Michelle," she said, looking down at me, "why don't you write in small letters?"

I just stared at her, not knowing what she meant. She waved my test in my face, the red marks of correction vivid and harsh, exposed for everyone to see.

"Small letters," she said slowly, as if I didn't understand. "You wrote all these words in capital letters."

I continued to look up at her. Since I'd written in capital letters all that school year and the year before, I didn't see why anyone should have a problem with it now. Looking more closely at the words that she held two inches from my face, I saw that she hadn't corrected any spelling. And yet the paper was covered in red, because what she *had* done was rewrite every single word in small letters.

"Michelle," she said, with a hostile edge to her voice, "do you even know *how* to write in small letters?"

And it must have occurred to us both, and to everyone else, that I didn't.

Around me, I heard snickers. One boy hissed, "What a dummy!"

Miss Anderson shook her head and looked at me distastefully. "They must not have taught you very well over there in Japan."

But they did, I wanted to tell her. Thanks to my mother, I could read and write more kanji than any other child in the Japanese school, even those who had two Japanese parents. I knew characters that fifth graders didn't know. I had learned the math that she was teaching us two years before and had always scored first in my class. But I didn't tell her any of this; it wouldn't have helped.

Instead, I just sat there silently while she declared in a loud voice, "You're going to really have to work to catch up with the rest of the class. They probably should have held you back another grade."

That afternoon when I got home from school, my grandmother was already setting the table for company. It was Friday, which meant that Jim Riesling would be coming over for supper. But to my surprise, several of the other coffee shop regulars showed up, too—Earl Watson, Ray Davis, and eventually Uncle Pete, who was a little late, as always. They had come to discuss the Garretts. Because I was the only one who'd actually seen one of them, I was included in the conversation. They let me sit at the dining room table with them while my grandmother ate alone in the kitchen. Normally I would have been thrilled at such an arrangement, at being included in the circle of men. But it didn't feel like such a privilege that day. Grandma had made my favorite supper—chicken-fried steak, peas, and mashed potatoes—but my food sat untouched while they questioned me. Beneath the table the dog lay on my foot, my only anchor to something gentle and comforting.

"What does he look like?" Earl said, leaning across the table. "I asked Kevin but that boy don't know his ass from a hole in the ground."

"What do you mean, what does he look like?" said Ray. "He looks like they all do—black and ugly."

"Did he try to talk to you?" Earl pressed, ignoring his friend. His eyes were red from anger or beer, and he leaned so close I could see the veins lacing through them. The light shone off his bald spot, which was ringed with the same black hair as his son's. I looked down to avoid his stare and my eyes settled on his arms. There was a curved, protruding scar on the inside of his right wrist, just where his shirt sleeve ended.

"No," I lied. "I only saw him in the cafeteria."

"He ate with you?" Uncle Pete asked, surprised. He was generally so good-natured that it was troubling to see *him* troubled, to see his handsome face screwed into an angry scowl.

"You know, we don't need to do this," Jim said, dropping his hands heavily on the table. "Let her be. He has nothing to do with her."

"He has something to do with *all* of us, even Mike here," said Charlie, and the others nodded. I didn't like the expression on his face—it was angry and impatient—so I looked past him at the faded reproduction of the Last Supper, and then to his right, at his gun case. It was like a small wooden hutch for china, lifted up and nailed to the wall. Two shotguns and a rifle leaned with their barrels in grooved slots, their muzzles pointing up toward the ceiling. His pistols—a Colt .38 Special and a

Smith & Wesson .357 Magnum—hung from metal hooks in the back. On the top shelf were my grandfather's sharpshooting trophies and Brett's trophies from field trial competitions. Surrounding the handguns, taped to the wood, were yellowed old newspaper clippings from Charlie's marksman days, and from his time as a baseball player in the amateur leagues.

It bothered me that my grandfather was upset about Mr. Garrett. I had known that he didn't think particularly well of blacks—I'd heard him say that they were lazy and dependent on welfare, and he seemed to think sensational stories of crimes committed by black people were an indictment of the entire race. But I'd taken these remarks in the same vein as his grunting disapproval of bell-bottoms, or hippies, or war protestors—as general displeasure with difference, a resistance to the world shifting around him. I hadn't really thought he was serious. And it was one thing to hear his opinions about people *out there*, on TV. It was another to see him directing those feelings toward a real person, someone I knew.

"Listen," Earl said, and his eyes were piercing. Although it had been over a year since he'd met me, I don't think he'd ever really looked at me before. "If you see him at school, don't talk to him. Don't talk to him, don't smile at him, don't treat him like he belongs. He needs to understand that he ain't welcome here, and everybody in town has to let him know it. That means *everybody*— even you, little girl."

I looked down and moved some peas around my plate. I wondered if he'd given a speech like this about me when I first came to town. One way or another, the message had been conveyed—Earl's wife and sons never talked to me.

"I heard the wife's got people seeing her," Jim said now, and I was relieved that the men's attention had been drawn away. "She's been helping a lot of patients at the clinic."

"Must be people from out of town," my grandfather remarked, and he was probably right. It was hard to imagine anyone from Deerhorn going to see her, but people from larger towns like Wausau and Steven's Point might have felt less uneasy. And those towns had a few black residents too, maybe some who were willing to come all the way to Deerhorn to be treated by a black nurse. She might even have been seeing some black soldiers who were home from the war, since there was no veterans' hospital in the area. I knew, though, that the other men weren't happy to hear this.

"Well, the buck's losing customers, that's for sure," Charlie said. "Mike told me there was only ten kids in Janie's class today."

"He sounds like a nice enough fellow," Jim said, seeming almost defiant. "I heard he offered to give some extra help to kids who were having trouble with their schoolwork."

"Help?" Earl said. "From a nigger?"

With this reproach, Jim settled into silence. He leaned back in his chair and crossed his arms, eyes cast down at the table. I'd always wondered if my grandfather and the other men tolerated some of his unconventional views—like his belief that women should be hired as police officers and that draft dodgers shouldn't have to serve jail time—because they didn't take him seriously. But now he was even less aligned with them than usual. After the other men left and we moved into the living room, Jim barely said a word, working slowly on a single beer and staring blankly at the television. He was joined in silence by my grandmother, who didn't speak to Charlie, but whose sudden, unusual attention to me—a hot chocolate, an extra piece of pie after dinner—let me know she wasn't pleased about what had happened that evening. I wasn't feeling very sociable either, and as soon as the Friday Western was over at nine, I escaped into my room.

The room I slept in was actually a guest room, and that's exactly what it looked like. Because we'd all assumed my stay was going to be temporary, my grandparents hadn't changed it when I arrived. The furnishings were heavy and wooden, pieces they'd inherited from their families, and the wardrobe was full of my grandmother's winter clothes. Although the old furniture was big and mismatched, I liked it; it felt substantial and permanent. And I especially loved the old bed. It was huge and enveloping, and that night I dove straight into it, rolling around on the handmade quilt.

I wanted to forget the last few hours; I wanted not to feel how I felt. And because it wasn't comfortable, all of a sudden, to be in that house, I pulled myself up out of the bed and looked at the postcards I'd tacked to the wall. They were from my father, from his various stops on his way out west the year before—Des Moines, Topeka, Denver, Salinas, Salt Lake City, and Reno. At first, they all said more or less the same thing: *I hope things are good there. I haven't talked to her yet.*

When he arrived in California, though, his writings

had changed. He *had* talked to her, eventually; he'd found her in Sacramento. Then he followed her to Stockton, San Francisco. For a while the letters—they'd turned to letters once he was more or less settled—included descriptions of where he was staying, whatever odd local radio or newspaper jobs he picked up, the new friends he made or the older ones with whom he'd reconnected. *You're going to love it here,* he'd written from San Francisco. *You'll feel right at home. It's wild and beautiful and everyone can be who they are.*

He'd say a bit about my mother—*I talked to her on the phone the other day,* or, *I caught up with her outside the place she works*—and always tried to sound upbeat. He promised that he'd come and get me soon, that we'd all be together again.

But as the months passed he began to refer to her less, or with a different tone—he hadn't seen her in a while, he wrote at one point, but he was sure that he'd speak to her soon. She gradually faded from his letters until finally, a couple of months before, he stopped mentioning her altogether. Then he had written from Kansas City, worrying my grandmother. And now there was a new postcard that I hadn't put up yet, which had arrived just that week from Springfield, Missouri. He was on the move again, but heading east, maybe toward Wisconsin.

Although I tried not to dwell on it, I missed my father. He wasn't a bad man, or even a particularly bad parent—I had good memories of him bouncing me on his knee and ruffling my hair, and singing songs while he fried bacon and eggs in the morning. He was gentle and big-hearted, and he cared about things being right in the world. It was just that he wasn't centered, the way that Charlie was. He couldn't really focus on anything, except on the one thing that he could never hold, my mother. Even when the three of us were still living together, she had seemed to be leaving already. I could still recall her perfume and her high, impatient voice—but I couldn't, despite the pictures in the attic, conjure her face at all.

I didn't want to think about my mother, though, so I got up and went over to the bureau where the postcard from Springfield lay. It was a picture of a Civil War–era cannon in front of a church, against a backdrop of clear blue sky. *I'm staying with some friends I met this summer at the music festival*, my father had written. *I've got a job here with a radio station starting next week, and I'm going to save some money. As soon as I do, I'm coming to get you—and then we can go back to California!*

There was a hopefulness to this postcard that was different, that seemed real this time, and it raised my own hopes too. I thought about writing back, but as usual, there was no return address. In my shirt drawer were half a dozen letters I'd written, waiting for when I'd have a place to send them. If he was staying in one place long enough to work and save some money, maybe that time would be soon.

But while I stood looking at the postcard, I felt jumbled, confused. As unsettled as I'd felt at the dinner table that night—and as uncomfortable as I felt with most of the people in town—I still loved living with my grandparents. The everyday routines of their house and their lives, the meals and chores and evenings at home, were comforting and solid. And I loved wandering in the country; I loved my life outside, I loved playing and biking with the dog. It was a different kind of life than I had with my father, and with both of my parents; living with them had been shifting and uncertain. I wasn't sure I was really eager to go back to that life. But I did want to feel like they wanted me.

Thinking about all of this, I felt a sudden surge of loneliness. Then I heard scratching at the door. When I opened it, I found Brett there, ears lifted in concern and questioning. I leaned over and petted him on the head, kissed him on the snout. I brought him into the room and invited him to jump up on the bed, which he did, and then I hugged him until I drifted off to sleep.

FOUR

During the fall of 1974, time seemed to move both faster and more slowly than usual, with each event brightened and magnified like the leaves on the maple trees, which were bursting then with color. I remember that time vividly, the particular tensions in the air, the way that all of us faced the morning with a heightened awareness, as if we were preparing ourselves for whatever the day might bring. The uneasiness in town was sharpened by events in the larger world— the resignation of the president, long lines at gas stations, the kidnapped heiress who was still missing even though her captors had been killed or arrested, the escalating crisis in Boston. Everyone seemed to be on edge, and at nine years of age I felt suddenly old, as if I knew that the things I was witnessing then would propel me into an early adulthood.

But there was more to those weeks than tension and difficulty. Some good days were mixed in, too. And as those days grew increasingly rare, I held on to them more tightly.

The Saturday after I'd been questioned about the Garretts at dinner, Charlie and I loaded the car up with several bats, two gloves, about three dozen baseballs, and headed out into the country. My grandparents' car was a lime-green '64 Pontiac LeMans, so big it could have fit eight people in its long bench seats, one short of a starting lineup for a baseball team. The car had clocked 22,000 miles in the ten years they'd owned it, just slightly more than I rack up now in a single year in California, and it's a measure of my grandfather's view of the world, of his essential satisfaction, that he never saw reason to drive more than fifty miles from Deerhorn, and then, really, only to hunt.

That day, he sat with his right arm thrown across the back of the seat and his knees spread wide, so relaxed he might have been sitting in his living room. His left hand rested lightly on the bottom curve of the wheel, even as we hurtled along at eighty miles an hour down a two-lane country road. I wasn't scared because everything about the way he held himself made clear that he had this powerful machine completely in his control. Besides, I was eager to reach our destination. There was a baseball field about ten miles into the country, which used to be the home of the Deerhorn Bombers until the new ballpark was built close to town, and which now served mostly as a practice field for the boys who still lived out on the few remaining farms. It was at the far end of a pasture that backed up to the woods, and deer would wander into the outfield at dusk. Charlie drove me out there sometimes when we knew the place would be empty to work on my batting and fielding. We always brought Brett with us, and as we approached the field that morning, he raised his head to feel the rushing air against his face, the wind lifting his black ears like sails. When we pulled off the road onto the gravel parking area he began to circle and whine, as eager as Charlie and me to be outside.

Is there any place more perfect than a baseball field in autumn? Anything better than the smell of the grass; or the crisp, cool air; or the red and yellow leaves against the clear blue sky, which was paler now than it had been in the summer? I didn't think so, and this field was my favorite. Because it wasn't used as much as the fields in town, there weren't any worn spots in the grass, and the infield was perfectly level. The backstop was simple—about fifteen feet tall and thirty feet wide—not one of the huge, imposing structures they had put on the newer fields. The dugouts were just benches behind a six-foot fence, and the bleachers along the base lines were made of wood. The outfield wall, which was painted a fading Brewer blue, had a few old ads from businesses in town—Dieter Tires, Ronnie's Bar and Grill, the *Deerhorn Herald News*. Past the third base line was a wide, unbroken view of the countryside—the slightly rolling hills spotted here and there by stands of wood, a few red barns in sharp relief against the green of the fields. It was quiet there, so quiet you could hear the individual songs and conversations of the birds, the approach of a car on the distant highway. Any home run ball was hit into the woods beyond the outfield, where it became part of the landscape with the rocks and fallen leaves, maybe scaring a deer or two as it landed.

There was something about stepping out onto a baseball field that always gave me a thrill, as if some energy source, some element in the grass, entered my feet and moved up through my body and set off an extra charge in my heart. I knew that my grandfather felt it, too. He was grinning as we unloaded the gear and carried it to a spot along the first base line. And seeing his worn Brewers cap and the muscles that still lined his arms, I could imagine him at eighteen or nineteen years old, driving out to the country with a duffel bag and glove, just looking for the next field, the next game.

We played catch for a few minutes to warm up. Brett followed the flight of the ball through the air and ran back and forth, barking, between us. Then my grandfather sent me out to the shortstop position. He stood at home plate and threw the balls up for himself, hitting them as they fell. He sent ground balls, line drives, and pop-ups across the field, moving me left and right, making me charge or take balls on a hop or run backwards to keep them from flying over my head. I was a fairly good fielder for a nine-year-old—proficient at judging hops and even backhanding grounders—although I still flinched at very hard-struck balls that whirred straight at my head. Brett waited patiently through this barrage, sitting between first and second at the second baseman's spot so he could watch but not be in the line of fire. He knew not to chase balls that were intended for me. But if I couldn't handle a scorching grounder or a high line drive and the ball went past me into the outfield, he'd chase after it, sprinting full speed, as if he planned to pick the ball up, turn, throw it back toward the infield, and cut the base runner down at home plate. But once he actually retrieved the ball the urgency was gone; he'd trot casually outside the third base line, lifting his head as he readjusted his grip, supremely proud of himself, and drop the ball at my grandfather's feet. Then he'd run back out to second base and wait for my next miss.

After thirty minutes or so of fielding, I would take up my bat and Charlie would go out to the pitcher's mound.

At first he'd just throw the ball straight across the plate until I could hit it consistently. Sometimes he'd yell out instructions—move up in the batter's box, don't let your shoulders fly open, take your step toward the pitch a bit sooner. Batting is about muscle memory and repetitive motion, and you have to get to the point where you're moving perfectly and acting without thought. If you think too much about any part of the swing—the position of your hands on the bat, the timing of your step, the relative movement of your hips and shoulders—you can break the rhythm and throw everything off. When players, even professionals, get into a hitting slump, it's often because they're thinking too much, breaking down the various parts of their swing until it becomes a series of separate, fallible mechanical actions instead of a unified expression of grace. At nine years old, I already knew this. Sometimes I could hit beautifully, as if the ball sought out my bat. And other times I couldn't hit a thing.

But that day I was able to connect. After my grandfather was sure I was swinging smoothly and consistently, he started mixing up his pitches a bit, moving them inside and outside, higher and lower, offering curveballs and change-ups to test my eyes and my timing, even throwing the occasional splitter. He'd been a pitcher as well as a third baseman, so he could make all those pitches, and sometimes, on my more futile batting days, I'd believe he was trying a little too hard to get them past me. I wasn't as good with these more difficult pitches, swinging way out in front of the change-ups and on top of the splitters that looked like strikes but then dropped precipitously just before they reached the plate. But when I *did* connect, when the ball hit the center of the barrel of the bat and flew out into the field, I felt a sense of joy and freedom as powerful and true as anything I've ever experienced. If you have never felt the resistance and connection of a bat hitting a baseball; if you have not heard the crack of the bat split an autumn afternoon; if you have not watched that ball sail through the open air and settle into the fresh-cut grass, you have missed one of life's purest feelings of achievement. Hitting a ball is like catching a piece of the sky and sending it back up to itself. It's like creating your own crack of thunder. And stopping a ball—especially a grounder you have to reach for, or a line drive that should have flown past your glove—is like catching a bolt of lightning.

We were out on the field practicing hard, both covered in a sheen of sweat. By now, my grandfather had stripped off his short-sleeve shirt and was pitching in his undershirt. (It's funny how even the simplest things can change with time and context. Those shirts—which then were simply part of the working man's unglamorous uniform—have now taken on a hip, modern masculinity, as well as the more descriptive name of "wifebeater." This, even though the men I knew who wore them—my grandfather and Uncle Pete—were as likely to hit their wives as they were to give up beer or hunting.) But for all of our exertion, our efforts didn't feel a bit like work. For Charlie, there wasn't a real distinction between work and play, anyway, or at least there shouldn't have been. In his mind, if something wasn't enjoyable, it wasn't worth doing, and this held true even for the things he did to make a living. He'd taken pleasure, he said, in cutting out perfect pieces of leather for shoes; in watching freshly plucked chickens move down the assembly line. And there was no mistaking the pleasure on his face when he played baseball with me, or when he was walking through the woods at dawn with his shotgun in hand. All work should feel like play, he said, and all play should involve hard work. This was a lesson I learned well, and still adhere to. The things I do for fun, I do with effort and dedication, and the things I do for work must always involve some pleasure. I can't stay focused at my job unless I'm enjoying myself. And as I sit here at my desk I'm wearing a wool Dodgers hat because of something else that Charlie told me, which is that all serious work should be done in a baseball cap.

That day, we were out there for more than two hours before Charlie said we should start to think about going back. Then, just after I'd hit one last ball, we heard the faint but growing sounds of approaching birds. I looked up over the woods, and there they were—a large flock of birds, a hundred or so, flying in a jagged V formation. They were well up in the sky, but not so far that we couldn't hear their chorus of honking, the deep-throated calls they made to each other and announced to the rest of the world. Their V was uneven, left flank longer than the right, and when they were almost directly overhead, a few birds from the longer line broke out sharply to the left, shifting because of instinct or wind patterns or the sun into a more southerly direction. They gradually became the head of an entirely new V, the birds on either side of them assuming positions downwind. Then slowly the rest of the flock fell into line, the ones that had headed the previous pattern forming the new right flank; the ones who'd made up the rear flying double time now to catch up and form the flank to the left. In a minute or two the entire flock had completely rearranged itself. And as they flew off further away from us we could still hear the honking, their arguments and debates, their calls of life.

We simply stood and watched them go. There was something about them that made me want to take off my cap, and when I looked at Charlie, I saw that he had done exactly that. He gazed up at them not with the hungry look of a hunter, but more like a man admiring a landscape or a beautiful woman. Even Brett sat and watched them, ears erect but body still, tongue hanging out in a happy pant. Somehow, we all knew it was the end of our day. My grandfather came over then and rubbed my head.

"Those were Canada Geese," he said, "heading down south for the winter."

"Where do they go?" I asked.

He watched them as they became indistinguishable spots in the sky. "Down to Kentucky, I think. Or Missouri. Those geese come down from Canada along the Mississippi Flyway. They take the same path every year. They mate for life, and when they have babies, the whole family stays together until the young ones are grown. They even make the first few migration trips together so the parents can teach them how to do it. What we were looking at just now was a whole little town of them."

I stared up at the sky long after I could no longer see them and thought about my grandfather's words. Those young ones had it good. But I didn't, even with my parents gone, feel like I had it so bad—not when I lived with my grandparents, who fed and sheltered me;

not when my grandfather towered over me and warmed my days like the sun. Besides, my father was closer now, and chances were he'd be there soon. "I haven't seen you bring one home," I said.

"They're not for hunting," he said, bending over to pat the dog. "I mean, you *can* hunt them, but I don't. Never have. There's something about the idea of breaking up those families." He smiled. "Plus, they'll fight you, boy. They're not helpless little birdies. One time a dog of mine, a German shorthair I had when your pop was just a kid, made the mistake of getting too close to a nest. We didn't even know it was there. We were out fishing and the dog, Jackson, was sniffing around 'cos he was bored. He practically stepped right on a nest that had five chicks, and then suddenly this big male comes back from his patrol and starts screaming and honking like the dickens. Well, old Jackson just about jumped out of his skin, and then the gander came straight at him. Beat the hell out of that dog with those big strong wings—the poor dog just cowered and covered his head. By the time I chased the bird away, he'd got pushed back fifty feet. He was so embarrassed he couldn't look me in the eye for a week. Was pretty much ruined for hunting after that."

I looked over at Brett, who was watching us, ears erect, wondering what was going to happen next. Charlie must have known what I was thinking.

"Now *that* dog," he said, nodding at Brett, "that dog wouldn't have had any trouble. He would've thought the gander was playing, and body-checked him right back. Probably would have gone and tried to warm the nest of babies. Probably would've cuddled right up with the goose and the gander."

Brett lifted his head and looked at us even more alertly; he knew we were talking about him. I gave him a ball to carry and helped my grandfather load our equipment back into the car. Brett's eyes were already getting that bloodshot look they got when he was tired, and both of us were fast asleep by the time we hit the town limits. Then I felt Charlie jostle me. "Wake up, Mike, wake up!" He'd pulled into the Kmart parking lot, and I didn't know why we were stopping until I smelled the bratwurst cooking; someone had set up a grill in front of the store. That woke me up fast and we tumbled out of the car. We each ate two brats smothered with ketchup, mustard, and sauerkraut, and my grandfather had a beer. After we finished he said, "Don't tell your grandma—she'll be sore at us for spoiling our appetites." He gave me a crooked grin, a bit of sauerkraut stuck in his teeth. I felt like the luckiest kid in the world.

My sense of well-being lasted into the following day. I didn't even mind that we were going to church, which normally would have filled me with dread. Church was the one thing we did for my grandmother; it was clear that our attendance was important to her. She was religious in a deeply felt, personal way that had little to do with conventional displays of belief or the expected social mores of church attendance. No, faith was something my grandmother harbored in private, like secret love. Sometimes I'd catch her reading the Bible when I came home from school, and she'd quickly slip it into a drawer. My grandmother's feelings for Jesus were intense almost to the point of being romantic; the only times I ever saw passion in her face were when she looked at her carving of Him on the cross.

But she didn't actually speak much about her beliefs; she just made us go to church, as if simply by putting ourselves in His presence, we'd grow to love Him, too. Charlie's feelings about the church appeared to be more dutiful than religious, and although I believed in God, I did not believe, as my grandmother did, that He could redeem the sins of man. My grandmother didn't try to shape my views herself, although she had, one day the previous spring, enlisted the efforts of her grandniece Geri, whose own brand of faith was more exacting, and who'd driven all the way over from Steven's Point to try and save my soul.

"You have got to give your life up to Jesus, child," Geri had said in her booming voice. She sat on my grandfather's sofa, facing me, while he paced back and forth in the dining room. My grandmother had put me in her own recliner, where I felt tiny and enveloped; she had pulled a chair up in front of the television, which was turned on but soundless, and was looking back and forth between Geri and me.

Geri continued. "I'm only telling this to help you, Michelle. Your father ain't done his job of it."

I looked at a spot on the floor directly between us. But even out of the corner of my eye I could see her short, stubby body, her baby-blue suit, the plastic feather in her dime-store hat.

"Devote your life to Lord Jesus the Savior, and He will pull you out from the flames of oblivion."

My grandmother broke in. "Now, Geri, don't scare her."

Geri looked at her. "Aunt Helen, I'm only trying to help salvage what's probably already beyond salvaging." She turned back and fixed me with a heavy expression. "You're a half-breed, child, with dirty yellow blood, but Jesus can save you."

My grandfather came storming into the living room. "Now wait a minute, Geri. You just hold off a minute. You don't talk like that to my grandchild in my own damned house."

She looked up at him, eyes flat. "Charlie, you may have no concern over the state of this child's soul, but I do." She turned to my grandmother. "He doesn't have Jesus in him either, Helen."

My grandfather leaned over her, fists clenched. "What the hell makes you think—"

"That's probably why Stewart got confused," Geri sniffed, ignoring him. "That poor lost boy. First he goes and marries a Jap, of all things. And then they have a child . . ."

"Now, Geri, I don't think . . ." my grandmother said, rising.

". . . and then he just runs off and *leaves* her."

My grandmother stared at her, hurt and surprised. "But he's coming back," she said. "He's coming back for her soon."

Geri gave her a look of infinite patience. "Oh, Helen. Do you really believe that?"

There was a heavy silence for one moment, two. Then my grandfather thrust his finger toward the door. "Get out," he said evenly. "Get out of my house."

She glared at him, kissed my grandmother, and left through the front door. Neither of my grandparents moved. I looked past them at the television, where a lumbering, muted Elvis Presley sweated and sang, heaving in his sideburns and his bright white suit. We heard Geri's car start up, heard it pull away.

"Crazy bitch," Charlie said when she was gone.

But whatever Charlie thought of Geri or of my grandmother's faith, he never argued about going to church. The morning after we played baseball, I put on a pair of clean pants and a blouse—I never wore a dress—and met my grandparents in the kitchen.

We drove to church and found that Mass was being held outside, in the park across the street. This made me think the same thing I had thought during the summer—that I liked God better when the weather was warm. I saw a few of my classmates, including Missy Calloway and Brady Grimson; but while they noticed me, they didn't say hello. Several other people saw me, frowned, and steered their children away.

We found Uncle Pete and Aunt Bertha under a tree about forty feet in front of Father Pace. I was surprised that they had gotten there ahead of us. Uncle Pete was usually late for everything, to the annoyance of the women, but it was impossible to really get angry about it because he was always so cheerful, so happy to tell you about the great half-inning on TV or the fishing hole he'd found or the project in the woodshed that had made him lose track of time. But he was there before us that day, and when we approached, he pinched my cheek, slapped Charlie on the back, and moved over to make room for our chairs.

Church was not my favorite place to spend a Sunday.

I don't know whether my resistance had to do with the Mass itself, or with how the church leadership had responded to my parents and me. My father still believed in God, I knew, but his faith had changed, or maybe his God had, to one who cared about the poor and unfortunate and who welcomed all His children. That was not the God worshipped in Deerhorn. When my parents had tried to come to Mass during one of their visits, a deacon had told them in no uncertain terms that the church did not acknowledge their marriage. And the first time my grandparents had brought me to church the previous year, that same deacon had informed them that I wasn't welcome. This news wasn't exactly taken kindly by my grandfather, who'd pressed the deacon on his reasoning, and then, upon hearing that my mother's non-Christian background made me ineligible to be a Catholic, had responded—right there in church, loud enough for the whole congregation to hear—that the deacon's pronouncement was "bullshit." The result was that I stayed for the rest of that service and was allowed to come back the next week. My grandparents never spoke to that deacon again, and now rarely even spoke to Father Pace. But they were Catholic, and there was no other Catholic church in town, so they still took out their money when the collection basket came around, and still showed up for ten o'clock Mass.

A few minutes after ten, Father Pace stepped up and adjusted the microphone. He was a tall, thin man, with dark hair that sprouted from the backs of his hands and thick eyebrows that looked like living creatures growing out of his forehead. He didn't smile much, not even during the meet-and-greet session after the service was over, and he was not—if this is any measure of how people thought of him, or didn't—the subject of conjecture or gossip. His sermons were usually long and dry, too abstract to hold my attention; I'd look around and be relieved to see the other kids falling asleep or poking the ground for insects.

That afternoon, though, after the usual preliminaries and a short reference to the Bible, he looked out at the audience as if trying to make contact with everyone in the park.

"Sons and daughters, brothers and sisters," he began, "we are living in a time of extraordinary change— a time when the proper roles of men and women are being upended, a time when communism is spreading unchecked, a time when the American way of life is being threatened by enemies both inside and outside of our borders. We are living in a time, my friends, when faith itself is under siege. Sometimes change is difficult, sometimes it is necessary, and sometimes it's just plain wrong."

People shifted in their seats, unsure where he was going but mildly interested.

"And the latest travesty is occurring as we speak. Our Irish brethren in Boston have had a storm set loose upon them by the Godless decrees of judges and politicians."

Now, the shifting and whispers stopped and the entire crowd was paying attention. In the distance, I could hear the sounds of traffic, but nothing—not even the squirrels—was making any noise in the park.

"Every evening on the news," Father Pace continued, "we see horrific scenes of Catholic children being forcibly bused to schools in the darkest corners of the city. We see white neighborhoods being infiltrated by whole busloads of outside forces."

I sat up straighter now myself. I knew what he was talking about—I too had watched the images of busing in Boston, the protests, the angry and violent crowds. But what Father Pace was saying was at odds with what I had observed. Is this really how he saw things? Did other people think this, too?

"What's at stake for these Irish people, these good Catholics," he went on, "is more than just a question of whether their children can attend their local schools. What's at stake is their ability to *define their own lives*."

He leaned into the microphone and his voice boomed across the park. "No one but *God* should determine how we lead our lives. We have every right to decide who we live among, who we worship with, and how we educate our children. People were made differently for a reason—*a reason!* Those judges and politicians in Boston, those heavy-handed liberals, have forgotten that simple truth. *And now we're facing a similar threat right here in Deerhorn!*"

He stood up straight and scanned the crowd, his large hands gripping either side of the lectern. Now everyone was rapt, including the children.

I couldn't believe what he was saying. I couldn't believe what was coming from his mouth. While Father Pace would occasionally comment on current events, from the PCP overdose of the pharmacist's oldest son, to the young women who were taking advantage of the sinful new law allowing the murder of unborn babies, to the robbery scandal involving the fire department, to the happy return or sad loss of soldiers who'd fought in Vietnam, this seemed different, like he was challenging his entire congregation. And he kept on going.

"In Boston, the Catholic parishes are accepting families whose children need a refuge from the public schools. We believe this is a generous and appropriate response. Some of you have already moved your children to our school, and I want you to know that more of you are welcome. And likewise, I'm calling upon our good Catholic doctors in town to take on a few more patients, so that people won't have to go to that Godless clinic."

He lowered his head now, his eyes nearly closed, and spoke in a firm, soft voice. "We may not be able to control the circumstance that has been thrust upon us, but we *can* control our response to it. None of you has to sit there and take it."

And he went on to invite people to approach him after Mass if they wanted to enroll their children in the Catholic school. Then he began his regular sermon. It didn't seem, though, that anyone paid very close attention. The crowd was abuzz with his unexpected pronouncement and no one could stay still.

I couldn't believe that Father Pace had talked about the Garretts. Without ever mentioning them by name, without even speaking the words Negro or black or teacher or nurse, he'd made his position—and the position of the church—very clear. I didn't understand how he could do this—how he could reconcile his usual words of doing right in the eyes of God with the stance he now condoned. But considering his church's reaction to my parents and me, I suppose I shouldn't really have been surprised.

Maybe if I'd been older, I might have had a better sense of how unsettled people were by all the changes going on in the country. Maybe I might have understood how what was happening in Boston was having effects that rippled all the way to Deerhorn. But the nightly images I saw on the news confused me more than anything. The sight of buses full of black children being pelted with rocks, of white children walking nervously through hallways full of black faces, of police in riot gear being taunted by white youths with baseball bats and hockey sticks, of the Irish city councilwoman speaking about the coming race war, felt as far away to me as the images of the disgraced president stepping off his plane, of the bombings in Cambodia. I did not understand what all the fuss was about. I couldn't comprehend why people were so upset, or what exactly they believed was at stake. It seemed strange to me even then, when I was a child, and I'm not sure that my perception would have been any different if I'd been twelve or seventeen instead of nine. What I might have had with age, though, was a greater appreciation for the seriousness of people's reactions. What I might have had with age was a healthier sense of fear regarding what was possible.

Later that afternoon, I ran into the Garretts. I'd been doing nothing in particular, watching the Packers game so I could be in the same room as my grandfather, when my grandmother asked me to go to the market to buy some milk and ice cream. The main strip of town, which included Jimmy's Coffee Shop and Earl Watson's gun store, was about six blocks away. The market, a small, five-aisle store that was the town's main source of gro-

ceries, was at the near end of Buffalo Street, across from
what used to be the Sears building and was now some
kind of storage place for discarded old appliances.

I liked to go to the market, or maybe I just liked how
important I felt when I was running an errand for my
grandmother, and there was one cashier, a dyed red-
head named Gloria, who always gave me candy. That
day, because I could handle the load with one bag, I took
my bike up to the store. I skipped inside and passed the
end displays of potato chips and Pabst, and as I turned
the corner into the freezer aisle, I almost ran right into
them—Mr. Garrett and the woman who must have been
his wife, a thin, dark-skinned woman of about his age.
He was leaning on the shopping cart while she opened
the freezer door and pulled out a carton of strawberry ice
cream. They were talking easily, unguarded, and when
Mrs. Garrett turned back from the freezer I saw how she
looked at him, eyes showing a pleasure I wasn't used
to seeing expressed between married people. She had
strong, high cheekbones and slightly hollowed cheeks
that were so polished and smooth they might have been
carved of stone. There was something in her bearing and
the set of her shoulders that made her look regal, even
there in the freezer aisle. She was wearing a neat blue
dress and carrying a handbag, as if they'd just come from
church. (And now I wonder—*had* they been at church?
Did they drive up to Wausau or all the way to Steven's
Point to find a community of other black congregants?
Because they couldn't have worshipped in Deerhorn, of
course. No local church would have had them.)

I stood and watched them as he poked her like a
teenage boy trying to get a girl's attention—and it was

hard to believe that these two people, this playful man and his dignified wife, had thrown the town into such frenzy. I didn't think they would notice me—I was so used to people ignoring me that I'd almost come to believe I was invisible—but as Mrs. Garrett turned back toward the freezer, she stopped in mid-movement.

"What?" her husband asked.

She nodded in my direction and he turned. When he saw me, his face broke into a smile.

"That's just Michelle," he said to his wife, and I was both scared and thrilled to realize he knew who I was.

"Oh, right," his wife said, and the guardedness that had started to come into her manner was gone again, and she smiled too.

"Hello, Michelle," he said gently, in a tone of voice he might use to coax a cat out from under a bed. He was looking right at me—they both were—and suddenly I felt exposed, painfully aware that there was no corner I could easily slip around, no crowd of people into which I could blend. I knew I should answer but all I could manage was a nod and half a smile.

"Are you here with your family?" Mrs. Garrett asked. Her tone was friendly, but there was something about her that made me want to stand up straighter, a self-assurance I wasn't used to seeing in a woman. "What are you looking for?"

I couldn't get anything out of my mouth—it was like the muscles in my throat had cramped up—so I gestured toward the ice cream. I took a few steps forward, opened the freezer door, and pulled out a frost-covered carton. It was strawberry, just like theirs.

"That's good stuff," Mr. Garrett said. "My wife and

I got some, too. Well, I'll see you at school tomorrow, Michelle. You have a good day, now."

I looked from them to the carton of ice cream and back again, wanting to speak, unsure of what to say. But finally I got so nervous that I just waved goodbye. Then I ran past them down the aisle, feeling their eyes still on me, and hurried to the counter to pay. My heart was beating a hundred miles an hour as I handed over the money and waited for Gloria to bag my item. After receiving my usual Peppermint Pattie, I biked home as fast as I could. I was so flustered that it wasn't until I mounted the stairs that I realized I'd forgotten the milk. But this I could handle—at the end of the block was the Cloverdale Dairy, and so I walked up and bought half a gallon.

After I'd given my grandmother the ice cream and milk, I took the dog up to the attic, to my father's old room, and thought about what had happened. I'd seen the Garretts, both of them. And they'd been nice to me. And they'd excused or overlooked my inability to speak, my awkwardness in their presence. I felt like I'd been let in on a secret, and I knew instinctively that I couldn't tell my grandparents about it, or anyone at school. But something important had happened; I felt like part of something. For the next hour and a half, before my grandmother called up for supper, I sat there smiling, thinking about my chance meeting in the store, holding it, turning it over like a jewel.

No one paid much attention when the following item appeared in the paper two days later:

Free Satellite Clinic to Open;
Will Serve Outlying Areas

As part of its planned expansion, the Deerhorn/Central Wisconsin Clinic will provide free care once a week at a satellite location serving the outlying areas of Deerhorn, a clinic official said today. The clinic will be open on Wednesdays, and will operate out of the old Carver Package Store building that is currently managed by Henderson Realty. "We want to be able to serve people who don't normally come into town for medical care," said Dr. Del Gordon, the clinic's chief administrator. "There are a lot of people out there on the old farms and in the backwoods who never see a doctor." Free services will be provided by licensed medical staff and students in the clinic's new nursing program, and will include immunizations, tuberculosis tests, mammograms, and physicals. The Deerhorn Central Clinic will be absorbing all costs of renovating the building, Dr. Gordon said. "We want to extend our appreciation to the town of Deerhorn and both our old and new staff for helping turn our clinic into the medical jewel of Central Wisconsin." The satellite clinic will be open from 8 a.m. to 7 p.m., every Wednesday, at 342 Besemer Road, just off of Route 5.

Deerhorn was not a generous place. Almost everyone in the town had once been poor, or had at least struggled hard to get by. Every family had stories of crops that didn't flourish, businesses that folded, farms that closed up as country people moved into town; and the Depression was still so fresh in the memories of my grandparents and their friends that it might have occurred within the last decade. Years before, a local boy—the son of a poor farmer, a veteran—had been elected to the House of Representatives, and had eventually become one of the most conservative members of Congress. People in town believed that if *they* had made it, if *they* had struggled and fought successfully to keep their heads above water, then everybody else could too. The people I had seen the previous week, living in tin shacks and cobbled together hand-me-down trailers, did not evoke their sympathy or sorrow. And so no one seemed to care that those same people would now have access to medical care. An institution whose presence the townsfolk resented was helping a set of people they chose not to see.

Those next few days at school, it seemed like the controversy around Mr. Garrett had settled down, or at least had leveled off. The number of students who came to his class held steady at ten or eleven. From what I could gather, no one from the school called the other students' parents to demand that they return; some of them had enrolled in the Catholic school. There had been talk that the two fifth grade classes might be combined, putting Mr. Garrett out of a job, but nothing came of it. Things were quiet. Miss Anderson had settled into a kind of tense determination, and we all started to learn again, at least a little. Monday, Tuesday, Wednesday rolled by, and I was almost lulled into believing that the school was accepting Mr. Garrett and that everything would be all right.

Then on Wednesday afternoon the telephone rang, just as we were sitting down for supper. My grandfather answered it and his expression grew darker. His fingers curled into a fist, which he placed on the desk.

"All right," he said into the phone. "Come over after supper and we'll get our heads together. Call Jim and Earl too."

He hung up and sat at the table in front of his empty plate. My grandmother, who'd been getting ready to bring in the food, looked at him expectantly.

"That clinic out there for the country people," he said. "That nigger nurse was out there today."

We looked at him, waiting for more.

"That *nurse*," he repeated, looking up at us now. "She gave people shots. She was giving them physicals. *She laid her hands on our children*." And as he said this he cringed, physically withdrawing from his words, as if from the actual hands he found so offensive.

I looked at my grandmother and saw her eyes open wide. "She shouldn't have gone out there," she said, sounding more surprised than anything, as if one of her friends had played out of turn in bridge. "They should have *told* us she was going to be working there."

"Those people had no warning," my grandfather said. "No warning at all. It just got sprung on them." He got up from his chair and walked out to the patio, letting the screen door slam shut behind him. My grandmother looked from the door to the table back into the kitchen, but it was clear we weren't eating just then. After a moment or two, she went into the kitchen and I walked over to the patio door. I opened it gingerly and peeked my head around the corner. My grandfather was sitting on the old worn couch they'd dragged out there, staring absently across the street at the Miller children as they climbed their apple tree in the fading light. He didn't speak or move when the door creaked open, so I stepped out and sat down beside him. It was mid-October and cool enough for sweaters, although neither of us had one on. Normally it would have been dark by now, but because of the gas shortage, daylight savings was in effect all year so there was still a bit of light. I waited for him to take my hand with his rough, callused fingers, but he didn't move; he just stared out the window.

"Junie Miller lets those kids run wild," he said, and I looked across the street. The two oldest ones, Jarrett and Karen, were up in branches fifteen feet off the ground; they were eight and ten, old enough to be climbing trees. But the baby John, who was only three, was trying to get up too, his little arms reaching futilely for the lowest branch.

"They're okay," I said, by which I meant that at least they—unlike so many other children in the neighborhood—generally left me alone.

"Jim Miller's gone so damn much," my grandfather continued. "And when he *is* here, all he does is drink beer."

Jim Miller was a long-distance truck driver, and it wasn't unusual for him to be on the road for two or three weeks at a time. I always knew he was in town because the big red cab of his truck would be parked in the Millers' front yard, dwarfing their garage. When I thought of his loud voice, though, laughing with the kids, the way he threw them over his shoulder and made them squeal with delight; when I thought how he was home at least part of the time, those kids seemed pretty lucky to me.

"Grandpa," I said now, "what's wrong with the nurse working at the clinic?"

He sighed and patted my hand and kept looking out

the window. "You wouldn't understand yet, Mike," he said. "Some things you've got to grow up to understand. But people don't like to mix with people different from them. They like to be with their own kind."

I understood what he was saying about the Garretts, about himself. But what exactly was my kind?

I couldn't ask him, though, because he was still staring out the window, and I knew it wasn't the Millers he was thinking about. Five or six times in the year I'd lived in Deerhorn, there had been tornado warnings on TV. Each time, my grandfather planted himself out on the porch, looking angrily out at the horizon as if daring the storm to approach. I usually sat with him through these hours-long vigils, despite my grandmother's pleas that we come inside and take shelter in the cellar. He would tell her to stop worrying, it would be all right, and then turn to me and wink and say, "Women." Then we'd sit together quietly and watch the sky. Twice, we actually saw the funnel-shaped cloud twisting across the horizon, hesitating, teasing, as if considering all the houses and trees on the ground before deciding which ones to touch down upon. But even when one funnel got so close that it ripped out a stand of trees two blocks away from us; even when we were looking at the storm eye-to-eye; even when I got so scared I covered my head with my arms and burrowed into his side, my grandfather would not retreat. He stood firm and stared the tornado down. He would not let it come any closer.

And that was what he was like that night, the night we found out about Mrs. Garrett and the clinic. He was looking out the window, staring straight into the face of the storm, and there was no way he was about to back down. The difference this time, though, was that he wasn't squaring off against an act of nature. The thing he was trying to hold at bay wasn't dangerous at all. I wondered if he had sat on the porch like this when he'd heard about my mother; whether he'd steeled himself against my parents' union. And I wondered if *he* was the reason my mother hadn't liked to visit; whether his influence, his legacy, were also why she couldn't stay with my father, or with me.

I sat outside with my grandfather for a good half an hour before the first of his friends arrived. It was Jim Riesling, who said, "This isn't an emergency, Charlie. We don't really need to do anything."

And my grandfather, as he often did when someone said something he didn't like, simply acted as if he hadn't heard him. In the next few minutes Earl Watson appeared, too. Ray Davis arrived a bit later, and eventually Uncle Pete. My grandmother made me eat quickly in the kitchen and then shooed me into my room, where try as I might, I could not make out the conversation. But the men stayed up late, talking around the dining room table, huddled together against the gathering storm. They didn't seem to realize that the danger was not *out there*, on the other side of the window. They didn't realize that the storm was right there in the room, contained in their own minds and hearts.

FIVE

Although no one would ever know it if they looked at me now, I was raised to live in the country. Now I have an apartment in a fashionable section of Los Angeles, close to restaurants and museums and nightclubs. Now I go to grocery stores to purchase my produce, and take my car into a shop for even simple repairs. The people here in L.A. would never believe what I was doing as a child, while they were going to the beach and playing soccer. By the age of eight, I knew how to shoot a gun. I could drive my grandparents' Pontiac, milk a cow, even operate a tractor if I had to, which I learned to do out on the old family farm still owned by my grandmother's brother. I knew back pain from bending over in my grandparents' garden, picking vegetables for dinner and canning. I'd helped scale fish, gut squirrels and ducks, string deer up by their feet in the garage. And while I never actually killed the game I ate and helped prepare, I'd been there when it was shot, with Charlie in the wild, stalking silently through the fields at dawn.

Charlie took me hunting with him and Uncle Pete over the strenuous objection of my grandmother. I don't know whether she disapproved because of my gender, my age, or fear for my safety, but Charlie prevailed, as he always did. I still remember being shaken awake at four

a.m., my grandfather already in his camouflage and hunting cap. If the game was pheasant, grouse, or ducks, the
hat he wore was army green. Later in the season, when
it was deer, he changed to fluorescent orange. I put on
a smaller version of his hunting outfit, left over from my
father's childhood. While I was getting ready, Charlie
gathered his ammunition and supplies. He'd take out
the shotguns—his Remington Wingmaster and my Ithaca
66—and load them into the back of the car. He'd pack
the food—roast beef sandwiches my grandmother had
made the night before, canteens of water, a thermos full
of coffee. Then we'd put Brett in the car and back down
the driveway, pick up Uncle Pete—who often slept in
the car—and drive through the pitch-black night, the
dog whining with excitement until we'd reached our
starting point for that week, twenty, thirty miles into
the country. If we were hunting for birds, we'd go to one
of the marshy areas east of town. For deer, we would
work our way deep into the woods, although not to
the makeshift deer stand that Charlie and his friends
had built; he would never take me to a place where
we might run into other, less careful hunters. We'd
walk quickly but deliberately through the cold fall air,
me taking two or three steps for every one of Charlie's.
The outfit I wore was more than twenty years old, but it
felt unused because my father had only worn it once or
twice. (It was bulky and utilitarian, made for function
instead of looks—not like the form-fitting camouflage
tops and girlish orange caps I see on young female hunters now, in California.) My father hated hunting—the
blood and grit, the suffering of the animals, even the
cold, dark mornings—and Charlie believed that part

of the problem with Stewart, his failure to turn into a proper LeBeau, was that he hadn't started hunting soon enough. By the time Stewart first went out into the woods, he was ten or eleven years old—and by then, he'd already been influenced by Helen and her womanly, book-reading ways.

I knew already that there was something very manly in holding a gun, in tracking and killing other living creatures. There was an exhilaration, a palpable tightening of the air, as the dog flushed pheasants, grouse, or ducks out of the tall grass, as the men tensed and fired their weapons. It was a heightened sense of excitement, the promise of possession and dominance, that I would have linked, had I been older, with the sexual. These men were never more alive than when they were just about to kill. When they shot something—a pheasant, a duck, or especially a deer; when they watched it struggle and die, there was no doubting their vitality or power. It was men at their purest, most primal state, the state of their highest fulfillment. Later, when they smiled into cameras with a string of captured birds, or stood together holding a buck, they were civilized again. They had assembled themselves for public consumption and the wilderness was gone from their eyes. But they loved those kinds of photographs, their conquest complete, and always brought a camera when they hunted. In so many of the old pictures I have of my grandfather, he's holding something dead.

But there was more to those men than violence. They also had a warmth and openness that I never felt from women. In my family, it was the men who were the nurturers. They were the ones—my father included—

who grinned widely when I did something funny, who bounced me on their knees, who ruffled my hair in affection. They were the ones who threw their arms around me and wrapped me up in bear hugs. It was Charlie and Pete who got angry when something happened to me at school; who held my hand when I was scared; who always seemed to welcome my presence. The women—my grandmother, my great-aunt Bertha, and even my mother, from what I remember—were more measured in their affections. Their nervousness, judgment, and frequent short scoldings always made me feel disapproved of, unfitting. They never touched me in a way that wasn't corrective. I don't know if they were frustrated with their own circumscribed lives, but I do know they couldn't imagine any other way of being. To my grandmother and great-aunt, the liberated women of the big cities, who worked corporate jobs or used child care or marched to demand equal rights, were as foreign and unknowable as the bowing, kimonoed women of Japan. They tried to bend and shape me—to fit the town, and to fit their image of what a young woman should do, which included boring things like cooking and sewing. But the men just let me be, and even their mundane tasks—like painting the house, or mowing the lawn—were more appealing to me, more active and exciting. To me, being a woman meant being limited, defined, and always stuck inside. Being a man meant having freedom, and I wanted that freedom. My grandfather was willing to give it to me. And even though he was disappointed in his own son and disapproving of his daughter-in-law, I knew that he was smitten with his grandchild. In several of the pictures I have from the time I lived in Deerhorn, my grandmother is looking into the camera. My grandfather is looking at me.

Charlie taught me how to really see and feel the world around me; there was so much I noticed and still notice because he revealed it. I remember, for instance, when I went out walking with Brett a few days after my grandfather and I sat out on the porch. A new letter had arrived that afternoon from my father, from Springfield, and he said he was coming home for Thanksgiving. He didn't say how long he was staying, or if he was taking me back with him. But he was coming. My father was coming. And just the thought that he was on his way, especially now, when everything in school and in town was feeling so tense and strange, had filled me with such anticipation and joy that I couldn't keep still.

I needed to move, to be free. So I rode out to the country and dumped the bike and walked with Brett through the woods. It was late October now, and each tree stood unembellished and bare with its leaves on the ground beneath it, like a woman who'd just stepped out of a colorful dress. We came around a stand of trees and entered a meadow with a small, dark pond in the middle. Right at the place where the land met the water was a small flock of Canada Geese. There were maybe thirty or forty of them, some in the water, some on land, sitting and resting or walking around, picking seeds and insects out of the grass.

Since the day we had seen the flock flying over the baseball field, I had read up on Canada Geese in the old encyclopedia my father had left in his attic room. I knew by now that the flocks not only traveled to the same place each year, but that they rested at the same spots along the way, like a family on a regular driving trip that always stops at familiar restaurants. And I also knew that, like the human family, the geese stopped more often when they were traveling with young ones, who couldn't go for such long distances—sometimes six hundred miles a day—without more frequent breaks. Although apparently their noise and droppings made them a nuisance to some people, others scattered seeds on their land to attract them. I don't know if that's what was happening here, but these geese seemed plump and contented. As Brett and I drew nearer, the dozen or so birds that were still on the land waddled quickly, but without much concern, down into the water. The whole flock moved away from the edge of the shore and into the middle of the pond. This was because we were there—to avoid us—and yet the birds didn't even bother to glance our way. They looked haughtily off in the other direction, as if our rudeness didn't warrant acknowledgment.

I stopped to admire them as they swam. They were beautiful birds. They had sleek black heads and white markings that looked like scarves, coming all the way up to their cheeks. Their long, graceful necks spread gradually into their powerful gray-feathered bodies. Even Brett seemed to understand that they were something special, because he, like my grandfather, declined to hunt them. Rather than sprinting through the grass to flush them, as he would have with pheasants and ducks, he simply stood and watched. He looked up at me occasionally to take measure of what I was thinking, and then turned back to consider the geese, working the jowls that nature made soft to carry birds without damaging their flesh. My grandfather had said that the parents migrated with their offspring, but by this time of year, I couldn't tell which was which. They appeared identical, interdependent, no individual need usurping the whole.

But as majestic as they looked in the pond and on land, it couldn't compare to what they looked like in the air. Their beautiful, shifting patterns, their throaty calls, were always new, and always exhilarating. Even now, when I see a flock of Canada Geese, I stop whatever I'm doing to admire them. They represent fall to me—the change, the loss, the arrival of a starker beauty. When they fly, a part of me flies with them.

School ended early the following Monday and we were all let out at lunchtime. I waited to leave Miss Anderson's class until the first rush of kids was gone, so that the hallway would not be so crowded. As I made my way toward my locker, I saw Mr. Garrett, striding down the hall and whistling as if he didn't have a care in the world. He was headed toward the teachers' lounge with a brown paper bag in his hand, shoulders high, eyes looking straight ahead. As he came closer, I was afraid he would talk to me—something that would surely be noted by the other lingerers in the hallway—but the feeling was immediately followed, like a gunshot and its echo, by shame. We locked eyes as he approached and the tune he was whistling sailed up briefly into a higher octave. But then, like a coconspirator who knew to keep his partner safe, he winked and passed by without saying a word.

I went home and had lunch with my grandmother. She made sandwiches with the ham that was left over from the night before, and I snuck pieces to Brett whenever she wasn't looking.

When I was halfway done she went back to her laundry, hanging linens and clothes on the clothesline that stretched across the yard, taking advantage of the Indian summer. After I finished eating I ventured out to help her. But then she went back inside to get more clothespins, and I heard her yell, "Brett!"

When I got there, Brett was licking his chops and the bottoms of his ears were coated in something greasy. I didn't need to be told what had happened: he'd stolen a stick of butter off of the counter and had eaten the whole thing, and he was looking very pleased about it.

"Darn dog!" my grandmother yelled. "Michelle, you need to keep him under control!" So I shut him in my bedroom—he was so happy with himself that he didn't even mind the confinement—and then left to avoid further scolding. Because I couldn't think of anything better to do, I walked uptown to look for my grandfather. I passed the grocery store where I'd seen the Garretts a few days earlier, crossed the railroad tracks that divided the near end of Buffalo Street from the main strip, and wandered into Jimmy's Coffee Shop.

I stood still for a moment just inside the front door. Halfway down the long counter a lone man sat reading the paper, and the two waitresses chatted loudly by the register. In back, I could hear the clanging of dishes being washed from the lunchtime rush. Other than the man at the counter, Charlie and his friends were the only customers. They were sitting in the big corner booth that had seats wrapped around three sides of the table.

Charlie was in his usual corner spot, with Earl Watson and Uncle Pete on either side of him. Next to Earl was John Berger, a tall, rangy man who owned the largest construction company in the area. A young man was with them too, a thin fellow in his early twenties, who appeared to be the only one eating. Except for him, all the men were leaning forward, looking serious. But when I approached the table, my grandfather brightened visibly. "Hey there, Mikey," he said. "No school today?"

I shook my head and managed to say that the teachers had a meeting. Then I stood in front of the table, not knowing what to do—there was no clear path to my grandfather and Earl and John Berger weren't moving. Charlie hit Uncle Pete on the shoulder, who hit the young man, and they both piled out of the booth to let me scoot across the orange vinyl seat and sit beside my grandfather. He asked if I wanted a Coke, which I did; Lorraine, the middle-aged waitress, brought one over. The men resumed drinking coffee, but they seemed a bit restrained, not calm and casual as they usually did when they sat around this table.

And then it occurred to me that they'd been talking about the Garretts. In fact, this was probably where they talked about them most, their social gathering transformed into a kind of meeting. I had interrupted their discussion, and they were having trouble shifting to easier topics. Finally, though, my grandfather cleared his throat and gestured toward the new young man.

"This here's John's oldest boy, T.J.," he said. "He did a couple of tours in 'Nam, and now he's moving back home from Milwaukee." He put his hand on my shoulder. "And this here is Mike, my only grandchild." The young man looked up from his sandwich and nodded, but didn't say a word. Despite the crew cut and the left-over military stiffness, he was unshaven and a bit bleary-eyed. I remembered what I'd heard my grandparents say about John Berger's oldest son—he also had a thirteen-year-old son named Cody, as well as a nine-year-old daughter, Harriet. What they'd said was that T.J. had always been a bit wild, which had probably served him well in Vietnam. As a teenager, he'd gotten drunk and unruly enough that Ray Davis's men had apparently had to escort him home on several unrecorded occasions. But he had straightened out, moved to Milwaukee for a while, and enlisted in the army, and now he had finally come home.

"He could've stayed in the big city," said Earl now. "But the city couldn't offer you nothing, son, that you couldn't get here in Deerhorn, ain't that right?"

"Nothing but a whole lot of trouble," said T.J., taking a gulp of his Coke. Although he was on the skinny side, he had a certain physical ease I've always associated with men who use their bodies to work. And my impression was confirmed when John cleared his throat and said, "He's going to come and work with me until he gets himself settled. He's got a girl, you know, and they're having a baby."

There was a general murmur of approval and T.J. grinned widely, as if he'd accomplished something un-usual. "That's good, that's good," said Earl. "There's nothing like being a father. It'll change you, son. Put everything in your life in the right place." There was a friendliness to his manner that I'd never seen before, a warmth he must have reserved for those he approved of. He took a sip of his coffee and asked, "So how was Vietnam? I'll bet you burned up in those swamps. Did you kill yourself a whole bunch of gooks?"

I looked up at the men's faces, surprised, but there was no reaction except for T.J.'s chuckle. "That was *your* war, Mr. Watson. What we had was Viet Cong. And yeah," he smiled. "I did kill me a bunch of 'em." And here I thought—although I couldn't be sure—that he looked for a second at me.

"My years in the army were the best years of my life," Earl said. "You were surrounded by good men, doing the country's work, and you always knew exactly where you stood."

"It's *still* good, I guess," said T.J., scratching his neck, "but things have changed since your time. Now, there's no telling who you might get thrown in with. I mean, there was a lot of good country boys, but we had some sissy city boys, too. And a whole lot of niggers and spics."

Again I looked for a reaction and again there was none. The men all nodded and shook their heads.

"They mix everyone up now, I guess," his father said. "Throw the coloreds right in with the white men."

"That happened in Korea, too," Earl said. "But it's gotten worse now, what with the army needing recruits, and all this garbage in the last few years about niggers and their rights. People don't understand. You give a nigger a gun and let him fight, and pretty soon he starts to thinking he's as good as a white man."

Then Uncle Pete turned toward the window and said, "Funny you should say that. Look."

We all followed where his finger was pointing and saw an older man walk by the coffee shop, holding a

leash in his hand. It was Darius Gordon, the retired lawyer, farmer, and unofficial town historian who'd been
a baseball hero when my grandfather was a boy. But I
knew immediately why his appearance sparked Uncle
Pete's interest, and it wasn't because of his youthful he-
roics or his knowledge of the town. It was because his
middle son, Del—Dr. Del Gordon—was chief administrator of the Deerhorn Central Clinic.

T.J. Berger sprang up with more speed and force than
I would have guessed his thin body could muster. His
father stood up too, and then Earl, and my grandfather
and Uncle Pete. They all walked to the door quickly and
I followed closely behind; by the time I was outside, Earl
had called Gordon's name. The old man turned around
and his dog turned too, a beautiful gray-ticked English
setter. When the dog saw all the people, she drew herself up and growled softly. Gordon quieted her with a
quick tug on her leash and a short, low, "Hup!"—and
the dog licked her nose and sat down.

"Hello, Earl," he said. "What can I do for you?" Now
that all the men were standing together, I saw that Mr.
Gordon was the tallest. He must have been eighty or
eighty-five, but with his thick head of gray hair and upright posture, he looked and moved like a much younger
man. He still hunted and fished, and since his wife had
died, he spent his summers in a cabin next to Cortland
Lake with its abundant supply of bluegill and crappies.
When he reached up, quick, to save his hat from a gust
of wind, you could still see the grace and fluidity that
had made him, for four years, the second baseman for
the Cincinnati Reds.

Now that Mr. Gordon was facing him, Earl seemed

to hesitate. For years Mr. Gordon had been the only lawyer in town and that afforded him a certain standing, which was multiplied because he still farmed his own land and had helped other families hold onto their farms, too. He was educated, and a baseball hero, but he had no airs, and that combination of qualities earned all the town's respect.

Even my grandfather seemed different as he approached his old idol. He faced Mr. Gordon directly but stood back on his heels, allowing the older man his due space. "Hello, Darius," he said evenly.

"Hello, Charlie. What's going on, fellas?"

Charlie looked a little uncertain now, as if it had taken all of his bravery just to get him outside. He waited for an especially loud car to pass before saying, "Well, everyone's stirred up about that teacher, you know."

"That's right," said Mr. Gordon, looking at me. "Is he teaching your class? No, I suppose you're too young for fifth grade."

It was so unusual for me to be addressed by an adult that I looked behind me to see if someone else was there. I didn't answer, but Mr. Gordon didn't notice. My grandfather, though, put his hand on my shoulder protectively. "He's not, but she's seen him. Ain't that right, Mikey?"

I nodded.

"Well, his wife works over at the clinic," Mr. Gordon said, as if we didn't already know; as if word had not already traveled, like a virulent strain of the flu, all over town and into the country.

"Yeah, that's what we wanted to talk to you about," said Earl. He did not seem particularly affected by the cold, nor by the status of the man he was speaking to. "We were just in Jimmy's having our coffee, and John, he says, 'I wonder what old Darius thinks about that nigger nurse working in his son's clinic?' And I says, 'I don't know, John, let's ask him.' And then we look out the window and there you are."

Mr. Gordon held his coat shut and choked up on the leash. "I don't think *anything* about it."

"Well, why'd he let her in there?" asked Earl, leaning forward, cheeks red from the biting air. "And why's she out at the country satellite? Just 'cos folks are poor doesn't mean that any damn thing should be let loose on 'em."

"She's a top-rate nurse," said Mr. Gordon. "Del worked with her down in Chicago. When he took over the clinic, with the expansion and the nursing school and all, he wanted to bring in good staff."

"You mean he *brought* her?" Uncle Pete asked. "On *purpose*?"

"Yeah, he did. So what?"

"Well," Earl said, "we just think he should have known better."

Mr. Gordon turned his head slowly and looked Earl in the face. "There's gonna be a *lot* of new people coming into town, Earl. You might as well get used to it."

Listening to this exchange, I remembered what I had heard about Del Gordon. He'd spent most of his adult life outside of Deerhorn, going to college in Madison and medical school in Chicago. He'd been a military doctor during the war in Korea, and then had lived in Chicago until recently. Charlie and his friends must have thought about that too, because now Earl said, "See, this is what happens when people leave Deerhorn. Folks come back here confused."

"My boy," said John Berger, putting his hands on his hips, "didn't come back here with no mixed-up notions."

Mr. Gordon raised his eyebrows. He was a gentle man, but now he had been pushed, and it was clear he did not appreciate it. "Well, I wouldn't hold up *your* boy as a model."

T.J. Berger stepped forward, fists clenched, as if he'd forgotten that the man who'd just insulted him was old enough to be his grandfather. His father, glaring at Mr. Gordon, held him back.

"He's just saying," Charlie put forth, trying to calm the situation, "we'd of thought you taught him different than that."

Mr. Gordon sighed. "Look. I'm not saying I would've done the same thing. But he's a grown man, Charlie. What do you want me to do? I stopped taking him over my knee fifty years ago." He paused. "And besides." Here he looked meaningfully at Charlie. "*You* know how hard it is to keep hold of your kids."

Something rippled across Charlie's face and his body grew tense; I could feel it through his hand on my shoulder. He was in conflict; I knew that, everyone must have known that. Because as much as he hated the way my father lived, as much as he disapproved of my mother, how could he totally reject their union when it had produced me, whom he loved? Still, my presence there was proof of Stewart's choices. I kept waiting for Charlie to stand up for my father. I kept waiting for him to say that his boy was coming back, that he was on his way home, but he didn't.

118 🌟 Nina Revoyr

"Well, you better let Del know," said Earl, "that folks in town are real unhappy with what's going on up there. *Real* unhappy. Especially now that she's going out to the country and treating white people." He said "treating" as if it meant injecting them with poison. "You know what it's like when folks get upset around here. There's no telling what might happen."

Mr. Gordon heard the threat there, and he lifted his chin, looking down the length of his nose. "I'm not saying I would have done the same thing," he repeated. "But the clinic's going to bring a lot of good to this town. It's going to help business, it's going to help construction, it's going to create jobs. My son is trying to bring in the best people he can. And I believe that he knows what he's doing."

Earl walked up so close I thought he might touch him. "You better shut that coat tighter, Darius. I think the cold's affecting your head. Or maybe you're just getting senile."

"Get out of my face, Watson," said Mr. Gordon, and I knew that despite his age he would not be afraid to fight. "Get out of here and go do something useful with your time."

That night, we were awakened by a phone call. I didn't know what the sound was at first, and I was so asleep it was like I was hearing it underwater. I only began to surface when I heard the creaking of my grandparents' door, the heavy padded footsteps of my grandfather. He left the door open between the hallway and the dining room, so I heard him clear his throat, pick up the receiver, and say, "Hello?"

I figured it was Pete or Earl, both of whom went out drinking and occasionally came home late, or Ray, who was sometimes on duty. But whatever they were calling about—probably a new development at the clinic or at the school—Charlie wouldn't be happy about being awakened. He was quiet for a moment, and then he said, "Do you know what time it is?"

I looked at my clock face, and by the light of the moon, I could see it was 12:27. I waited for him to say that whoever it was, Pete or Earl or Ray, should call him back later, or that he'd see him in the morning at the coffee shop. But what he said was, "She's asleep. I'm not going to wake her up."

My eyes flew open and I sat up in my bed. Charlie was quiet, and when he spoke again, his voice sounded terse. "Well, she's home every night and all weekend. Wanting to hear from you. And then you wait till after midnight to call."

Now I heard a softer set of footsteps, my grandmother's. She came down the hall and went into the dining room, pulling the door closed behind her. I heard her muffled, questioning voice, followed by his sterner, lower one. But I couldn't make out the words anymore, so I crawled out of bed and carefully made my way out of the room. I stepped quietly down the short hallway, stopping in front of the door. It wouldn't close all the way, so I put my ear up to the crack, which wasn't big enough to see through but enabled me to hear.

"Yes, we got it," Charlie was saying. "Yes, the postcard too. It's good you're in one place for a while."

"Ask him when he's coming," my grandmother said, and although I couldn't see Charlie, I could picture him waving her off, gripping the receiver and frowning.

"She's fine," he said. "She's no trouble at all. About twice as big as when you last saw her. She's looking forward to you coming for Thanksgiving, you know. Your mother is too." Then he was quiet for several moments. I heard some shuffling, as if he was walking or turning in place. When he spoke again his voice had a harder edge. "Well, make up your mind, son. Are you coming or not?" Another pause, and now he was breathing so hard I could hear him from where I stood. Then: "You can't keep saying you're doing something if you're not going to do it. You can't keep getting her hopes up. It's not fair."

More quiet, and then his voice so loud I jumped back from the door. "I'm *not* being hard on you! I'm just telling you how it is! It's not just *you* you've got to think about. You've got a *child* here, remember? And she needs you to—"

He stopped abruptly. Then he said, "God*damn*it!" and slammed down the phone, and I knew that my father had hung up on him.

"Charlie, keep your voice down," my grandmother said, but my grandfather didn't answer. He'd hung the phone up with such force that it made the desk shake, and either that, or my grandmother's getting up and moving toward him, caused the door to open a couple of inches. I hid my body behind the wall and peered through the open crack, and saw something I had never seen before—my grandfather sitting down with his head in his hands, fingers working through his thinning hair. My grandmother stood in front of him and gently put her hand on his shoulder. I expected him to shake it off, to tell her to leave him alone. But they both stayed where they were.

I felt strange and confused standing there, seeing them like this, so I slipped back to my room and then back into bed, where Brett was still snoring on his pillow. My father had called—I couldn't even remember the last time he had called—and it was clear that he wanted to talk to me. Sure it was late, and sure he and Charlie had argued. But he wanted to talk to me, wanted to see me, and they had talked about Thanksgiving. He would come after all of this, wouldn't he? I knew he would come. There was no way he would have traveled so far, gotten within striking distance, if he weren't headed back to Wisconsin. If there had been any question about it, maybe the fight had even helped. Maybe Charlie had shamed him into keeping his promise.

The next morning at breakfast, my grandparents were both subdued. They were quieter than usual, not talking about the goings-on in town or their plans for the day, and Charlie hardly touched the eggs and sausage on his plate. I kept waiting for them to say something about the call, about my father, but neither of them mentioned it. They were both especially kind with me, my grandmother letting me put more brown sugar than usual on my oatmeal, my grandfather refilling my milk glass. I thought maybe my grandmother would mention the call after school, when Charlie was gone to the coffee shop, but she didn't. Neither of them brought it up at supper, either. By the next day, I realized that they weren't going to tell me, and I didn't know what that meant. All I knew was that my father might be coming, that I might be seeing him soon. And I was starting to hope that, when he left again, he'd think about taking me with him.

SIX

A few days after my father called, I stopped at my locker to pick up my scarf and gloves and was a little late in getting outside. By the time I made it out to the playground, Missy Calloway was sitting on my bench with Jessica Brown, speaking in her most teacherly voice about the math test we'd just finished taking. I continued past them, beyond the kids playing handball and hopscotch, and headed for my second favorite spot. There was another wooden bench around the corner of the building, toward the front of the school. This square area of concrete, to the right of the swings, did not have any grass or equipment. Because there was nothing to play with it was usually empty; because it faced east, it was sunny through lunchtime. I liked to sit on that bench sometimes, away from everyone else, and lean my back against the wall. This physical distance made me less self-conscious about being alone; at least here, out of sight, I wouldn't get teased for it. But if someone approached me in a way that seemed like trouble, I could just slip around the corner, back in view of the teachers.

On this morning, though, when I turned the corner, my usual space wasn't empty. Several boys—they looked like third and fourth graders—had surrounded another boy I recognized as Billy Coles, one of the children from the trailers in the country. He was sitting on the bench, back pressed flat against the wall, the four other boys standing around him in a semicircle. One of them was leaning over him, finger pointing in his face; Billy kept trying to back up but there was nowhere to go, so he just slipped a little further down the wall. Although Billy wasn't small and didn't seem especially weak, he was often clipped on the head or shoved into the lockers when he made his way down the hall. He had a voice that was always on the edge of a whine, and he often scuffled with other boys. But this confrontation was clearly one he hadn't invited; he looked scared, and his eyes were darting between the other boys' bodies, looking for a path of escape.

Other than me, Billy was the most unpopular child at school. He had dirty-blond hair that was jaggedly cut, with a ponytail half a foot long. His face and clothes were often streaked with dirt, and his shoelaces were always knotted and clumped, where they had broken and been tied back together. His fingernails were always dirty, and his nose often ran; I'd seen teachers recoil physically when they had to touch him. Billy had several equally dirty brothers and sisters whom I sometimes saw in town—at the ice cream parlor, or the movies, or in the grocery store, anywhere businesses were giving something away for free. His mother was a small, silent woman who came to the market to buy groceries with food stamps. His father was tall and skinny, with tied-back hair as long as Billy's; I sometimes saw him picking through garbage cans on the outskirts of town, and we'd both turn our heads away, embarrassed. Billy was not the only child at school from the country trailers—once

a week a group of them were marched into the gym for
a bath—but because he butted heads with the kids from
town, he was the one who drew the most attention. I'd
never particularly liked him myself—he was one of those
children whose own self-pity provokes as much irritation as sympathy—but right then I wanted to say, just
slip to the left. Turn the corner and you'll be safe.

"You stink, Billy," said the boy who was leaning over
him, and I saw that it was Dale Davis, Ray Davis's son.
Dale was a decent, popular boy, and not a known bully.
"Why don't you go take a bath or something?"

"He don't *have* a bathtub, Dale," said another boy,
Walter Kale. "He's got to take 'em here."

"Oh, that's right," Dale said, as if this was news to
him. He was dark-haired and compact like his father,
but there was a self-assurance in his manner—even at
age eight—that his father seemed to lack. "You don't
have a bathtub, or a car, or even a bedroom, ain't that
right? Hell, if it wasn't for the bus that brought you to
school, we wouldn't even know you were out there."

Billy grimaced, as if these words were a physical as-
sault. "Leave me alone, Dale," he said miserably.

"You want me to leave you alone, huh?" said Dale,
standing up straight and crossing his arms. "I'll bet you
didn't tell that nigger nurse to leave you alone."

Now I understood. Dale usually didn't bother the
country children, or any of the outcasts, really. But he'd
been listening to his father. And his father knew that
people had started going to the clinic.

Billy looked up at him now, and his expression neither confirmed nor denied Dale's suspicion. Still, Dale
stepped in close again. "It's true, ain't it? She was out

there, wasn't she? She was out at that clinic they made from the store."

"I *had* to go there!" Billy protested. "I was getting sick to my stomach and my head always hurt. I didn't know the nurse was gonna be a nigger!"

"So now you're a nigger-lover, ain't you, Billy?"

"No."

"She touched you everywhere, didn't she?"

"No!"

"And I'll bet you liked it, too!"

They began pushing him, poking him, trying to get him to react, emboldened by his anguished "Stop it!" and awkward attempts to defend himself. Their focus and excitement intensified with each passing moment, and then all four boys pressed around him so tightly that I could no longer make him out between their bodies. Billy's cries and the excited shouts of the boys who surrounded him were noticed by kids on other parts of the playground, who began to rush over to watch.

Then, out of the corner of my eye, I saw a large adult figure come around the side of the building. It was Mr. Garrett. He must have been on recess duty that day, and he came whipping around the corner faster than I'd known an adult could move. A couple of the newcomers shouted out, "Run!" and the boys who'd cornered Billy all scattered, like flushed birds who fly in no particular direction in their desperate attempt to escape. Even Billy took off, as panicked as all the others.

"Hey!" yelled Mr. Garrett, grabbing this way and that, but the boys slipped through his grasp. "Hey, you're going to hear about this later!" He turned toward the bench where Billy had been, looking at me for a moment, then looking back.

And then, right after our eyes met, we both saw something else—one boy who hadn't gotten away. He was sprawled out on the pavement in front of the bench, and it looked like he'd tripped on the thick link chain that secured it to the playground. He pushed himself up into a sitting position and I saw that it was Kevin Watson. His black hair was falling over into his eyes and he was trying to catch his breath. Kevin pulled down the sleeve of his jacket and looked at his forearm—there was a large red scrape, and seeing this, he promptly began to cry. He had always cried easily—I remembered the tears that followed his scolding by a teacher in the cafeteria the year before—but in this case tears were warranted. It looked bad—a deep scrape maybe four inches long, blood running down his arm, bits of dirt and rock pressed into the open flesh. When Mr. Garrett saw this, he gave up on the other boys and came rushing to Kevin's side. He knelt down on one knee and placed his hand on Kevin's shoulder.

"Are you all right, young man? Let me take a look at that," he said, and the sternness of his voice from a few minutes before was gone, replaced by a tone of concern.

"No!" Kevin cried out, flinching from his touch. "I'm fine! I'm fine! Leave me alone!"

And there was something other than pain in his voice, something more than the irritation that children sometimes feel in the face of unwanted attention. What it sounded like was fear.

Mr. Garrett must have heard it too. He backed off

a bit, but still stayed close. "It's all right, son. I'm only trying to help. Now let me have a look at your arm."

Kevin's face was covered with tears. His left hand was holding his sleeve up and cradling his right elbow, exposing his arm to the air. And when Mr. Garrett inched closer, gently curved his hand around Kevin's elbow and tilted up his forearm, the boy didn't flinch or pull away. The skin around the wound looked dry and cracked, and the flesh of his fingers was sickly white. Mr. Garrett carefully pulled out a few of the pebbles, and then unfolded his handkerchief, pressing it just below the wound to wipe away the running blood.

"It's going to be okay," he said. "It's just a bad scrape. Now let's get you up on your feet and we'll take you inside."

Kevin nodded. He wasn't looking at Mr. Garrett, but he wasn't crying anymore either. Mr. Garrett held out a hand to help him, but Kevin refused it. Since his right arm was still elevated to keep the blood from running down, he turned to his left, pressing his hand to the ground to brace himself as he got his legs set under him. And as he rolled that way, facedown, back end higher than the front, his jacket and shirt edged up his back, exposing ten or twelve inches of skin. There was just a flash of something that shouldn't have been there, several dark strips of color. Then the clothes came back down, and they were gone. I looked at Mr. Garrett's face, and saw that he had seen them, too.

"Kevin," he said, and now his voice sounded different. "Stand here for a second. Let me look."

And maybe Kevin thought the teacher was still talking about his arm, because he didn't move away or protest. Maybe he'd forgotten what his clothes concealed, so accustomed was he to carrying his secret. Or maybe he knew exactly what was happening and wanted someone, some adult, just to see. When Mr. Garrett lifted the back of the jacket again, what he uncovered was a network of dark, thin marks, some just an inch or two long, some the entire width of Kevin's back. Many of them were long-healed, hardened and raised; they looked like a game of Pick up Sticks affixed to his flesh. But some were fresh—scabbed over, or still open, oozing tiny spots of red. I did not see how the blood hadn't soaked through his shirt. I did not see how he could lean back in his chair.

Kevin had turned away from me, so I couldn't see his face. But I saw Mr. Garrett's. When he let go of the jacket and straightened up, he looked like he was going to cry. The muscles in his cheeks were jumping, and his eyes were pained. When he spoke, it was in a heavy voice I hadn't heard before.

"Kevin, who did this to you?"

Now Kevin twisted away and took hold of his arm again. "No one! Leave me alone!" he said, and then he ran away, back across the playground and toward the building. Mr. Garrett stood and watched him for a moment, and I had a sense, then, that he was taking measure, trying to figure out what to do. He lowered his head and shook it slowly, pressing his lips together. Then he straightened up and walked across the schoolyard.

In the years that have passed since 1974, I've often wondered what would have happened if Mr. Garrett had kept his knowledge to himself. He could have let Kevin go home without telling anyone what he had seen. He could have just minded his business and let people go on as they always had. If Mr. Garrett had turned away from what we both saw that morning, it might have stayed a secret forever. For surely I would never have revealed such troubling information. I would never have said a thing.

That evening, after supper, there was the now-familiar knock at the kitchen door. This time, though, it wasn't Earl or a group of Charlie's friends. This time it was Ray Davis, by himself. When my grandmother pulled the storm door open, Ray was standing there in the olive pants he always wore on duty, along with his police department jacket. He had taken off his wide-brimmed hat, and he stood holding it against his chest as if apologizing in advance for his visit.

"Good evening, Helen," he said. "I'm sorry to bother you, but is Charlie at home? I need to talk to him. It's important."

She hesitated—these unannounced visits were wearing on her—but then she stepped out of the way and said, "Sure, Ray. Come on inside."

He met my grandfather in the dining room—Charlie, drawn by the knock and the voices, had already gotten up. But when Ray responded to his suggestion that they sit down at the table by saying, "No, Charlie, I think it's best we discussed this in private," I knew that he was there about Kevin Watson.

My grandfather took a moment to reply. "All right," he said. "Well, let's go out on the porch then."

This was late October, and the temperature was now down in the forties. My grandfather put on his shoes and a barn coat, and Ray kept his jacket on, and after my grandmother had given both of them beers, they stepped through the door off the living room and out onto the porch. The front porch actually led, of course, to the front door of the house, but no one used that door except the mailman and salesmen and sometimes Charlie, who'd stand out front in the evening, stick two fingers in his mouth, and make a sound as loud as a factory whistle to call me home. But as little as the door was used, the porch was used often. For my grandmother, it was a place to let her pies cool. For my grandfather, it was a place to keep an eye on the neighborhood. It also gave him a place to hold private conversations.

In this second function, though, it was probably less effective than he realized. When he didn't completely shut the inner door, as he didn't this time, leaving it open a crack for the sake of light or heat; and when I was perched on the very end of his couch, I could, if I concentrated, generally hear the conversation. I had done exactly that just two nights before, when my grandparents had gone out there after supper to talk about my father. Now, with my grandmother in the kitchen washing the dishes, listening was not very difficult. They began by discussing the weather, which had changed from autumn glorious to prewinter gloom, and Charlie must have been sitting in the chair furthest from the door because his voice was harder to follow. Then Ray cleared his throat.

"Steve Baker called from over at the elementary school today. Someone told him about some whipping marks on Earl's boy, Kevin." He paused, and I could picture him gripping his beer can more tightly. "It was . . .

well, it was that new teacher, the colored one. He got a look at Kevin's back on the playground."

Silence from my grandfather. Then: "*That's* what you came over to tell me?"

"Well . . . Charlie. It could cause Earl a problem. If the teacher officially reported it, we'd have to investigate."

"Well, did he?" He sounded angry and impatient.

"No," said Ray. "The teacher told Baker about it, and Baker convinced him to let him handle it. He called me directly instead of going through the department. And now I'm trying to figure out what to do."

My grandfather took a moment to answer. "Well, what would you do if it was somebody else?"

Ray sighed. "Get the kid looked at, I guess. And if it's as bad as they say, I'd have my men go and pick up the father."

"But it's *not* someone else."

"No," Ray said. "It's Earl."

And for the first time his voice seemed to loosen a bit, as if something he was holding tight was slipping free. I thought Ray Davis was generally a decent sort, too uncertain, maybe, too deferential to be the face of the law. And it occurred to me that although Earl was his friend, he wasn't sure about the best course of action. Maybe he was looking to Charlie for permission to go talk to Kevin and question his father—maybe that would give him the courage he needed. But if so, he didn't get it, because when Charlie spoke again, he said, "That nosy bastard. I knew those niggers would bring nothing but trouble."

Ray didn't respond. Maybe he was still thinking about what to do, but Charlie's stance on the matter was clear. His voice was more distinct now—he must have been facing Ray, or his anger added volume to his words.

"They got no right to tell a man how to raise his children. Or what he can or can't do in order to discipline 'em. Hell, I took Stewart over my own knee when he was a boy, and now it looks like I didn't do it near *enough*."

"We all do that, Charlie. But this is different."

"Earl's own daddy was tough on him," Charlie continued. "*Too* tough, some folks might say. I know Earl had a hard time of it, but it kept him in line. And now he's just trying to keep his own boys out of trouble." He paused, and I remembered the scar on Earl's arm, about the size of the end of a cigar. When Charlie spoke again, his voice had the tone of a command. "Don't talk to the boy, Raymond. I'm sure it's all blown out of proportion. Just talk to Earl, and let him know what's going on."

When Ray spoke again, he sounded resolved but not happy. "So you think I should just tell him that people are looking out?"

I could almost see Charlie nod. "Yes. That's what you'd do for me, Ray. That's what you'd do for any of us. Or else why even bother to call yourself a friend?"

Ray was silent, and I could imagine him looking down the street, the lights coming on in the living rooms all along Dryden Road. "I don't even know how to bring it up, Charlie," he said finally. "I mean, how do you tell a man . . . ?"

"Tell him they're sticking their black noses where they don't belong. Tell him you know who's in the right here, and that you're going to stand by him. This is bullshit, Ray. You know it is. This is bullshit, and you need to put a stop to it."

But when the men came inside, I wasn't sure from Ray's expression that he knew it was bullshit at all. He had the chastened look of a young man given an unpleasant task by his father. He left quickly, maybe to see Earl Watson, and then Charlie went into the kitchen for another beer. My grandfather was angry and preoccupied; he'd been in a sour mood already and this had made things worse. Neither my grandmother nor I dared to approach him. And when he came back to the living room, where she and I had already gone, he lay down on the couch, turned on the TV, and didn't speak a word to either one of us.

I don't know what Ray said to Earl, but I know he said something, because the next time I saw Earl he was drawn-in and tense, even more ill-tempered than he'd been all fall. I wouldn't have chosen to be around him, but my grandfather had taken me with him, as he always did, to run his Saturday-morning errands. After we'd picked up a rake and trash bags at Kmart and a tailpipe at the auto supplies shop, we pulled up in front of Earl's gun store. Charlie said, "'Lo, Earl," by way of greeting as we walked through the door, and then he sat down in one of the folding metal chairs that Earl had set up by the counter. He patted the other chair to indicate that I should sit.

"'Lo, Charlie," Watson answered, not acknowledging me. "Hey Jake," he yelled, "bring Charlie here some coffee!"

I'd thought Earl was alone, but after a minute or two, Jake Watson came in from the back office and handed my grandfather a Styrofoam cup. At first I wasn't sure he had noticed me. But then his thin lips curled into a smirk, which gave me a little spasm of fear. Jake sat on a high stool behind the counter and crossed his arms, looking at me, and I thought of the times during the summer when I'd passed him and his friends out near Six Mile Creek, sitting on top of their cars and smoking pot or drinking beer. If they saw me, they'd stir themselves enough to throw rocks, and I'd bike past them as fast as I could. Although Earl didn't know—I assumed—about the pot and the rock throwing, he had to realize that Jake got into trouble. From what I heard, he'd been suspended from the high school more than once for fighting or for arguing with his teachers. Now, looking back, it's tempting to explain Jake's behavior as anxiety over the war, especially since some of his older friends had been drafted; especially since one of them had come home without his legs. But the war had ended more than a year ago, and so his surliness couldn't be blamed on the threat of the draft.

The gun shop was set up like a jewelry store, with a U-shaped glass counter and wide display cases against the two side walls. Above the cases were advertising posters for some of the store's best sellers—Remington, Smith & Wesson, Ithaca, and Colt, even one for Italian Berettas. Earl had inherited the store from his father and then expanded the business; he also taught gun safety classes out at the firing range, including a class specifically for kids. I had taken the class myself the previous fall at Charlie's behest, shooting round after round with a little .22-caliber single-action army revolver. The gun seemed small and insignificant compared to Charlie's heftier pistols, but I'd liked the feel of it, the warmth of the metal, the sense of contained power. From there I'd graduated to a .410-gauge shotgun to prepare for bird hunting, which was almost easier because I could brace the butt against my shoulder.

There were no customers in the store that day, which was unusual—it was a week before the opening of deer hunting season, one of the busiest times of the year. Earl was cleaning a used Colt 1911, dabbing polish onto a cloth and gently stroking the barrel. He worked with focus and pleasure, not speaking to us yet; then he turned and put the gun back into the display case. The longer-barrel pistols, as well as the rifles and shotguns, were in the cases against the wall. The smaller handguns were in the counter displays in their felt-lined cases, as harmless and still as watches. Earl ran his eyes over his entire inventory almost tenderly, as if the guns were living things that required his care. His eyes were red and the lines in his forehead and cheeks looked deeper than usual. Then he turned toward us and placed his fists on the counter.

"Got a new Browning Citori over and under you might want to look at, Charlie," he said. "Best wingshooting gun I've ever seen."

My grandfather sat with his hands cupping his knees and his legs spread wide, slouching a bit, totally at ease. "I'm getting too old for wingshooting, Earl. Those birds get smaller every year, and they move too goddamn fast. Deer are better for me now—they're a bigger target, so I can actually see 'em. You going to make it out with us next weekend?"

Earl nodded. "I hope so. Trying to figure out whether to open next Saturday. I'm usually in the store the first day of the season, but I sure would like to get out there."

Charlie nodded. "Well, come with us then," he said. "Pete and I fixed the ladder going up to the stand, so even you could get your big ass up there now."

"Well, I'll try to get my new part-time man to come in so I can go. And this season," he said, pulling himself up straight, "I'm going to take my boy out with me." I looked at him, and so did my grandfather. It was clear which boy he was talking about, and which one he wasn't, and his knowledge that we knew how he divided his sons turned his face red, and tightened his fists.

"Kevin's just too soft for hunting," he said by way of explanation. "He can't even put a worm on a hook."

But the mention of Kevin's name let something new into the store, like a draft bringing in a foul odor. My grandfather looked down, embarrassed.

Earl said, "Ah, hell," and turned away in disgust, and slammed the display case shut. When I glanced over at Jake to see his reaction—his face showed nothing—I realized for the first time how much he looked like his brother. He too had lush black hair that was a bit long. He too had a compact body and short, stubby fingers, but he was put together differently, with more strength and ease, and on him the bushy hair and stockiness suggested power, not disarray. No one had ever knocked him over or taken him down a notch. No one had ever looked at him and found him lacking.

As the silence continued between the two men, I knew that Ray had talked to Earl, but that my grandfather hadn't. I wondered if they'd speak of Kevin, or if the presence of Jake and me would stop them. Either way, I wanted to be out of there. Earl scared me now, even more than he had before. I kept remembering the scars on Kevin's back, the oozing of the still-fresh wounds. I couldn't imagine a person doing that to someone else, especially not a parent to a child. My father had never raised a hand to me, my mother either—something I'd never even thought about before but that now made me think I was lucky. I glanced over at Charlie to see if he was going to say something. But just then, Earl looked out the window and exclaimed, "Well, I'll be god-damned."

I turned toward the window, and saw what he saw—Mr. Garrett walking alone on the other side of Buffalo Street. It seemed that he too was out doing Saturday errands—he was carrying a couple of shopping bags—and I wondered why his wife wasn't with him. I felt my grandfather sit up straight beside me; felt the air sharpen to a fine, dangerous point. Earl's face contorted into an ugly mask of itself. Never taking his eyes off Mr. Garrett, he stepped out from behind the counter. He walked out through the front door and onto the sidewalk.

Mr. Garrett didn't see him at first. He was walking leisurely, stopping to look in store windows, swinging his bags in a big, loose arc, like a boy who'd just finished running an errand for his mother and was dallying before he went home. He was dressed more casually than usual, in jeans, a green canvas jacket, and sneakers. But the jeans only drew attention to the length of his legs, and revealed muscles you couldn't see when he wore dress slacks. Watching him, even from a fifty-foot distance, I thought, what an impressive-looking man.

But that's not what Earl Watson was thinking. Jake got up off his stool and followed Earl out the door, my grandfather an arm's length away from him. I stood and walked over to the doorway. And from that proximity I could see the look on Earl's face, the sheer and open hatred. His eyes were narrowed and his lips pressed tight, and a small spot appeared in the center of his cheek, stark white against the darkening red. His fists opened and closed and I could feel the tension radiating off his body.

Mr. Garrett must have felt something, too, for now he looked across the street and saw us there. And he must have seen me first, because his face softened a bit—but then his eyes settled on Earl. I don't know if he knew who Earl Watson was, if he knew this was Kevin's father. But the hostility in Earl's face was unmistakable. Mr. Garrett looked at him for a long, hard second. Then he nodded slowly—an acknowledgment more than a greeting—and continued down the street.

The next Wednesday after school, I took my bike from the garage and headed out into the country. It was dreary outside, cold but not unbearable, the beginning of the long haul into winter. The trees seemed worn and tired; the fallen leaves had all turned limp and brown. The ground was muddy from a recent rain, and the cold had caused the mud to coagulate into hard brittle lumps, which made for a bumpy ride. I'd left Brett at home—this was something I needed to do by myself, and besides, I wasn't going to the park. Instead, I rode all the way out to the satellite clinic, where I knew Mrs. Garrett worked on Wednesdays. I didn't know why I wanted to see Mrs. Garrett; I just knew that I had to go there, had to see her after the Saturday stare-down between Earl Watson and her husband.

The clinic was in a building that had once been a package store next to the original highway. When the old highway became obsolete with the opening of Route 5, the store, without its main source of customers, had failed. This all happened long before my time, but I knew that the store had tried to revive itself at various times as an auto supplies shop, a feed store, and even a bar, until finally all commercial efforts stopped and the building was left to deteriorate. I had passed it occasionally on my rides into the country, and I had never, in my short time in Deerhorn, known it to be anything but a boarded-up place with empty beer cans strewn in front and tall weeds sprouting up through the cracks in the stairs.

But as I approached the old building—which was about half a mile east of Route 5 on Besemer Road—I was amazed by the transformation. The boards had been replaced by plain but functional windows. The cracked stairs had been removed, replaced by new stairs with metal railings. The old wooden sign, which had been painted over countless times to reflect the building's different incarnations, was gone, and in its place was a brand-new sign, with bold red and black letters, that said, *Deerhorn-Central Wisconsin Satellite Clinic.* And for the first time in all the times I had seen this place, there was evidence of people—cars in the parking lot; two mothers talking at the bottom of the stairs while their children played peek-a-boo around their legs; figures moving behind the new windows. It was a remarkable change. The building didn't look very big from outside, and I couldn't picture how it might have been laid out. But it was bustling with activity. I noticed, through the wide front window, a row of people in what must have been the waiting room, and as I stood with my bike at the edge of the parking lot, several more people came out the door. I recognized Sammy Tyler, one of the trailer children and a third grader who got marched to the showers with Billy Coles every week. I wondered what might have been wrong with him, remembering the strange growth on his cheek, his graying teeth, the spots of thinning hair. As the Tylers moved to the end of the parking lot and walked down the road, I realized why there were so few cars for the number of patients waiting inside—because not many of the country people owned them.

Good things were happening here; even I could see that. I wanted to take a peek inside of the building, so I slowly walked my bike closer and looked around the corner. There was another door and a window maybe five feet off the ground, with a pile of cinder blocks nearby. I was standing there thinking about moving the blocks closer to the window when the side door opened and Mrs. Garrett stepped out. She didn't see me at first— she looked tired and preoccupied—so I watched as she closed the door behind her, pulled her blue coat shut against the cold air, and leaned heavily on the railing. Then her eyes met mine, and she jumped.

"Goodness, Michelle, I didn't see you there," she said, as casually as if she talked to me every day.

I gripped my handlebars and fought the urge to pedal away. "I'm sorry. I didn't mean to scare you."

"Oh, so you *do* talk." She smiled, and her face seemed warm and open. Her hair was pulled back into a tight, neat bun, and as she turned her head I saw again the structure of her cheekbones, the full lips, the confident set of her jaw. "Park your bike," she said now. "Come over and sit with me."

And even though I'd biked out there specifically to see her, even though I'd made the trip for the purpose of talking to this woman, the invitation to actually do so put me into a nervous fright. This was typical of me at nine years old, and is still typical of me now: I want to understand and experience things, but only from a distance; only while I still hold a part of myself away. I did what she instructed, though—rested my bike up against the wall and went over to the stairs. She sat down on the top of the steps, but I stood there at the foot of them, hand curled over the rail.

"So what brings you out this way?" Mrs. Garrett asked.

I looked at her hands. They were graceful, able hands, impossibly long. On one finger there was a wedding ring, and on her other hand a heavy ring that looked like my father's ring from college, which my grandmother had kept as a testament to his unfulfilled promise. And I had the strangest sensation, then, of wanting to feel those hands upon me. But all I did was shrug my shoulders. "I don't know."

"It's at least three miles from town," Mrs. Garrett said. "That's quite a trip for a girl your size."

"I do it all the time," I said, my pride flaring suddenly. "I go out to the state park almost every day in the summer."

Mrs. Garrett smiled, glad to get a rise out of me. And she probably knew full well why I was there. "Well, that's good," she said. "It probably keeps you out of trouble."

A car pulled into the parking lot, and we both watched as it kicked gravel up and turned into a space. Then Mrs. Garrett fixed her eyes on me. "How long have you lived here, Michelle?" she asked. "Have you been here your whole life?"

"No," I said, letting go of the railing and hugging myself against the cold. "I was born in Japan. I just moved here last summer. Well, I guess the summer before last."

"Japan! That's quite a ways away. And you live now with your grandparents?"

I nodded.

She seemed to hesitate before asking the next question. "And where are your mother and father?"

To my surprise, I felt my eyes fill with tears. "They're not here," I said. I looked at her shoes, the door, my bicycle. "My mother left, and my father went out to look for her. But he's on his way back now. He'll be here soon." I made it sound like she'd just gone up to the market and hadn't returned in the expected time. But three years had passed now since my mother had left, and more than a year since I'd last seen my father.

Mrs. Garrett nodded as if this story was not surprising to her. "I lived with my grandparents, too," she said. "My father worked for the railroad, and my mother was a live-in maid, and so my grandparents had to take care of us. My parents would come and stay with us whenever they could."

"Why did you come here?" I asked suddenly, and I realized that this was something I'd been wondering for weeks. Mrs. Garrett looked taken aback for a moment, but then her expression turned thoughtful.

"I had a chance to make a difference here, with the clinic growing and the new nursing school. Also, I like the man I'm working for, Dr. Gordon. I knew him before, in Chicago. When he asked me to help him, it was too good a thing to pass up." She laughed. "I never thought Joe and I would end up in Central Wisconsin, but I suppose you didn't, either."

"But," and now I ventured a look at her, "a lot of people here don't like it." As I said this it occurred to me that she was the only woman I knew who wasn't a housewife, or a teacher, or a grocery clerk. There must have been other nurses at the clinic, of course, but I didn't know who they were. And Mrs. Whipple, the nurse at school, seemed more adept at applying bandages and administering hugs than providing any substantive care. Plus, Mrs. Garrett had been brought specially; she'd been handpicked by the head of the clinic. She seemed above the other nurses, more important. And from the vantage point of adulthood, I wonder now—was part of the town's animosity toward the Garretts related to their jobs? It was bad enough, in people's eyes, that a black couple had moved to Deerhorn at all. How much worse was it that the Garretts did not conform to their ideas of what black people could be? That they were professionals, with more education and skill than almost all the white people in town?

Mrs. Garrett nodded and sighed, and just for a moment the lines deepened around her eyes. "I know, but we couldn't let it stop us, Michelle. If you only do things to make other folks happy, pretty soon you'll end up doing nothing." And now her face took on a defiant expression that reminded me of her husband. "Besides," she said, "we're not just rolling over for these people. The more they push, the more determined we are to stay."

I looked at her and wondered if she really knew what she'd gotten into. "Aren't you scared?" I asked her.

"Aren't *you*?"

I thought about that for a moment. I thought about what I'd just said—that people didn't like that the Garretts were there. The same thing had been said about me, I knew, and also about my mother. Had *she* been scared, discouraged, and was that why she hadn't come back? Had she felt a level of hatred and threat that was greater than what I'd experienced? Even with the dirty looks and harsh words I'd endured, even with the fights and the rocks, there was something that kept me from thinking that I was ever in real danger. Maybe it was because I knew that as much as people might disapprove of me, their actions stopped at a certain point because of Charlie. But there'd been nothing protecting my mother, and there was nothing protecting the Garretts, and I knew that better than anyone. I was a daily witness to the hatred they inspired, which was both similar to and more intense than the hostility directed at me.

Just then, the door opened and a middle-aged man came out. He was wearing a white coat and carrying a clipboard, and he moved so quickly that both of us snapped to attention. "Hello," he said absently in my general direction, not really seeing me. Then he turned to Mrs. Garrett. "Betty, we need you in here. There's a kid with a 103-degree fever."

"Well, looks like my break's over," said Mrs. Garrett, standing up. She smiled at me. "Nice talking to you, Michelle."

SEVEN

On the first day of deer hunting season, my grand-father's alarm went off at three-thirty. I wasn't going with him—he didn't want me out in the woods on opening weekend, which attracted so many of what he called "drunk once-a-year hunters" who were trying to get away from their wives—but I still got up to watch him get dressed. He pulled on his camouflage jacket, which was covered with dark green splotches that looked like wet leaves, his lace-up hunting boots, and a thick orange cap. In a leather bag he carried over his shoulder he packed binoculars, knives, a compass, rope, his lunch, and ammunition—cylinders, encased in bright red plastic, that were longer and thicker than my fingers. He opened the gun cabinet and took out his deer hunting rifle and some heavy rope to reinforce the stand. Charlie seemed agitated this morning, not exhilarated like he usually was before a hunt. I wanted to ask what was wrong but there was something in his demeanor, in the way he threw his gear around, that made me afraid to bother him with questions. I knew, though, that any anger he felt was bad news for the deer. At four o'clock he left to meet his friends.

All day my grandmother worked the house, worry-ing. Charlie had been shot once years back, by a hunter who mistook his movements for a deer. He was proud of

that scar, pulled up his pants leg and fingered it sometimes when he had too much to drink. My grandmother
washed the dishes extra hard that afternoon, vacuumed
like she was punishing the carpet. At lunch she even
opened a can of beer and drank it out of a juice glass.
She kept looking at me like she was about to say something, but then appeared to decide against it. I didn't
know why she was acting so strange. I stayed up in the
attic with Brett and did my best to stay out of her way.

A little before three p.m. a loud honk announced the
return of the hunters. My grandmother and I rushed outside just in time to see Uncle Pete's brown pickup truck
pull into the driveway, followed by my grandfather's
Pontiac. In the bed of the truck two deer were laid out
on their sides, back to belly. Uncle Pete and Earl got out
of the truck, looking more businesslike than happy; Jake
was with them but he stayed inside the cab. Ray Davis
and Jim Riesling were in Charlie's car; they tipped their
caps at us as they got out and made their way over to
the truck bed. My grandfather rushed into the garage to
lay newspaper on the floor while Pete and Earl dragged
out the first deer. Uncle Pete grabbed its front legs and
Earl its hindquarters, and they both swore at the flies
that swirled around the carcass as they shuffled with it
toward the garage. It was a midsized young male. Two
small horns protruded out of its head with three points
each, like a series of bent, twisted fingers. Even from the
steps I could see its open brown eyes, the tuft of white
in its tail, the soft black velvet nose. I could see the dark
red blood, vivid and obscene against its golden fur. Every two feet a drop of it hit the pavement.

They took it into the garage. There they tilted it,

hindquarters up, while my grandfather tied a thick rope around its legs and strung it up from a wooden beam. It swung back and forth, its front legs extended as if reaching for the floor. The three men smiled now and wiped their hands on a towel; they looked at the deer with expressions of satisfaction and power and something very close to lust. My eyes traveled down the length of the deer's body to the paper on the cold cement floor. The blood dripped in slow-spreading circles.

As soon as the men turned to go back out to the truck, my grandmother went inside. I stayed on the stairs, though, inching closer to the driveway. As Jim and Ray pulled the second deer out of the bed, a doe, their expressions were much more sober. I remembered then one of my grandfather's steadfast rules: never hurt anything female. He must have known I was thinking this, because he came toward me as his friends lugged the body to the garage. "Earl got her by accident," he said. "He was aiming for the buck, but once he hit her, we had to take her down."

His face stayed impassive as they carried her by. She was smaller than the buck, with lighter hair, a smear of blood against her shoulders and flanks. They were holding her upside down, waist level, and there beneath her tail I saw the vulva, exposed, each fold open and distinct in the afternoon sun. They strung her up by her hind feet, next to her mate. I didn't want to look at this, so I glanced back into the bed of the truck, where bits of fur and blood and feces were crusted onto the metal. Some blood-soaked newspaper fell out of the back and fluttered noisily away toward the street.

The other men left then, all except for Pete, who always stayed behind to help gut the deer. Usually I liked to be there when Charlie did this kind of work. I'd sit for hours next to his work table down in the cellar, watching him pluck feathers off of ducks, bone and clean fish, slice up rabbits and deer for freezing. (And now, when I see signs up in deer hunting country for *processing deer*, I feel like the hunters are cheating, not abiding by one of Charlie's other cardinal rules: you should always take care of what you kill.)

But that afternoon, something didn't feel right. My grandfather was always happy this time of the day, tired but still full of energy. He loved to come home after a successful hunt, loved the transformation of his kill into food. Today, however, he was somber, and his mood seemed to be about more than the fallen doe. While Pete stayed in the garage to set up buckets for the blood, I followed Charlie down to the cellar. He washed his hands in the sink, dried them, and then opened his storage cabinets, pulling down three carving knives and placing them on his work table. Then he glanced up and saw me and gave me a sad smile. "You want to help us out with this, Mike?"

"Can I just watch?"

"Sure. Sure you can." He looked down, and he seemed to be avoiding my eyes. That scared me, so I finally asked my question.

"Grandpa, what's wrong?"

He fiddled with the handle of one of his knives and tilted his head, not quite looking at me. "Well, Mike. Well. We got a letter from your dad yesterday." He put the knife down and scratched at something on the table. "He said he left Missouri and was headed west again.

He was in Denver, on his way out to Fresno. He said the job in Springfield didn't work out, so he had to get back to where he had some contacts. He told us to say . . ." he trailed off, and I knew what was next.

"He isn't coming, is he?"

Charlie looked me full in the face. "No, Mike," he said. "No, he isn't."

I just stared at him, and he kept looking at me sadly. We stayed like that for several seconds. Then he reached out with one hand and tried to pull me toward him. I wriggled out of his grasp and shook my head no.

I had to get away, I had to get out of there, so I ran up the stairs and out the front door. My bike was lying in the front yard where I'd left it earlier in the day, and I bolted down the driveway and picked it up. I started to pedal away without knowing where I was headed. I couldn't go out into the country, which would be over-run with hunters, so I rode up to Buffalo Street. But there were plenty of hunters right there in town, their pickup trucks taking all the parking spots in front of the coffee shop and gun store. I veered off of Buffalo and over to the park by the church, figuring correctly that it would be empty. And there I picked up rock after rock and threw them as hard as I could. When I saw the flicker of a squirrel's tail high up on a branch, I started throwing at the squirrel, not really to knock it down, not really to hit it, but because it gave me a place to aim.

I wanted to hurl those rocks until there was nothing left to throw. I wanted to get out whatever was inside me. Because throwing those rocks, like biking—like the running and lifting and hiking I do now as an adult— was not only about working the body, but exhausting the mind. And my mind was filled with things I didn't want to think about. My father had been planning to visit for Thanksgiving, and now he wasn't coming. He was supposed to come and get me, but he wasn't going to. All of the hope and anticipation I'd felt over the last few weeks was collapsing under the weight of itself. I didn't know what to stand on; I didn't know where to turn, and I had nothing left now to look forward to.

On top of that, even the things that had felt like solid ground were shifting beneath my feet. I had just biked away from Charlie and Pete; for the first time I was running away from them. This was new, because in the past I had always wanted to be near them; there was no better place to be than in their company.

But in the last few weeks their company had begun to feel less safe. What I had always seen as their strength and fortitude had crossed over into something different, unfamiliar. I couldn't go home, and I couldn't go out to the country; I could not figure out where to be. And so I stayed in the park hurling rocks at the trees until I was too tired to think anymore.

Deer hunting season only lasted three weeks, but that fall it felt more like three years. My grandmother kept me from taking the bike out after school and on weekends, wisely preventing me from heading out to the woods where the shooting seemed to go on day and night.

But this was the worst possible time for me to be trapped inside. I couldn't sit still with the news about my father; I didn't want to think about it. I couldn't stand to look at his postcards, either, so I took them all down, hiding them in the back of my shirt drawer. If he wasn't coming back to Wisconsin for Thanksgiving, then when was he going to come? Why was he headed out west again? Did it have something to do with my mother? This possibility was the only thing that helped ease my disappointment. I held on to a sliver of hope that maybe this was all a part of a bigger plan. But in the meantime, the days I was stuck indoors were a slow, cruel torture.

Throughout those weeks my grandfather was gone more than usual, spending time at Earl's gun shop before he came home for supper, and hunting on the weekends when his friends were off work. When he was home, he tried to entertain me—telling me stories of hunting adventures from seasons past, letting me sit on the end of his couch while he poked me with his feet. But none of this could break through my somber mood. Every day I wondered if there'd be word from my father, a call or letter saying where he'd settled for the moment, some indication of what would happen next. But there was nothing, and Charlie's efforts to cheer me up didn't help, and as much as I wanted to go to him, to give over to his caring, something was holding me back.

He could sense this, I think. Sometimes I'd look up at him and find him staring at me intently. But if he knew my disappointment was about more than my father, if he sensed that I was feeling uneasy even there, with him, he didn't mention it. The only thing that gave me comfort through this time was Brett, and he definitely knew that something was wrong. He was even more attached to me than usual; he wouldn't let me out of his sight. When I was sleeping he would curl himself around my head, and now, when I opened my eyes in the morning,

I'd find him already awake, looking down at me with his ears perked—worried, protective—until I rubbed his head and told him good morning, and that he was a good dog, and that everything would be all right.

In mid-November, on the last Friday of deer hunting season, Jim Riesling came over as always. We had just settled down in the living room—except my grandmother, who was finishing up the dishes—when the telephone rang. She came out of the kitchen to answer it, wiping her hands on her apron. When she picked up the phone and heard what the caller had to say, she bunched the apron in her fist.

"Charlie," she said, "you'd better come here. This is Ray, and he's over at the clinic. They've got Kevin Watson—he was taken there this afternoon—and now they've called in social services."

Charlie pulled himself up off the couch and went into the dining room, looking so angry that I shrank back in my chair. Jim kept his eyes on the television screen, wearing an expression I couldn't decipher. After my grandfather took the receiver, he stared down at the desk where the telephone was and mostly listened to Ray, sometimes breaking in with things like "When?" and "What now?" and "Why can't you do something about it?" He stood through the entire conversation, one hand clenched around the receiver, the other curled into a loose fist that he tapped lightly on the desk. I saw the tense muscles in his arms, in his back, and now, thinking of my grandfather, of what he was like, I imagine how hard it must have been for him—a man so used to solving things with his strength and his will—to be confronted by something he couldn't solve physically. Then he was off the phone and he kept looking at the desk for a minute, until my grandmother asked, "Charlie, what happened?" I had come into the dining room, and Jim had stood up, and Charlie turned slowly to face us.

"Earl took Kevin to the clinic this afternoon, the emergency room. And somehow things got twisted around and they called in social services."

Jim's face was set, his voice even. "And then they called the police?"

Charlie shook his head. "No, that's the thing of it. They *didn't* call Ray. They called the county sheriff."

Jim looked beyond Charlie, somewhere past his shoulder. "Well, the clinic is a county operation, even if it's in town. So maybe they always deal with county law."

Charlie shook his head. "It's plain disrespectful to the local police for the county to butt in that way. They flat-out bypassed Ray and his men."

"Maybe it was because they knew that Ray wouldn't do anything about it."

There was an edge to Jim's voice I'd never heard before, and Charlie must have noticed it, too. He looked at the younger man and asked, "Whose side are you on, anyway?"

But Jim just raised both hands and turned away. In the silence left by his refusal to talk, my grandmother asked again, uncertainly, "What happened?"

Charlie took a moment to gather himself and stop glaring at his friend. "Well. Those social workers talked to Kevin I guess, and the sheriff's deputy talked to Earl, and they decided that it was all a whole bunch of nothing and released Kevin back to his dad. But they kept the boy there for hours. Scared the hell out of him, it sounds like. Ray got wind of it sometime in the afternoon and went over to talk everyone down."

"So it turned out all right?" my grandmother asked. And I knew this was what she really wanted to know—that everything would be all right; that nothing terrible had happened; that her life and Kevin's life and the life of the town would go back to the way it had been. Her world did not include things like fathers being questioned by the law and children talking to social services. It had barely expanded enough to include a grandchild like me.

"Yeah, everything's all right," my grandfather said. "Ray said Earl was heading home, so I'm going to go over to meet him. Mike, get in the car. Maybe you can keep Kevin company while I talk to Earl and Alice. Jim, do you want to come with us?" He was looking at his friend as if this wasn't a real question, as if of course Jim was going to come with us.

But Jim just shook his head. "I'll pass on this one, Charlie."

Charlie glanced at him, his open mouth betraying his surprise.

Jim asked, in a soft voice, "What happened to Kevin, anyway?"

Charlie looked the younger man straight in the eye. "His arm," he said. "He broke his arm." Then he turned and headed out to the car.

The Watsons lived on the other side of town, way out on Warren Road, past the restaurants and stores, beyond the theater. Their family, like my grandparents', had moved in from the country, although their arrival in Deerhorn preceded the Wilkes's and LeBeaus' by a generation. Earl and my grandfather had always been close, and Charlie considered Earl the toughest of his friends—the best bow hunter, which required more endurance, skill, and stealth than hunting with guns; the least affected by the elements; the most impervious to pain. Earl's toughness, Charlie said, had been honed by his time in the military and his years of trying to live up to the demands of his stern, exacting father. But by the time I knew him, Earl's life seemed pretty good. He and his family lived in an area of sprawling two-story houses set on parcels of three or four acres. His house was bigger than my grandparents', with an extra bedroom here, a family room there, and a wraparound porch where the men would drink beer in the summer after a long day of fishing at Treman Lake. When we pulled into the driveway and parked—Earl's car was not yet there—I really looked at the house for the first time. It was immaculate—the grass and bushes clipped, the picket fence freshly painted, the concrete driveway long and new-looking, without the cracks that split the driveway at my grandparents' house. And yet the light that shone from its windows and from the front porch seemed cold somehow, not warming. The place looked cheerless and official, almost too carefully presented. It didn't suggest safety, but enclosure.

My grandfather had brought Brett and me along but didn't speak to us as we waited. I don't think he really expected me to keep Kevin company—he knew we weren't friends, and neither of us was easy with other people. I think he just wanted me with him. In this, he treated me like I too was a faithful dog—a companion whose presence was desirable but didn't warrant conversation. I don't know if he wondered what I thought of what was happening, or if it occurred to him that I might have an opinion at all. He did assume—and he was right—that I'd never talk about what we did or saw, not even to my grandmother. My allegiance to him was complete.

After we'd waited about twenty minutes, Earl's gray Buick pulled into the driveway, passed us, parked up closer to the house. Earl got out slowly and Charlie met him between the cars, on the edge of the well-kept grass. From the quickness of his movements, it was clear—as I'd thought—that he expected me to stay in the car. So I sat in the backseat with my arm around the dog and cracked the window so I could hear. Because the porch lights were bright, like the lights of a prison yard, I could see everything that was happening.

Kevin stayed in his car, too. His profile was just visible through the dirty back window, and he sat there looking neither upset nor excited, just waiting for whatever would happen next. And as I looked at his round cheeks and his too-long hair, I found myself suddenly feeling angry at Kevin, annoyed that his problems had upset everybody and pulled my grandfather into this mess. It was not his fault, I knew that; I knew he was being hurt. But I wished—and I was also ashamed of this wish—that the Watsons' problems had been kept to themselves.

Earl's expression was hard and resolute, prepared to take whatever my grandfather said. Which was: "You all right? Ray called me from the clinic."

Earl's face relaxed a little and he ran his hand over

his bald spot. He must have known that it was far past time for pretending everything was normal.

"Yeah, I'm all right. They ask so many damn questions, try to make you feel like a crook. And they scared Kevin half to death."

Charlie grunted and the two men stood together, as firm and steady as a couple of oaks. "Last I checked a man had a right to take his son to the doctor without throwing people into a panic about it."

Watson pulled out a cigarette and lit it; the red tip bobbed up and down as he spoke. "That's right," he said. "The boy had an accident. *You* know how clumsy he is. Can't walk across the room hardly without bumping into something. And today, Alice was out somewhere, and he fell down the porch stairs."

"Broke his arm, Ray said?"

"Yep, broke his arm. A clean break. They put a cast on him, should be healed up in a couple of months. Then he'll be good as new."

I watched my grandfather absorb this; watched him decide it was true. And from the distance of adulthood, I wonder if his reaction was connected to what had happened with my father. Because whatever Earl may or may not have done, at least he had stuck around. At least he was here with his family. Charlie stood still for a minute, then nodded, and the two men were one—of a piece and of the town, against whatever outside force might threaten them.

I wanted to tell my grandfather to step away from Earl. I wanted him to come back to the car so we could turn around and go home. And then suddenly I remembered something from the previous fall, one of the times that Charlie and Pete had taken me bird hunting. Some-how we'd gotten separated and I'd ended up with Pete; Charlie was nowhere to be found. But then we heard a stirring in the tall grass ahead of us; Pete cocked his gun and Brett ran forward for the flush. Instead of pheas-ants, though, a strange man emerged from the grass, and the unexpected sight of him way out there in the marsh so startled me that I almost turned and ran. He wore a tan barn jacket and carried a shotgun, and I didn't rec-ognize him until Uncle Pete lowered his gun and said, "Holy Christ, Charlie. I almost fired."

That night, at Earl's house, I had the same disorient-ing feeling—my grandfather was right in front of me, but I didn't know him.

"Who got it into his mind to call the sheriff?" he asked now.

Earl shook his head and spat out a mouthful of smoke. "Who do you *think* did it, Charlie? Who the hell do you think? It was that black bitch married to the schoolteacher."

Charlie looked at his friend with a new intensity. "I thought she worked out at the *country* clinic."

"She does, but only on certain days. Rest of the time she's at the main shop."

Charlie put his hands on his hips and shook his head. "You didn't see her when you took Kevin in?"

"Hell no," Earl said. "If I'd a seen her, I would've made somebody else look after him. But they sign you in at the front desk of the emergency room and then they take the patients into the back. They made me stay in the waiting room, and I didn't know what was hap-pening until the sheriff's deputy came out and talked to me. The only reason I know it's her is that I saw her later—she stood behind the glass window and pointed me out. The bitch was looking at me, Charlie, like she had something to say about it. And Kevin told me it was her who examined him." He took a deep breath and clenched his shoulders. "They shouldn't have let her, not after what the husband did. The two of them have got it in for me."

This new information made my grandfather raise both his arms like he wanted to grab somebody and shake them. I thought of him again on the phone a bit earlier, my sense that he didn't know what to do with his body. I saw a light go on from inside the Watsons' house, and then the figure of Mrs. Watson looking out the window. The two men stood frozen in their tableau until Charlie said, "We've got to do something about this."

Earl nodded. "Damn *right* we've got to do something," he said. "It's bad enough those niggers are here at all. But now they're messing with my family."

They stood silent for another minute. Then the front door opened and Alice Watson stuck her head outside. She was still a pretty woman, or you could see that she had been, but the years of worry and silence had worn her away, like a house grayed by the buffeting winds. She wasn't from Deerhorn but from Wausau, sixty miles away, and now I wonder if even that slight displacement made her feel too isolated to stand up to her husband. The age difference might have made things difficult for her, too. Earl had married late, when he was almost forty, and Alice was nearly twenty years younger; she seemed even smaller in her husband's presence than my grandmother did in Charlie's. But I couldn't believe that she'd approve of his behavior. Now she said, "Earl, why don't you bring Kevin inside. I'm sure you're starving and I've got supper ready."

With that the men parted ways, after a last promise from my grandfather that they'd "figure something out." Earl walked over to his car, pulled open the door, and said, "Come on, boy," and Kevin slowly got out of the passenger's seat. And at that moment I wondered what it must have been like to be Earl Watson's son—to be the gentle, drawn-in child of one of Deerhorn's most prominent men. There were so few models, such strict expectations, for the boys and men in town. The most admired, like Earl and Charlie, were strong, fearless, and totally sure of themselves, without a hint of complication or softness. Here and there was an exception—like Darius Gordon, who was more genteel than the norm but whose athletic and hunting credentials placed him well beyond reproach. But that was about the extent of the acceptable variations. It wasn't clear what happened to other men and boys who diverged from the town's standards. Like Kevin, like the boys and men who lived out in the country trailers. And also like my father.

I don't know if Kevin realized I was there but he avoided looking in my direction; he moved slowly with his head hanging down. I saw the cast on his left arm, the sling over his shoulder. I saw how small he looked next to his father. I saw how he tried to hold his body away from Earl, even as he got within his reach. And I saw how Earl touched him—not with a comforting hand on the shoulder or a guiding touch on the back, but with his fingers gripped around the back of Kevin's neck. He

led his son up the driveway like he was dragging an er-
rant pup, and Kevin looked just that helpless. I felt another wave of annoyance then, followed by a thought so
clear and troubling that it made my stomach hurt. I realized that Kevin's weakness didn't stir compassion, but
contempt—from his father, from other kids, even from
me. And this realization moved me to anger—toward
Kevin and toward myself—as I understood how vulnerable this made him. I wondered what Kevin was thinking as he walked toward the house. I wondered what he
was walking back into.

EIGHT

That Saturday night, we got our first snow of the year. And it was a good one, a full-fledged storm that began in the evening and dropped a foot of fresh powder by morning. Just looking out the window and seeing the world covered in white lifted my spirits a bit—despite my disappointment that my father wasn't coming, despite the scene at Earl's house. When I went outside and let the snow fall on my face and my hands, I couldn't help but feel better.

We had to go to Mass in the morning, but as soon as we were back, I took the dog and headed out to the nearest woods. A few people had already been out for a walk, so there was a path I could follow without sinking in up to my knees. Brett ran along the trail for a while and then went bounding off into the powder. I tossed snowballs for him to catch, and then threw some at a tree, where they left white spots ten feet up along the trunk. Brett barked and jumped futilely, trying to reach them, all four legs off the ground. I felt guilty for misleading him and pulled him away, encouraging him to run out ahead of me.

He refocused quickly. He picked up a long branch and carried it down the trail, holding it in the middle like a tightrope walker's stick, just an inch above the surface of the snow. Farther up there were trees on either side of the trail, and Brett ran smack into them, each end of the branch catching one of the trunks. He bounced back from the force of the impact and looked confused for a moment. Then, taking a few more steps back to rev himself up, he ran forward and tried again. And again the thunk of the branch against the trees. He tried three or four times with increasing force, until finally the branch broke and he was left with only half of it, which he held by the far right end. Past the obstacle of the trees now, he ran along gaily, with his head tilting left from the weight of the branch. Then the loose end caught on something and planted in the ground, and he flew rump over head like a pole vaulter. He landed upside down in the powder off the trail, which was so deep he vanished completely. All was still for a moment. Then he sprang directly from his back to his feet, his entire body covered with snow. He was so obscured by white I couldn't see his black fur—but I saw the happy pink tongue sticking out of his mouth; and the joy in his body as he started to buck, like a bronco, shaking the snow from his body. Once free, he let off an exclamatory bark and bolted down the trail.

It snowed more on Sunday night, and as I walked to school the next morning, I again felt the exhilaration that a snowfall always brought me. It even carried me safely past the house of Jeannie Allen, the girl who often harassed me. Her father was shoveling, clearing a path from their door to the sidewalk, but Jeannie was nowhere in sight. As I walked by, she pushed her curtain aside and stared at me, but she didn't come out of the house. I took a deep breath of relief as I walked by

Mr. Allen, who nodded hello, and continued down the street.

At school, it felt almost like a holiday. All of the kids were talking about building snowmen and having snowball fights, and Miss Anderson had a hard time calming everyone down. It seemed especially cruel that we were stuck inside that day—but finally, it became clear that Miss Anderson was moving ahead with her lessons. No one answered questions, not even Missy Calloway; we were all staring out the window at the snow. No one fell for our teacher's attempts at discussion. And it was this unusual, depressed silence that made it quiet enough for us to hear a strange sound in the hallway.

First the clomping of heavy boots, moving steadily down the hallway. Then the whoosh of thick winter coats. This was no group of students walking late to class, or even teachers, who always seemed to move lightly. It sounded like an army, and as I turned toward the open doorway, I saw that in some sense it was. A group of four men was walking by, stone-faced and with clear purpose. Earl Watson was one of them, and Uncle Pete too; the others were Bob Grimson and John Berger. When I saw Earl and Uncle Pete I expected Charlie to be with them, but to my relief, he was not. I say relief because it was clear to me exactly where they were going. My classmates all murmured nervously, except Brady Grimson, who stood straight up and said, "Dad?" Bob Grimson might have paused for a moment, but then he kept on walking. "Dad!" Brady called out again, more urgently this time, and then he ran out to the hallway. Several of our classmates shot out of their seats and scrambled to the door, ignoring Miss Anderson's command to stay seated. I got up too and fell in behind them.

"Dad, what are you doing?" Brady asked. He'd run toward his father and then stopped abruptly as the whole group of men turned to face him. In their dark, bulky jackets and red plaid hats; in their thick-fingered gloves and heavy boots, they looked as big and unassailable as a mountain range.

"Go back to class, son," Bob Grimson said. He was generally an easy-going man, who worked long hours at the diner he ran with his wife and never took vacations, but he looked tired today, gray-faced and grim.

"But what are you doing here?" asked Brady again.

Mr. Grimson was quiet for a moment. The other men watched him, adjusting hats and gloves and tugging on their jackets. Uncle Pete avoided my eyes and I wanted to hit him, I wanted to hold him—I knew he wouldn't have come here on his own. "We're going to watch him teach," Mr. Grimson said finally.

"What?"

Now Earl stepped forward, looking bigger than ever in his thick green winter jacket. "We're going to watch the nigger teach," he said roughly to Brady. "Law says we're allowed to sit in the classroom and watch our children's teachers teach."

"But Dad," Brady said, turning back to his father, "he's not my teacher."

The men were silent for a moment while we all absorbed that fact. Miss Anderson came and stood behind the children in the doorway.

"He's here with me and Earl," said John Berger, pulling off his big gloves. "I'm here because of Harriet, and

he's here for Kevin. They're supposed to be in Mrs. Hebig's class next year, so we want to see what's going
on. And you'll get to the fifth grade too, all of you, in a
couple of years."

I pondered this. I knew that parents could sit in and
observe a class; Missy Calloway's mother had done so
the previous year. But I also knew—we all did—that
none of these men had ever, not even when they'd been
invited for a student conference or open house, stepped
foot inside the school before.

"Come back to class, children," Miss Anderson said,
and I was surprised by her tone. She sounded scared.
She herded us out of the hallway and back into the classroom as if away from the scene of an accident.

If we'd been having a hard time paying attention
before, now it was impossible. I wanted desperately to
sneak out and run down the hallway, watch what happened in Mr. Garrett's class. I wanted desperately to
tell the men to leave him alone, especially Uncle Pete.
Everyone in the class had forgotten the snow; we were
all listening, for what we didn't know. But when an
hour passed and no sound had come from the end of
the hallway, we settled back into the rhythms of Miss
Anderson's voice—not listening exactly but no longer
straining to hear something else.

I didn't see the men leave—they must have gone out
the back—but I heard later that they hadn't stayed for
long. "He was shaking," Charlie told my grandmother, re-
peating what he'd heard from Uncle Pete. "John opened
the door and they all walked in, and the nigger's eyes
popped out of his head. They sat down in the chairs and
just stared at him."

I tried to imagine those big, full-grown men sitting in those child-sized chairs, a scene that might have been comical under different circumstances.

"He asked what they were doing, and John, he says, 'I want to see what kind of learning my daughter's going to get. Far as I can tell, I've got no reason to keep her in this school.'"

"Did he ask them to leave?" my grandmother asked.

"Yep, and they quoted the law at him, said they were exercising their legal rights. Pete said the fella was so scared he kept dropping his chalk, and none of the letters he *did* get up on the board was straight. They stayed about half an hour, they said, and then they figured they had got their point across. Pete waited outside, and five minutes don't pass before the nigger comes out front while the kids are still in class and stands there and shakes his head." My grandfather seemed satisfied with this result. "We're getting to him," he said. "I think they're gonna break."

But he didn't—*they* didn't—at least not yet. The whispers at school the next day were at first about Mr. Garrett—about how his hand had shaken as he wrote on the board, and how tight and nervous he'd sounded as he tried to give his lesson. Everyone knew that he'd left the classroom soon after the men were gone, to get himself back together. Mrs. Hood's first graders had seen him out the window, shaking his head, just as Uncle Pete had related.

The next day, Miss Anderson came to class looking grim. It wasn't until years later, when I was an adult, that I wondered what Mr. Garrett's presence was like for the rest of the teachers—whether they were just as

uncomfortable with him as everyone else; whether they
looked at him or spoke to him in the teachers' lounge at
lunch; whether they called each other in the evenings
at home to discuss the day's events. For them, the Garretts' presence must have been troubling and surreal.
The conflict in Boston, and earlier, the events in the
South and in Washington, must have seemed totally
foreign to them, the struggles of a different world. The
civil rights movement had never reached Deerhorn, and
now, because of the clinic, some of the changes it had
made possible were happening right there in town, very
much against their will. The Garretts were alone now,
the first black couple. But would there be others, coming after them? And this was happening on top of all the
other shifts and changes of the time—the war, women's
rights, Watergate, drugs, and now the fall of the president that people had hoped would somehow restore the
order. Did any of the teachers threaten to resign from
their jobs? Whether or not they did, nobody actually
quit—in that town, good jobs were not easy to come
by, and teachers made more money than most everyone
else.

I did wonder even then, though, what it was like
for Mr. Garrett. When I saw him in the hallway or out
on the playground, he seemed different, more guarded
and watchful, his sense of ease gone. Did other teachers say hello when he passed them in the hallway? Did
they stop their conversations when he was near, or keep
talking like he didn't exist? Did he go home at night and
share stories with his wife about how people whom he'd
never hurt in any way still treated him like he carried
the plague? And of course I wondered these things, if he

experienced these things, because I had gone through them myself.

But that morning, I see in retrospect, Miss Anderson was troubled not only because of what was happening, but because she knew it would continue to happen. And it did. At about ten-fifteen, before recess, I heard heavy boots in the hallway. And we saw two unfamiliar men walk by down the hall in the direction of the fifth grade classrooms. Everyone saw them, although no one rushed to the door this time. We all knew where they were going.

At recess, some of the more adventurous boys in class ventured down the hallway. When they came back they reported that they saw the two men—fathers of children in the first and second grades—sitting in the child-sized chairs. The class was empty otherwise; Mr. Garrett and the children were outside. But the men were seated there, unmoving, rooted like trees, and I knew when I heard this description that they'd be staying there all day.

The next morning, a little earlier, another two fathers walked by. Again, they stayed in the room all day, not leaving the school until we were released at two-forty. The next morning it was a set of parents—Casey and Sally Borham—and the morning after that, two more fathers. We heard afterward that Mr. Garrett no longer seemed so nervous; he just went on with his lessons as if the adults weren't there.

But the students were rattled. They were caught off-guard when Mr. Garrett called on them, stuttering out inadequate replies; and even the usual chit-chat between subjects or after recess had dwindled down to nothing. This discomfort, the adults insisted, was because of the *teacher's* presence, not theirs. According to my grandfather, people were putting off housework, taking time from their jobs, rearranging their schedules to show up at the school and sit in on Mr. Garrett's fifth grade class.

I still don't know why Charlie wasn't among them. Maybe he was too old, but that didn't seem right; his age didn't stop him from doing anything else. Maybe as much as he talked about the Garretts, he wanted to keep a distance from the actions against them. Or maybe, on some level, my presence at the school prevented him from going. Maybe he realized there were parallels between their troubles and mine. I hope so; I hope this could be true. I just don't really know. What I do know is that he took a vicarious pleasure in people's efforts to unsettle the Garretts. And they were going to keep on doing it; they were going to keep sitting in on Mr. Garrett's class until all available parents had taken a turn. Then, they would simply start over.

It wasn't until the Saturday after the second week of visits that I discovered that not everyone approved of them. I went uptown with my grandmother in the early afternoon to do the weekly shopping, helping her fill the basket with seven days' worth of vegetables and meat, beans and flour and coffee, all the staples she used for her simple, hearty meals. We didn't talk much, my grandmother speaking only to tell me to fetch a box of cereal or to stop squeaking my shoes against the slick linoleum. But our silence was companionable; there just wasn't a lot to say. We didn't have as much in common as Charlie and me.

After my grandmother paid and the bagger boy had packed up all the groceries, she pushed the cart out to the parking lot. And there we ran into Darius Gordon, who was walking toward the entrance of the market. He was wrapped up tight in his long tan coat, a green wool cap pulled down over his ears. He had a look on his face that suggested that his thoughts were far away, and wherever they were, it wasn't pleasing to him. He didn't see us until he'd almost walked into our cart, and even then it was not until he mumbled his apology that he realized who we were.

"Oh hello, Helen, Michelle," he said, his breath visible in the cold winter air. "I'm sorry, I'm getting slow on the uptake in my old age."

My grandmother smiled. I knew how much she liked Mr. Gordon; she always said that he was a gentleman. "That hardly describes you, Darius. You're one of the sharpest men I know."

"Well, not so sharp that I didn't let myself run out of coffee. And it's hard for me to get started in the morning without it."

"Where's your Lucy?" my grandmother asked.

"Oh, at home in her dog bed. She didn't appreciate the thought of coming out in this cold weather. She's not much for the outdoors at all, actually, which is strange for an English setter. She doesn't run headlong into the world the way your Brett does."

At this, he looked at me, and I felt a double rush of pleasure—because he spoke to me, and because he praised my dog. Then he turned back to my grandmother. "Did you have a nice Thanksgiving?"

My grandmother hesitated. How could she answer

that? My father's absence had defined the whole day, and all the food and beer and talking, all the football and television, couldn't cover the silence of the telephone, the emptiness of the mailbox, the extra seat at the dining room table. As soon as the meal was over I had gone out with Brett and walked until I couldn't feel my feet.

"Yes," she said. "Pete and Bertha came over, and between us we ate the whole turkey. Michelle here helped mash the potatoes." She paused, and I knew she was keeping herself from looking at me, trying as hard as she could to sound normal. "And how about you?"

"Spent it with Del and his wife," Mr. Gordon replied. "It was nice enough, but holidays are for children. A bunch of adults sitting around and staring at each other gets tiresome after a while." He looked at me again, warmly. "You're lucky to have a grandchild, Helen. Especially lucky that she's staying with you. Del and Karen, I think they got too caught up in his career to think about having a family."

They were silent for a moment, as the subject of his son's job lay between them. And that made me stop feeling sad about the holiday and start thinking about the clinic, which of course made me think about the Garretts.

Mr. Gordon's mind must have turned in this direction too, for now he raised his eyes again and carefully asked, "Have you heard about what's been happening at the school?"

This was not a real question, I knew. Of course she had heard. What he was really asking was, what do you think of it?

My grandmother wouldn't meet his eyes now; she looked down at the cart. "Yes," she said. "I've heard all about it."

Mr. Gordon paused, and when he spoke, his voice was gentle. "They're crucifying that man, and he did nothing wrong. In fact, he did exactly what he was *supposed* to do."

My grandmother shivered slightly, and I wasn't sure it was from the weather. Her warmth toward Mr. Gordon was gone; she had retreated back into herself. "I think people are upset about them not minding their own business."

"And the wife, she followed the letter of the law. There was nothing she *could* do but make a report."

My grandmother said nothing to this, so Mr. Gordon continued, a little more strongly now. "And it's not just the showing up at school anymore. The wife told my son that a strange car's been driving by their house, a gray Buick. A couple of nights ago someone fired a shot over their roof." He leaned uncomfortably close now, his wrinkled hand gripping the cart. "*Earl* drives a gray Buick," he said, and his cheeks had turned red. "He's gone too far, Helen. He's losing control. You've got to get Charlie to stop him."

My grandmother stepped back and flinched as if he'd reached out to strike her. "They had no business coming here, Darius. They had no right. They've brought on all this trouble themselves." But even as she said this, I heard the uncertainty in her voice, as if she were speaking someone else's words and not her own. And in her face I saw a fissure, an opening, and I wasn't sure what it meant.

Mr. Gordon pulled himself up straight again, but he kept his clear eyes on her face. "It's not just about them anymore. It's about Earl, and that little boy. Who's getting worked up about what's happening to *him*?" His face had turned even redder, but he didn't seem to feel the cold. "My son looked at the X-rays, Helen, and he agreed with the nurse. And you put that together with what the teacher saw, and there's no way they couldn't call social services."

And now my grandmother shook her head and her lips began to quiver. "But it's Earl, Darius. It's *Earl*." She paused, started to speak, stopped, and started up again. "He's sat at my dining room table and eaten my cooking. He's sat next to Charlie at the coffee shop. He's gone hunting with Charlie and Jim and the others for more years than I can count." She gripped the handle of the shopping cart as if holding on for her life. "And I remember him as a *boy*, Darius, when we were all young, working with his daddy at the gun shop. I remember the day he came home from the war, the day he married Alice." She looked up at Mr. Gordon's face, and her eyes flashed with anger and pain. "How can you ask me to believe this about him? How can it be true?"

Mr. Gordon didn't answer her; he just lowered his head. My grandmother, the floodgates opened now, continued. "But Kevin's arm, and those scars on his back . . . couldn't there be another explanation?" She looked down at her gloves and sighed, and in the long moment before she spoke again, I was aware of the traffic going by, the shouted greetings of a teenage boy, the creak and bell of the automatic door sliding open as someone came out of the store.

"I just don't think I can make Charlie see it," she said. "Even if it was someone else who reported it, Darius, he's never going to go against Earl. And the fact that it was the two of *them*—well, that's just fuel on the fire."

And now Mr. Gordon looked back at her and their eyes met, and something passed between them—some kind of understanding or acknowledgment. I was stunned by what I had heard. For I knew now that she believed him. She believed what Mr. Gordon was telling her, which meant she believed the Garretts. She believed that Earl Watson was harming his son, and in this conviction, she was going against the explicit, active belief of my grandfather, who thought that the Garretts were lying. Or maybe he didn't really think they were lying; maybe he just thought that things were being exaggerated.

And there's this last possibility also. There's the possibility that Charlie knew full well that Earl was hurting Kevin and was choosing to defend him anyway. This I could not entertain. This I could not fit into my image of him, and so I simply chose to ignore it. Because I always saw Charlie as my defender, as an honorable man who didn't live in a world that allowed harm to come to children. It didn't matter whether it was me, or a stranger, or Earl Watson's son. There are things that good men do not tolerate.

Whatever the case regarding Charlie's stance on Earl, my grandmother didn't agree with him. And seeing her doubt, seeing her tacit agreement with Darius Gordon, made me realize that I didn't know her as well as I thought. What else did she have her own mind about? How else did she diverge from her husband? And what had it cost her all of these years to be his silent wife, his constant supporter, with no opinions of her own; no way to make a space that was separate from him?

I don't know whether she said something to Charlie, but I do know that it was right around this time that the house got very quiet. My grandparents didn't engage in their usual chatter over coffee and toast in the morning. At supper, we all sat silently around the dining room table, speaking only to ask for butter or salt. In the evenings, my grandmother stayed in the kitchen to listen to a radio program or read her Bible—she no longer kept it hidden—and I wonder how much of her withdrawal had to do with her religion, with her belief that there are greater loyalties than allegiances to friends. As the tension in the house increased she grew more open, more defiant, displaying her faith as if she were flaunting evidence of a new, attentive lover. Even Brett seemed to pick up on the change in the atmosphere—he would go from one of them to the other, licking their hands and whining, as if begging for them to make up. Then one Friday afternoon when my grandmother set out the usual extra plate for Jim, Charlie told her she should take it away.

"Why?" she asked, genuinely surprised.

"Because he's not coming over tonight."

She picked up the plate, half-turned back toward the kitchen. "That's too bad. I was going to make his favorite tuna casserole. Well, I guess I can just make it next Friday."

Charlie was lying on the couch, and he sat up so he could look at her. "You don't need to, Helen. At least not for him. He's not coming over anymore."

She turned all the way around and looked at Charlie

hard, and he met her eyes with defiance. And I realized and saw *her* realize exactly what this meant—that Darius and Del Gordon weren't the only ones in town who disagreed with what was happening to the Garretts.

NINE

The classroom visits stopped soon after that, seemingly on their own. I learned later by eavesdropping on the teachers at lunch that Mr. Baker had put an end to them—not out of any concern for Mr. Garrett, but because the constant presence of strange adults was becoming a distraction. It was upsetting the students, alarming the teachers, causing trouble all around. And he was worried about the declining enrollment—not only in Mr. Garrett's fifth grade class, but in the fourth grade classes below it, because parents were already making arrangements with parochial schools in the event that Mrs. Hebig did not return. So gradually things returned to normal, or as normal as they could be.

Except that my comfortable invisibility of a few weeks earlier had vanished, and everyone discovered me anew. I don't know whether the increased attention was a spillover of the hostility toward the Garretts, or if, with the classroom visits coming to an end, people needed a place to channel their anger. And I don't know if the change was related to the latest news from overseas. The North Vietnamese Army was on the move back into the southern part of the country—and suddenly, the other kids were giving me colder, harder stares. I was being called names again—Jap, Chink, Gook—

and getting pushed around more in the hallway.

And going to church wasn't any more pleasant than going to school. At Sunday services that week, no one would sit next to us, which really meant next to me; they'd pause briefly when they saw me sitting in the pew and then continue down the aisle. Even Father Pace greeted me with a bold and naked stare, which Charlie noticed and returned with a glare of his own.

But if church was hard for me, it had also gotten awkward for Earl Watson and his family. Earl was almost feverish as he shook everyone's hand; his wife waited silently behind him. Next to her was Jake, who looked uncomfortable in his jacket and tie, and Kevin, who kept his watery blue eyes on the floor. It seemed to me that some of the greetings that Earl got were less than enthusiastic; that a few people appeared to change direction when they saw him; that there was something veiled or distant in their eyes. Deerhorn was a small town, and word of his troubles was likely to have traveled all over, from the bars to the beauty salons to the feed and tack store where the farmers came in from the country. Maybe I was imagining all of this, though, and everything was normal. Maybe everyone would have stood by him no matter what was being said, especially given who had started the talking.

My grandfather remained steadfast in defense of his friend. If anything, as the days went by without further word from my father, he grew even stronger in his convictions. But because of the new silence between him and my grandmother, because she no longer welcomed some of his friends in the house, Charlie was spending more and more time at the gun store. He went there now between his two trips to the coffee shop instead of coming home, which meant that when he left the house at eight in the morning, we didn't see him again until supper. If my grandmother was unhappy with this new arrangement, she didn't show it; she just worked harder around the house and spent more time with her Bible. When Charlie did come home, we'd eat supper without talking; then he'd lie down in the living room to watch TV while my grandmother retreated back into the kitchen.

It didn't feel right in the house anymore. Between not hearing from my father, and the absence of Charlie, I was lonelier than ever. The silence between my grandparents was heavy, uncomfortable, full of disappointment and mistrust. I'd never seen this before, never known them not to agree, and I didn't like to be there inside of it.

The dog was as unsettled as everyone else. He watched me all the time now, even more closely, his brown eyes filled with concern. Wherever I went, he needed to be touching me, and I wasn't sure if it was for my reassurance or his own. One day he went after a loose dog in the neighborhood, and then, a few days later, he bared his teeth at the mailman. We both needed to be outside, to run out the agitation, but it was December now and so cold most days that even three layers of clothes and a heavy coat was no defense against the biting air. I had to stay indoors whether I liked it or not, even though the cold outside was easier to bear than the chill inside the house.

The only time I left was to go to school, and that was becoming more difficult, since Jeannie Allen had suddenly rediscovered me. I'd managed to avoid her for most of the fall—maybe she, like everyone else, had been distracted by the Garretts—but on Tuesday morning, Jeannie was waiting for me at the edge of her yard like she was defending her house against an invasion.

"You better go another way," she called out as I approached. "No niggers or Japs allowed on this road."

I didn't answer and tried to figure out what to do. Jeannie was a big girl, half a foot taller than me, and my encounters with her the previous spring had left me with bruises on my knees from when she'd thrown me on the ground, and a black eye from when she had punched me. Her family, for some reason I never learned, was avoided by other people. At school, Jeannie had two equally outcast friends; the three of them clustered together on the playground and in the cafeteria and tried not to draw attention to themselves. But here, out of school, she was master of her domain, and as soon as I got close enough she lunged. I sidestepped her, swinging my body as far as I could to the left, and her fingers grabbed the end of my jacket.

"Where do you think you're going?" she asked as she swung me around, and I went with the motion, not resisting, flying like a cat, thinking that she might lose hold of me.

"Let go!" I yelled out, and then I struck down just like Charlie had taught me, a hard chop above her wrist, where the arm is tender and vulnerable. Jeannie howled and let go of me and touched her hurt arm. I jabbed left, and she reached out again, but by the time her arms came together on the empty air, I'd drawn up and taken off to the right. She was off-balance, almost falling, and I was past her.

* * *

My run-in with Jeannie made me remember another difficult trip to school. That earlier trip had been several years before, when I was still living in Japan. My father usually walked me to the English-language school in the morning, and then a teacher's aide or one of our neighbors would walk me to the Japanese school after lunch. But on this day, for some reason, my father couldn't go, and so my mother had to take me instead. She didn't speak much as we passed by the stores close to our apartment—the bicycle shop, the fish market, the ubiquitous noodle houses—and unlike my father, she didn't hold my hand. She wore high heels and an outfit straight out of a fashion magazine, with a scarf around her neck and big, dark glasses. As we walked through the noisy, crowded sidewalks of Tokyo, people turned to stare at her, and I remember feeling nervous and also a bit proud to be in the company of such a glamorous woman.

When we got to the English-language school, the teachers welcomed my mother warmly and scurried about as if they were receiving a celebrity. They told her how well I was doing—I could write the entire English alphabet, and spell out my full name—but when they showed her one of my drawings, she glanced at it indifferently, as if it were a letter in a language she couldn't read. They looked from her to me and back again, curious, perplexed, and I could see they were trying to make sense of her beauty in relation to my plainness. Other parents—expatriates from England, Australia, New Zealand, America—arrived with their children; they dropped them off with kisses and hugs and spoke easily to each other.

That stopped when they got to my mother. They greeted her politely, some spoke a few words, and she replied in her easy English. But it was clear to everyone, even to me, that she was out of place here. Not because she was Japanese—that would have been too easy an explanation, and besides, these were all foreigners who had chosen to live in Japan. And I don't know that it would have felt any less awkward if she'd taken me to the Japanese school, which she didn't; the usual teacher's aide would do that. No, the disconnect was something much more fundamental than nationality or language or race. My mother did not know how to relate to other parents or to teachers; how to behave in a place that focused on children. She did not know how to exist in a world where she wasn't at the center of everything.

In early December, finally, there was one nice day—a day when the sun briefly made an appearance and the temperature cracked forty. Feeling as sprung as I would have on the first day of summer, I took my bike—once again leaving Brett behind—and rode the three miles out of town. I followed my usual route along the back roads, passing the park but not entering it. I went by the turn-off for the trailers too, then turned onto Besemer Road, not slowing down until I reached the satellite clinic. The parking lot—like the side of the road—was ringed with dirty snow, which had been pushed there by the plows after the most recent storms and was speckled with gravel and mud. There were three cars parked in front of the clinic, and through the windows I could see the shapes of people moving inside. I circled back and waited behind a small stand of trees so that people coming out wouldn't see me. I waited there an hour, although it felt more like ten, and each time the door opened I stood straight up, but the first time it was somebody taking out the trash and the next time it was a mother and her boy. Then finally, just as the cold was starting to get to me, the door opened and Mrs. Garrett came out.

She sighed and pulled her blue coat tight against the cold, as she had the first time I came to see her. But this time, she reached into her pocket and pulled out a cigarette. She lit it and then stood holding it in her right hand, her left arm keeping the coat closed around her. I couldn't read the expression on her face, but it looked like her thoughts were heavy. I wondered what she had felt the day she reported Earl, what she felt going to work every day. I wondered if she and her husband were wearing down, as my grandfather and his friends believed. And from the distance of almost forty years, I wonder this too: why exactly had the Garretts come to Deerhorn? For the sake of their careers? I knew that the clinic expansion provided an opportunity for Mrs. Garrett, but surely they could have found good jobs in Chicago. For the quiet rural life, far from the noise and stress of the city? Or to get away from something? It seemed an odd choice to move to Deerhorn, even if you factored in Mrs. Garrett's connection with Del Gordon. But maybe they weren't really aware of what they were getting into; maybe they had no sense of how bad it would be. The truth is, I'll never understand what led to their decision. We never really know why anyone does anything.

I do know, however, that they occupied a space in my mind I hadn't realized was there. It wasn't just curiosity, or attraction, or loneliness, or allegiance, but a need to have them like and acknowledge me. I admired them—for what they'd achieved, but also what they'd endured; they'd risked more than me, and bore their hardships gracefully. I fully realize that behind the image they projected, they could both have been rife with faults and imperfections. Maybe Mr. Garrett never put the toilet seat down. Maybe Mrs. Garrett never called her mother. Maybe they drank too much or littered or were petty and jealous; maybe they weren't the good people I imagined. I will never know who they were beyond my limited perceptions, and in not knowing, I realize that my picture of them will always be incomplete. It's a picture I've burnished to an improbable sheen because I knew them when I was a child, because they were good to me, and because I see them through the lens of time and sadness.

Mrs. Garrett's cigarette had burned down to a nub, and I was afraid I'd miss my chance if I waited any longer. So I pedaled out from behind the trees and rode into the parking lot. I must have shot out more quickly than I'd intended, because I didn't see the deep pothole at the top of the driveway—my front tire caught it and the bike came to a dead stop, catapulting me over the handlebars. As I flew, my leg got tangled and I came down on the gravel, my right ankle caught and twisted in the back wheel. I cried out in surprise as much as in pain, and felt more than a little embarrassed. But the fall must have looked spectacular, because it brought Mrs. Garrett running down from the landing, yelling, "Michelle!" and then, "Shit! Shit!"

She reached me in what seemed like an impossibly short time and disentangled me from the bike. "Are you all right?" she asked as she helped me roll over into a sitting position. Her hands seemed both to check and position me—putting me into place while also feeling for any obvious fracture. Nothing hurt except my ankle and I told her so.

"Okay," she said, "let's get you inside." And with that she helped me stand—right foot not touching the ground—and then lifted me as easily as if I were a cat and carried me toward the front door. She had one arm under my legs and the other beneath my back; my arms were around her neck for support. I remember being surprised that such a slight-looking woman could handle my weight so easily. And as I became aware of her thin shoulders, her strong hands, even the press of her breasts, I remember thinking that I couldn't recall the last time a woman had held me. Had this trip lasted more than about twenty seconds, I might have gotten far too used to it. But it was over as soon as she carried me through the door. She set me down, and then there I was inside the satellite clinic—the place that had been the topic of so much speculation, the target of so much disapproval. Inside, two other adults—one man, one woman—stood blinking their surprise.

We appeared to be in a kind of reception room with a desk near the door and some upholstered chairs, a few nondescript paintings on the walls. There was also a desk and file cabinet against the far wall; the work and waiting must have occurred in the same space. Once inside, I was reminded of how small the building was, especially since it had been divided to make separate rooms.

"She fell," Mrs. Garrett told the two other people, as if that explained my presence. "I'm going to take her into Exam One." And with that she led me into one of the subdivided rooms and sat me down on the raised exam table. I wondered what other people had thought when they found themselves alone with her. Were they nervous or uncomfortable, as they often seemed with me? Were they scared? Or were they perfectly all right? Did they avoid her eyes or shrink back as she approached? Did some people refuse her help altogether? I was sure they did; I was sure that some people would rather endure their pain and illness than subject themselves to her touch. And how did she deal with their reactions to her, the extra level of anxiety her patients might feel? Was she comforting and soothing? Was she annoyed?

I tried to push these questions out of my mind and focus on what was happening. At Mrs. Garrett's direction, I slid far enough back on the table that my leg was supported. She unlaced my boot carefully and eased it off of my foot. Then she rolled down the sock and I felt a flush of embarrassment at the ring of dirt just above where the sock had covered. But Mrs. Garrett didn't seem to care. She cupped my heel gently and stood over my foot, examining it from every angle. And while my ankle did hurt—I could already see the purple gathering under the skin—I also liked the feel of her hands on my foot, administering their care.

"You sprained it pretty badly," she said, and her voice sounded clear and firm in the space of that small room. "But I don't think you broke anything. So let's put some ice on it and elevate it to hold down the swelling. I'll give you some aspirin for the pain, and when it's eased off a little, I'll wrap it up for support and send you home."

I'd never sprained an ankle before, although I've done it plenty since, playing pickup basketball in California. And it's so often the same ankle, with the swelling in exactly the same place, that I wonder if I'm just re-aggravating that original sprain, way back from my time in Wisconsin. But that day, despite the pain, despite the swelling that soon looked like a base-ball growing out the side of my ankle, I was all right, I wasn't scared, because Mrs. Garrett was there. And her ease and matter-of-factness as she pressed the ice against my foot, as she wrapped it all firmly in a tan Ace bandage, made me think that everything would be okay. She'd taken off her blue jacket when we got inside, and underneath it she wore a thin white coat with *Garrett* embroidered on the chest pocket, over long brown pants and a cream-colored turtleneck. Her skin looked very dark against the sweater and coat, and I watched her expression shift from concern to cautious optimism.

She sat down in a chair in the corner and looked at me directly. "Why were you biking all the way out here, Michelle?"

I shrugged and said the same thing I'd said the first time. "I bike out here all the time."

"But the last time I saw you the weather was still warm. Now the roads are all covered with snow."

I gave an exaggerated sigh, for what could I say? That I'd gone out there because I felt so bad about what was happening with her husband? Because I admired what she had done at the clinic and I just wanted to see her face? Because their standing up for Kevin Watson de-spite all the risks showed a concern that I desperately missed from my parents? Because I hadn't heard from my father in over a month, and my mother much longer, and I didn't know when I would? The truth was, I didn't really know why I'd gone out there. Maybe this, what was happening, was reason enough.

Mrs. Garrett must have known she wasn't going to get an answer, because she sighed and looked out the open door. "Boy, you never know what you're going to come across in this town," she said. "There's so much I didn't expect here. Didn't expect at all. And then you, today, falling off your bike and almost giving me a heart attack."

And now I looked across at her and knew why I had come. But because I didn't have the language to tell her what I felt; because I couldn't say "I believe you" or "I saw it, too" or "I know that you were right," what I said was, "Kevin Watson goes to school with me."

Mrs. Garrett looked up at me sharply, but her voice was even when she spoke. "Yes, that's right, he would, wouldn't he? Yes, I suppose that makes sense."

"His dad used to come to our house," I said, with an urgency beyond the meaning of the words. "Earl—his dad—used to come to our house. But . . . but . . . he doesn't anymore. My grandmother doesn't like him."

I turned away and looked at the counter with its containers of supplies—glass canisters with bandages and cotton balls, and flat pink tongue depressors.

"He's a good kid, Kevin," I said, although I'd never thought such a thing until just that moment, and wouldn't have put it that way if I had. "Kevin, I mean, he's quiet and all, but he's a real good kid."

When I looked over at Mrs. Garrett again, I was surprised to see that there were tears in her eyes. And then I felt the tears well up in my own eyes too, and when she said, "Yes, he's a real good kid," I couldn't hold them and they spilled down my face. Then Mrs. Garrett stood up, crossed the room, and put her arms around me, holding me as she stood beside the table. My shoulder was against her stomach and I turned into her and cried, and it was Kevin, but it was Charlie too, and also my parents, because they had left me and I knew that they were never coming back. But all I could manage to say again was, "He's a good kid," and Mrs. Garrett held me more tightly against her and whispered, "Yes, and you are too."

I don't know how long we stayed like that, but after a while I heard footsteps and then someone was standing in the door. It was the man I had seen when we first came in. He was middle-aged and of medium height, with receding brown hair, and I realized that he was the same man who'd come outside the first day I'd talked with Mrs. Garrett. "Betty, we're getting ready to leave, and we should figure out what to do with Michelle."

I was surprised that he knew who I was, but I shouldn't have been. Everyone did. In that town, I could never be anonymous.

"All right, Del," said Mrs. Garrett. "Well, her ankle's sprained and her bike's banged up, so I should probably drive her back. Joe's in Chicago for his father's hip replacement surgery, so I'm not in any hurry to get home." She moved a little away from me, but with her hand still on my shoulder.

He looked from her to me and back again and a muscle twitched in his cheek. "You better let me take her,

Betty. Her grandfather . . ." He stopped and they were both silent for a moment, and I didn't know what he was saying. And then it hit me like the gravel of the parking lot coming up to meet my hands as I fell: he didn't think it was a good idea for her to take me home, because of how Charlie might react.

Mrs. Garrett quickly pulled her hand off my shoulder as she realized this, too. "Oh," she said, as if she'd been stung. And in that one syllable I heard all the feeling she'd probably been trying to hold down for months—the anger, the loss of patience, the resentment at the town that had made her feel so unwelcome. "Oh, sure, of course," she said, sounding business-like, and colder. "Well, then I guess you should take her."

There was another awkward silence, and then she leaned down and put her hands on my shoulders and looked me in the face. "Dr. Gordon's going to take you home, Michelle," she said, her voice gentle again. "I've done as much as I can. Now you be careful and don't ride your bike on these icy roads. And stay off of that ankle until it heals."

She touched my cheek and smiled at me, her face both sad and angry, and I wanted to say thank you. But all I managed was "Okay" and then the doctor came over, picking me up to carry me outside. His touch was rougher than hers, less comforting, and he jostled me as he walked.

Mrs. Garrett opened the front door for us and then the door of his Ford sedan, and the doctor leaned down and placed me in the back. Then he loaded my bike into the trunk, got in, and started up the car, and I looked out the window at Mrs. Garrett in a panic—not because I was afraid he was going to do something bad, but because in the clinic I'd felt safe for a moment, and now I had to leave. I was going back out again, back into the world where nothing made sense and where no one—not even Charlie—could protect me. Then the car started and we were moving away, and Mrs. Garrett stood on the stairs in her warm blue coat, waving until we'd driven out of sight.

The doctor tried to make conversation but I didn't feel like talking, not even when he mentioned how much his father liked me and I realized that he was Darius Gordon's son. It didn't occur to me then that it was unusual for the chief administrator of the county clinic to be working at a satellite operation. And now I wonder: was he there to make sure that this new effort was getting off the ground successfully? Or was he there to protect Mrs. Garrett? At any rate, he took me home and carried me up the back steps, explaining to my worried grandmother (my grandfather was out) that I'd fallen on the road just out of town. I don't know whether he made up this story for Mrs. Garrett's sake or my own, but in the end, I didn't think much about it.

It was Mrs. Garrett I thought about, what she would go home and tell her husband when they talked on the phone that night. I wondered what she was thinking about as she held me, and who her own tears were for. Were they for Kevin, or me, or maybe herself, for what she and her husband were facing? I wondered what she'd do that evening, alone in their house—whether she'd read or watch TV, cook or finish up some work—and I felt a sharp and sudden longing to be in her company, to bask in her strength and the warmth of her presence.

But one thing I was sure of was that I'd visit her at the clinic again. Despite her warnings about the icy road, despite my fall, I'd go out there because of how kind she was, because of the way she made me feel. I'd go out there because there was nowhere else to go.

TEN

It was only two days later that the final call came. The phone rang around seven o'clock that night, and my grandmother came out of the kitchen to answer it. After she said hello there was a period of silence. Then: "I'll get him," followed by, "Charlie, it's Alice Watson."

Charlie got up from his couch and met her eyes. And from the look that passed between them, it was clear that things had taken an irreversible turn; that everything had come to a head. He walked into the dining room and took the receiver; as he listened, his expression grew dark. He asked, "When did they come?" and "Do you have enough?" and "Where is Kevin now?" He listened a little longer and said, "Sit tight, Alice. I'll be right over."

He hung up the phone and sat down heavily at the dining room table. "They arrested Earl this afternoon," he said, looking at no one in particular. "An ambulance came and took Kevin away, and then Ray's men put Earl in jail."

My grandmother, who'd retreated to the kitchen doorway, made a tentative step forward. "What happened?"

Charlie sighed and shrugged. "I don't know, exactly. She said Earl and Kevin got into it pretty bad today. Earl pissed off and yelling and Kevin crying. Someone must have called about it—I'll bet it was that nigger teacher again." He scratched at a stain on the table and then smoothed it over with his fingers. "And next thing you know the police and the ambulance are there, and both Earl and Kevin are gone, and Alice has been calling around all afternoon, trying to figure out what to do."

The room was quiet as my grandmother digested this. In the silence, I heard the ticking of the clock. Then I remembered something, and although I didn't normally speak up at such moments, my information seemed important.

"It couldn't have been him, Grandpa," I said.

He stared at me blankly.

"It couldn't have been Mr. Garrett. He's not here, he's in Chicago. He hasn't been at school all week."

My grandfather continued to look at me, and it took a moment for this news to sink in. "Well, it must have been *her*, then. It must have been the wife. Either way, it doesn't really matter."

We all stayed silent for a few more seconds. Then my grandmother asked, "So what now?"

Charlie put both his hands on the table and curled them into fists. "Alice called her brother and her parents and put the money together for bail. So Earl's on his way home, but no one knows where Kevin is. She called the clinic, but they're not saying anything. They won't even tell her if he's there." He sat still for a little longer and then he stood up. "Well, I guess I better go get my jacket."

My grandmother looked at him sharply. "Where are you going?"

He turned back to her, surprised. "I'm going to Earl's. Where do you think I'm going?"

She leaned over the table and said in a firm, unfamiliar voice, "Charlie, he's going to be all worked up. You think this is a good idea?"

He looked at her as if he wasn't sure who she was. "He's my *friend*," he said. "I need to help him. I need to help him get his son back." And with that he brushed past her and hurried to their bedroom.

I didn't wait. Knowing that he wasn't even thinking of me, knowing that my grandmother would forbid me if I asked, I grabbed my jacket, called the dog, and rushed out to the car. I jumped into the backseat with Brett right behind me, guessing that Charlie would be less likely to notice us if we were out of his immediate sight. Because there was no way I was going to miss what happened now, this night when Earl finally got what was coming to him. And my grandmother, perhaps distracted by her argument with Charlie, didn't even see me leave the house.

But I wish now that she had. There've been many times over the years when I wish she had stopped me and made me stay at home. Because maybe if she had stopped me I wouldn't have seen what I saw. Maybe some of the things that happened that night wouldn't have happened, or at least would have played out differently.

When Charlie got into the driver's seat, he threw a quick glance in my direction but didn't say anything. Maybe he was so focused on what lay ahead that nothing could draw his mind from it. Maybe he thought the worst had already happened. Whatever the case, we drove out to Warren Road in silence, and as we approached, I saw the imposing size of Earl's house again, the cold white façade, the porch that seemed more barrier than gathering place. And parked in the driveway was a Deerhorn police car, its lights still flashing, throwing rotating beams of red and blue against the house and out into the darkness.

When I think back to that night, I remember things I couldn't possibly have seen. That squad car, for example. For while I did see a squad car, it was—it *must* have been—the car that brought Earl back to his house after his family had posted bail. But what I remember is different. Different and so vivid that all the details I heard in the weeks to come, all the hushed conversations at home and at school, must have blended together with what I actually *did* see to create an invented memory. Because what I recall but couldn't have witnessed are Earl's angry, threatening shouts, his accusations that Kevin was trying to get him in trouble. What I recall is Kevin crying over and over again, "I'm sorry, Dad! I'm sorry!" I remember the sound of flesh striking flesh; of the sickening crunch of bone; of the high-pitched screams of both the boy and his mother, begging for her husband to stop. And I remember that this seemed to go on and on until finally the squad car was there, and three big policemen struck the door with their fists and dragged Earl out in handcuffs. I remember the ambulance too, the blue-smocked emergency workers bringing Kevin out, holding his arm gently against his side. I remember Alice Watson standing on the steps of her house, holding her head in her hands and sobbing. And I remember Jake circling the police car and cursing, until one of the policemen threatened to arrest him if he didn't shut up and get his ass inside.

Later, much later, I would learn the extent of Kevin's

injuries—not just from that night, but from all of the nights, going farther back than anybody knew. I learned about the thick, raised scars that were not only on his back, but also on his buttocks and thighs. I learned about the fracture that night to his arm, the same arm from a few weeks earlier; but I also learned about the long-healed fractures of his fingers and collarbone, and a leg from when he was thrown against a wall. I heard about the cigarette burns to the insides of his arms, the times his father made him stand in the corner for hours, so long that he soiled his pants. And I heard, we all heard, about the great lengths to which Earl Watson had gone to conceal his abuse. He always closed the blinds before a beating began. He avoided hitting Kevin in the face. He never did more in public than raise his voice at his son, the same as any other father would do. And no matter how angry Earl got, no matter how drunk, he never failed to take these precautions. He never failed to do what he had to do to keep up the pretense of normality. He was never so out of control that he forgot to protect himself. He was never really out of control at all.

But that night in December, I knew none of these things yet. What I saw was a squad car outside of a quiet house, and soon enough, Earl Watson got out. Ray Davis had been in the driver's seat and now he got out too and they both looked back at Charlie. Then Charlie opened the door and stood to join them, not saying—he didn't have to say—that I should stay behind. He approached his two friends slowly, as if conserving his energy to deal with whatever awaited him. And as he got closer, Earl looked at him with an expression I could see even by the light of the porch lamp. It wasn't anger exactly, or at least not anger by itself. And it certainly wasn't guilt or remorse. It was more like whatever Earl had kept wrapped so tightly had begun to pull loose, to come apart. His mouth was slightly open and his lips worked without sound. His face appeared pale, drained of blood. And his eyes, which I could see in the rotating arc of the police light, looked emptied out and black. Somehow this version of Earl was more frightening to me than the dour but talkative man I'd grown accustomed to. This version was not recognizable; there was no telling what he could do.

Ray and Charlie must have seen this too. Now Ray lay a hand on Earl's shoulder and said, "We better get you inside to Alice."

My grandfather said, "You just sit tight tonight, Earl. We'll take care of everything in the morning."

"You're damn right we'll take care of it," Earl said in a low voice, and I knew it wasn't Kevin he was thinking of. Then Ray, understanding this, looked his friend in the eyes and said something that surprised us all.

"Earl, it wasn't them. It wasn't the blacks who reported you." He sounded apologetic, even ashamed.

"Bullshit," said Earl. "Don't fuck with me, Ray. I know that nigger teacher has it in for me."

"Maybe so," said Ray. "But he's not the one who called."

"He couldn't have," my grandfather confirmed. "Mike says he's out of town."

Earl absorbed this for a moment. "Well, it must have been *her* then," he insisted. "Maybe she went over to the school or something, and—"

Ray just shook his head slowly, his shoulders sagging. Earl lifted his head and looked at him incredulously. Several waves of reaction washed over his face—disbelief, anger, confusion. He whirled around and looked at his neighbor's house to the east, then spun again toward the house to the west.

"Are you kidding me?" he asked now. "It wasn't them? Well then, who the hell *was* it?"

Ray looked down. "It was someone else."

Earl turned back to him, clenching his fists. "Who?" he demanded. "Who the hell would have done this to me?"

Ray shook his head, a pained expression on his face. "You know I can't tell you that, Earl."

"Who?" Earl demanded again, and he stepped so close to his friend that I thought he might strike him. But Charlie put his hand on his shoulder, just like he'd do to calm a spooked animal.

"It doesn't matter, Earl," he said. "It doesn't matter who it was. We've got to deal with what's in front of us, which is your son taken off by the county somewhere and you facing a judge in the morning."

Earl kept glaring angrily at Ray, and I considered the depth of the betrayal. Someone else—not the Garretts, not the mistrusted outsiders—had reported his abuse. Someone else who was part of the town—a neighbor, a friend—had sided with them and sold Earl out. And to rub salt in the wound, his friend wouldn't tell him who it was. Even Ray was in league with the enemy. After another few tense moments of silence, Earl slowly raised his fist. He pounded Davis on the chest and said, "*Fuck* you, Ray." Then he turned and walked into the house.

Davis left in his police car, and Charlie and I drove away in silence. But instead of driving home we went over to Hammond's, my grandfather's favorite bar. He had brought me here before on nights when he wanted to get out of the house; we'd share a Tombstone pizza while he drank a few beers and talked with whomever was there. That night, we took two seats at the bar and Charlie ordered a Pabst Blue Ribbon and a Coke for me. I sat on my stool and stayed quiet. The sense of privilege I'd felt when we'd come here before was gone, replaced by a feeling of dread. The night's events didn't quite seem real, and yet they were, and here was my grandfather drinking in silence because he didn't want to go home; because his friend was in trouble and there was nothing he could do except hope that it would pass.

The bartender, Janet, brought him another beer when the first one was done, soon followed by a third. And while she usually talked to Charlie, she didn't linger that night because she knew that he was in a bad mood. Behind us, we could hear the sharp crack of pool balls, the curses and laughs at shots that missed or went true. In front of us was the TV with the sound turned down—images of NVA soldiers with machine guns drawn, moving further into southern Vietnam. I watched my grandfather's profile in the mirror behind the bar and thought for the first time that he looked old.

We were there for maybe an hour before Charlie got up, sighed, threw some bills on the counter, and led us back out to the car. There, we were greeted ecstatically by Brett, who wiggled all over us both before settling down again in the back. Charlie decided to get some gas before we headed home. I think he was looking for any reason to stay away longer—away from the house, away from what was happening with Earl, away from any more bad news. But he couldn't. And it was there at the gas station, as he stood with the pump in his hand, that Alice Watson found us.

She screeched into the parking lot in the Watsons' other car, the old tan Chevy, and pulled to a stop right in front of us. She jumped out and rushed straight to my grandfather, her face contorted with fear.

"Charlie, Earl's gone," she said, her voice high and shaky. "I think he's out looking for that couple. I tried to hold him there, I tried to calm him down, but he just wouldn't hear it. He left about twenty minutes ago. And Charlie—he took his gun."

My grandfather didn't speak for a moment. Then he yelled, "God*damn*it!" and struck the top of the car with his fist, so hard that both the dog and I jumped. "Did you call Ray?" he asked, as he hurriedly replaced the pump and screwed the gas cap on.

"Yes, I called him first," she said. "He sent some of his men straight over to their house. Then I called Helen, looking for you. She told me you hadn't come home yet, so I drove over to Hammond's, and Janet said you'd just left a minute ago. I called Pete too and he's meeting us at Ray's. Ray said I should go to his place instead of waiting at home."

Charlie looked off into the distance and shook his head. "Damnit," he said again, softer this time. And then: "All right, I'll meet you over there."

He got back into our car, and Alice into hers, and we drove over to the Davis's house. Pete's pickup truck was already parked in front. Ray had opened the door before the cars even stopped, and as soon as the three of us stepped inside, he said, "We shouldn't have left him alone." He was standing in the entranceway and as we passed, I felt the tension coming off his body. Uncle Pete was wound up too. He stood in the kitchen working his fists as if he wanted to grab somebody. Into this scene of anxiousness, my grandfather brought his usual calm. "What's the latest?" he asked, and you could see the other men relax—not because anything was fixed or resolved, but because Charlie LeBeau had finally appeared and so the chances for a favorable outcome had improved significantly.

"It's bad," Ray said. And then again, "We shouldn't have left him alone." Over his shoulder, from the living room, I could see the faces of his three children—Dale, five-year-old Jessica, and the baby, Andrew Lee—looking on with curiosity. The last time I'd been to Ray's house was the previous Christmas, when he and Charlie had sat admiring Ray's new rifles, pointing them at each other across the living room while the baby crawled between them on the floor.

"Carrie Sorenson called awhile ago," Ray told us. "She lives over on Hanshaw Road down the street from the Garretts, and she saw Earl go up to their house. No sign of the buck yet, but he came out with the woman— with his gun to the back of her head."

Alice Watson gasped and began to sway; Pete went over and guided her gently to a chair. And in the wake of their reaction, I almost didn't notice that Ray had referred to the Garretts by name.

"Carrie saw this?" my grandfather asked.

Ray nodded. "Al Mueller did too—he told my guys who went out there. Earl took her and put her in his car."

"No sign of the buck?" my grandfather repeated, looking from Pete to Ray.

Ray shook his head. "He must still be out of town. We're keeping a squad car out at the house, in case he turns up."

Charlie closed his eyes and lowered his head for a moment. "Jesus Christ," he said. "Holy Mother of God."

"I don't think," said Uncle Pete uncertainly, "I don't think he'd *do* anything, would he? I mean, he's probably just trying to scare her."

And now Alice Watson looked up from the table, her tear-stained face stuck here and there with strands of her light brown hair. "This is *your* fault!" she cried out. "You could have stopped this! You could have stopped him the day Kevin went to the emergency room. You could have stopped him when they saw Kevin's scars at school. But you had to stick by him, be his *buddy*. You had to deal with this like *men*." Her face screwed up when she said this. "And instead of doing right by Kevin and me, you just looked the other way. I hate you. I hate this stupid, godforsaken town. Oh, Jesus, why did I ever have to come here?"

She burst into tears and buried her face in her arms, resting them on the table. The room was silent. For while she had been looking directly at Ray, she'd really been speaking to all of them. All of them were culpable, and maybe, in their silence, they were finally acknowledging this; maybe it was only then they really knew it.

No one answered Mrs. Watson; there was nothing

to say. In the momentary silence Ray's radio crackled, and he jumped up and went into the other room. When he came back, his expression was set and determined. There was no more hesitation or uncertainty. "Someone spotted Earl's car downtown," he said. "They couldn't peg which direction he was going—the car turned a couple of times, almost like he was lost or trying to mislead us."

"So what should we do?" asked Charlie. "It's not helping to just sit here on our asses."

Ray thought for a moment. "I've got all my cars out looking for them, but we could go out too. Alice, you should stay here with Maryann and the kids. Pete and Charlie can go out together, and I can go by myself."

"No," Mrs. Watson said, standing up. "I'm coming. That's my husband out there alone with that woman, and I need to be able to see him." The tears were gone and her jaw was set, and she was dead serious. It was as if grief had burned away the soft outer casing of her personality, and now she stood before us hardened and pure, prepared in a way she'd never been before to face her husband and put a stop to him. The men just looked at her, surprised, not sure how to respond. But finally Ray said, "Okay then, Alice, you come with me. Pete, you go with Charlie."

Both men nodded and then Uncle Pete asked, "Where do you think he'd go?"

"Well, my men are covering the main roads out of town," said Ray. "But I don't have any other ideas. Alice?"

"I don't know," she said. And then looking up quickly, "Well, there's his folks' place, up Route 5 toward Glenville. They've got acreage out there and an empty barn."

"What about the state park?" Uncle Pete asked. "No one would be there now."

"Or the gun shop or one of your fishing spots," said Mrs. Watson.

"Yeah," Ray said. "That all makes sense. He'd probably go somewhere he knows."

It was decided that Ray and Alice would go out to her in-laws' place, since she wanted, even if he wasn't there, to be the one to tell them what was happening. That left Charlie and Pete to check the park and the places in the country. Ray glanced from my grandfather to me and back again, and I knew he was thinking I should stay behind. But Charlie gave him a look that cut off any question before he had a chance to ask. As we piled back into our respective cars, Ray said, "You find him, you just try to keep him calm. Let him know there's a way out. Don't get him in a position where he feels backed into a corner."

This last exchange put a charge of fear in my stomach. Until now, I couldn't have imagined a situation where one of Charlie's friends was treated as a threat. And when Ray asked Pete and Charlie, "You both got guns?" I knew that we were living in a different new reality where anything was possible.

How had it come to this? I wondered as Charlie drove in silence, both men looking straight ahead out the windshield. How had they let it get this far? And what would happen now? I couldn't, even with what I had heard that night, believe that it could really get worse. And I began to wonder now about the Garretts—

if Mr. Garrett was on his way back to Deerhorn, if he had worried because he couldn't reach his wife. I wondered about Mrs. Garrett, what she must have thought when she opened the door and found Earl Watson there. The idea of that scene made my stomach turn over. I was scared for her, scared for what Earl might do. And I was scared for all the rest of us, too.

Charlie drove, as he always did when he and Pete traveled together, and the two of them hardly spoke—just an occasional word or half-sentence to indicate a direction, along with a quick gesture or nod of the head. Yet the two men seemed to understand each other perfectly, and it occurred to me that this was what they were like when they were hunting; the long familiarity, the years of tracking side-by-side making idle conversation unnecessary. The longest sentence that either one of them spoke was when Pete leaned forward to look out at the sky and said, "Full moon tonight. At least we'll be able to see."

Charlie grunted an acknowledgment and then turned off the highway and into the state park. It was empty at that time except for the animals. And it looked totally different now, at night, in the winter, than it had during my bike trips in the fall. The trees, so lush and green in summer and colorful in autumn, were a bare, dull gray. The meadow, where we could just make out the dark shapes of the bison, seemed vast and unforgiving. As the headlights searched through the darkness, the road they illuminated seemed unfamiliar, full of unexpected turns and digressions. At the turnoff for Treman Lake, Uncle Pete spoke again. "The lake's not frozen, is it?"

"No," Charlie said. "Not cold enough."

I wondered why they cared about the condition of the lake. Then the thought struck me, like a punch in the stomach, that they were thinking of the likelihood that a body could sink down in the water and settle into its concealing depths.

When we reached the lake, I saw that it, too, looked different now in winter. In the summer, children played on the sandy beach and fishermen dotted the rock-covered banks. Now, the built-in barbecues were closed and locked tight, and a lone boat was tied up to the rickety pier, rocking slightly with the movement of the water.

"Not here," Charlie said, and Pete nodded.

"Probably too easy to get to."

"Maybe Alice was right and he went out to his folks' place."

"But that'd be the first place we'd look."

Charlie swung the car around and drove out of the park. He hesitated for a moment at the exit.

"Where to?" Pete asked. "You think the cemetery? The clinic?"

My grandfather shook his head. "Too close to town. I think he was just driving down there to confuse us."

"What about the satellite clinic?"

Charlie thought about this for a moment. "I don't know. But it's worth a shot."

And it did seem worth a shot. It had a certain logic, because the satellite clinic, even more than the central clinic, had gotten under people's skin. They seemed to find Mrs. Garrett's presence there particularly offensive— out there where the people had no other recourse, where they had to take whatever care was offered. Out there where her presence was as surprising and dramatic as the deer that once raced down our school hallway.

My grandfather took a right turn onto the highway, heading further out of town. Again there was silence, and the growing sense of time passing, the uncertainty about what awaited us. As the buildings thinned out and the small stands of wood began to blend into each other, I stared out the window and feared for Mrs. Garrett. What would Earl do to her? Where had they gone? And why had he chosen her, taken her, when it wasn't even the Garretts who'd caused his latest trouble? But these were not questions I could answer then, and so I gathered up the dog and hugged him hard, burying my face in his fur.

When we reached the satellite clinic, Charlie pulled into the parking lot and trained his headlights on the building. The clinic was dark and the parking lot was empty. "Not here," said Uncle Pete unnecessarily.

But I looked at the building anyway, and remembered how it was in the daylight, with cars parked in the lot and the inside full of people. I thought of Mrs. Garrett standing on the front landing; I thought of her taking me inside. The place seemed abandoned now, or maybe it was just that night, the darkness that had settled over everything. In any event, as Uncle Pete said, no one was there, so Charlie turned the car back around. Then suddenly he hit the dashboard with his fist and said, "I know where he went."

I sat up straight and Pete looked over. "Where?"

"The deer stand."

And Pete said, "I'll bet you're right."

Charlie got back onto the highway and hit the gas

hard, sending the car up over eighty. Now that we had a clear destination, time shifted again, began to be measured in well-defined minutes that were rapidly escaping us. I watched the trees go by in a blur and held the dog tighter against me. I prayed that my grandfather was right.

I'd never been to the deer stand—the couple of times I'd gone deer hunting with Charlie, he'd taken me somewhere else—so I didn't know where it was or how long it would take to get there. But I knew it existed, because he'd talked about it at home—how they'd built a little elevated platform in the forest, covered with leaves and branches, nestled in a triangle of trees. They'd wait there for unsuspecting deer that were traveling through the woods. Below it, in a lean-to they'd also covered with branches, they kept coolers full of food and beer. And a little apart from it, a small depression in the ground where they placed the deer they'd already killed. The men had talked about this stand—the perspective it gave them, the modifications they would sometimes make—with the intensity and delight that their grandchildren might feel about a backyard treehouse. For some of them, spending time at the deer stand, away from their lives in town, seemed as much the point of going out to the woods as the actual hunt. The stand was their sanctuary, their recreation and escape. It was a place where they couldn't be reached by spouses or employers or anyone else who had a claim on them, and as soon as my grandfather had mentioned the deer stand, the air was charged with purpose and certainty.

We drove for what seemed like forever. Then finally we turned off the highway onto a small side road, and turned again onto a dirt and gravel road that seemed too treacherous and rough for the car. The bumping and rocking unsettled the dog, who sat up and started to whine.

"Quiet, Brett," my grandfather scolded, and I heard the tension in his voice. Both he and Pete were leaning forward now intently.

After several more minutes of the bumpy road, another slight turnoff. The trees were in so close they were scraping the car. The headlights reached only a few feet ahead, into impenetrable darkness. I thought that maybe we'd taken a wrong turn somewhere and were being swallowed up by the forest.

Then suddenly we were in an opening and the car came to a stop. The space was about twenty-five or thirty feet long and maybe fifteen feet across, and it was obvious that someone had been back here with an ax and cleared out the low-hanging branches. At the end of the space, its nose reaching into the forest, was Earl's big gray Buick.

Both Charlie and Pete jumped out of the car and quickly went around to the back. They opened the trunk, moved some things around, and slammed it shut again. Then Charlie opened the back door and looked me in the eyes.

"Stay here, Mike. Don't move," he said. And then he held something toward me, gesturing for me to take it, and I stared at it for a second or two before I realized that it was a gun. "Take this and keep the door locked. If Earl comes back, don't open the door, no matter what he says. This is a .38—do you think you can handle it? It's single action, just like the .22 you learned on. It's just a bit bigger, is all. Use both hands and keep your arms locked out so you can handle the kick when you fire."

I hesitated for a moment, and Charlie pushed it closer. "Go on, Michelle. Take it. You've got to take this now."

And so I took the gun from him, felt the cool weight of it in my hands, held it away from the curious dog. And in the moment before my grandfather pulled back and shut the door, I got a good look at his face. His jaw was set and his lips were pressed tightly together; he was ready for the task at hand. But his eyes did not look angry or fearful. They looked knowing and resigned. They looked sad.

Then he slammed the door shut and the two men were off, reduced to beams of light in the forest.

I sat in the backseat, holding the gun, adjusting to the silence after the sound of the men's voices, the commotion of the last sixty minutes. With the headlights off I became aware of just how dark it was; I couldn't even make out the hood of the car. The gun in my hands felt warmer now, but no less heavy; it was much bigger than the .22 I was used to. I wondered where it had come from—this was not the .38 from Charlie's gun case—and I realized he must have kept it in the car. I wasn't confident that I could fire this gun with any control, and I didn't know what to do with it now—whether to set it beside me, hold it, or put it away in the front seat. What I finally did was rest it against my leg, my right hand holding it in place. With my left arm I reached over and held my dog.

There is nothing more lonely than sitting in a car late at night in the middle of an unfamiliar forest. Although this was thirty-seven years ago now, I still remember the feel of the seat against my legs, how I suddenly became aware of a tear in the fabric. I remember the way the temperature began to drop inside as the air lost the warmth of the heater. I remember how the edges of the car became visible as my eyes got used to the dark; how the trees slowly took shape in the blackness. And I remember the weight of that gun on my leg, which was nowhere near as heavy as the weight of Charlie making me take it; the weight of knowing why it had to be taken.

By now, the beams of the flashlights had disappeared into the forest. I heard the sound of my breathing and tried to count, tried to sing, anything to keep myself from thinking too much about what we were doing there, what might be out there in the woods. Then Brett let loose a torrent of barks so sudden and loud that I jumped and felt the gun slip from my hand.

"Brett! What?" I asked. He went to the window, turned back toward me, and then barked again—loud and full-throated, lifting his head to let out the stream of sound. His bark had always been loud, but it had never sounded so insistent, so deafening, as it did inside that car. My heart was racing and I kept telling him to stop, to be quiet; I didn't know what he was barking at and the gun had fallen to the floor and I wasn't sure that I could handle it anyway. Finally he stopped, as suddenly as he'd started. My heart began to slow a little and I stroked his back to calm us both down. He looked at me—I could see better now—with his saddest, most soulful expression. I didn't know what he was asking me for, or telling me just then. But he looked at me that night like I was his best and only friend, and for a moment I began to feel safe again.

We sat there awhile longer, and then Brett started to whine and paw at the door and I felt a wave of relief; I understood that he just needed to pee. I thought about Charlie's instructions not to open the door. But Brett had been in the car for a couple of hours by then, and Charlie wouldn't want him to piss on the seat, and I didn't see anything wrong with letting him out for a second if I locked us back in again. So I unlocked the door and opened it and Brett jumped out. He went to the edge of the clearing. But instead of just sniffing around and lifting his leg, he trotted off into the woods. He headed the opposite direction from where Charlie and Pete had gone, and I wondered if he'd smelled a deer or raccoon. I waited a few seconds and then called out to him softly. He didn't come. But I heard a rustling sound nearby, Brett picking his way through the fallen branches, so I got out of the car to find him and bring him back.

"Brett! Damnit! Come here!" I cried out. I walked across the small clearing, trying not to look at Earl's car, and entered the woods where my dog had gone. Now that my eyes had gotten used to the dark, it was actually quite easy to see. The moon was full and the stars were out, and while I couldn't always tell where I was putting my feet, I had no trouble making my way between the trees. My ankle still hurt from my fall at the clinic, but I just gritted my teeth and kept walking. Ahead, I could hear my dog sniffing and panting, engaged in some ancient, blood-borne need to hunt. But each time I got close enough to reach out and grab his collar, he dodged me and ran off a bit further.

The woods were getting thicker now, and as the trees grew dense, their tops shut out more of the sky. I put my hands out in front of me to feel for branches. Once or twice I tripped over a twig or a rock and tweaked my sore ankle, but I managed to keep my balance. My dog was going further ahead, increasing the distance between us; I could still hear the panting and the twigs beneath his feet. But maybe because I was with him, maybe because I was so focused on getting him back, I wasn't as scared out there in the woods as I had been sitting in the car. At least I wasn't until I looked up and saw a light ahead, a torch or lantern that had no business being out there. And now I realized that this was what Brett had scented or seen, for that was exactly where he was headed.

I picked up my pace a bit, trying to catch up with the dog before he got too close to the light. Once, twice more I whispered, "Brett!" but he was on the trail of something, and wasn't listening. My heart pounded in my chest and I wanted to turn around, run away and go back to the car. But my dog was out there in front of me and I couldn't leave him. And maybe, just maybe, as afraid as I was, my curiosity was stronger than my fear.

When I got within thirty feet of the light, I saw that it was coming out of another clearing, like the one where the cars had been parked. This one was larger, maybe forty by twenty. I slowed down as I got closer, trying to make out the scene in front of me through the branches. On the left side of the clearing was a jagged stump with a lantern set on top of it. And off on the far side someone was moving, laboring, lifting things and replacing them again. I knew from his green winter coat and black wool cap that it was Earl Watson—but when he turned for a moment to grab another armful of branches, I was shocked by the sight of his face. The weak orange light of the lantern made his eyes look deeper set, and some basic human quality seemed burned out of them. I slowed down some more and moved forward as quietly as I could, and Brett too seemed to realize that caution was in order, because he stopped and waited for me. But the man in the clearing was involved in his work, and the branches he was moving were making noise as they scraped together, and then there were his own heavy grunts of exertion, and he did not hear anything else.

I crept closer to get a better look at what he was doing. I wanted to see if Mrs. Garrett was with him, but there wasn't any sign of her. I stood maybe twenty or twenty-five feet away from him now, when I was suddenly struck by the position I was in. I was alone in the woods with a man who had beaten his son and kidnapped a woman. I knew he had a gun, and I'd left mine in the car, and my grandfather wasn't there to protect me. All this knowledge made my heart and stomach lurch, and I knew that I had to get out of there. And I would have; I would have turned around and gone back to the car, if my dog hadn't run into the clearing.

To this day I don't know what he was doing. Was he simply running forward because he recognized Earl? Was he following his spaniel instincts and taking those last steps forward to complete the job of flushing his prey? Or was he just stepping out and announcing himself? It might have been that; it might have been as simple as that, for what Brett did was take a couple of bounding steps forward, pose in his "ready" stance, and let out a declarative bark. I called out, "Brett!"—I couldn't help myself—and now Earl spun around, looked at Brett, and then stared out into the woods.

"Who's there?"

I didn't answer and Brett stood staring at him, his tail erect and moving in small, tight circles.

"Charlie?" Earl called out now. "Charlie, is that you?"

Then he looked at Brett again and back out toward the woods and spoke in a different tone. "Mike, I know you're there," he said, quieter now. "You better come and show yourself, girl."

I could have just turned and run. I could have hobbled through the woods and gone back to the car, where the gun was, where Charlie might find me. But I knew that Earl was faster than me, and I wasn't going to leave my dog.

And there was something else, too. Maybe, despite the evidence that Earl was dangerous, I didn't think he could do any further harm. He was so familiar to me, so normal, and I didn't want to believe that evil appeared in such everyday forms. I didn't know yet that violence and hatred aren't things that exist outside us, looming threats that we can recognize and keep from our lives. I didn't know that they are everywhere, everywhere we look, in the hearts of the people we know and live with, and in our own.

I stepped forward into the clearing and my dog looked up at me happily, proud to show me what he had found. Earl was standing straight up now, his cap pulled back, the top of his winter coat unbuttoned. His coat and pants were streaked with dirt, and as he stood he brushed some leaves from his shoulders. His face—I could see it more clearly now—had an odd, calm expression. He didn't look frenzied, as he had earlier at his house. He looked like he had things well in hand. For a moment my fear subsided and I was lulled into thinking that everything would be all right, as if maybe there was some good reason he was out here in the woods, in the middle of the night, moving branches. But that ease vanished quickly when he shook his head and said, "You shouldn't have come out here, Mikey."

"I . . . I didn't mean to," I stammered. "Brett jumped out of the car, and . . . and . . ."

"You came with Charlie, I know. They're looking for me, aren't they?"

I nodded and didn't say anything. Beside me, my dog sat down with a grunt.

"And they're probably looking for that woman too, but guess what? They ain't going to find her. At least, not in the shape they want."

He laughed a sharp, bitter laugh, and I realized then that what I saw on his face was not calm at all, but anger—an anger so focused and pure and distilled that it had burned away all other expression. There were no rages coming, no tantrums, no loud bursts of fury. The anger in him was so thorough and consuming that it didn't need further expression.

"It's only her, you know," he continued. "He's out of town, like Charlie said. She said he went to visit his people." He gave that strange, bitter laugh again, and I realized with horror how he—and Charlie—had learned she was alone. "His people! Well, someone so damn caring, someone who's such a family man, should have shown more respect, don't you think? More respect for Earl Watson and *his* people."

Above us, an owl gave its three-part cry. The wind

rustled through the branches and I pulled my coat tighter. I wanted to point out that the Garretts had, in fact, cared for "his people"—they had cared about his son. But I knew that anything I said would increase the distance in his eyes. And besides, he just kept talking.

"They took Kevin today," he said. "They just up and took him away, and they won't tell me where he is, like I'm not even fit to talk to him. As if they have any right to tell me how to raise my own children! You don't *do* that, you understand? You just don't do that. And somebody had to account for it."

I was struck by what he said. Listening to him, I realized that what so offended Earl was not that his son was off in the care of strangers. It was that something of his had been taken. Something had been removed from him against his will, a possession whose fate he believed he should control completely. He would have been angry, too, if someone had taken his car or one of his pistols. That it was Kevin who'd been taken wasn't substantively different. It was simply a matter of degree.

"But it wasn't them who reported you!" I protested, and as soon as the words were out I regretted them.

Earl stared at me now like he was startled that I'd spoken, like he was surprised to find me there with him at all. "What did you say?"

"It wasn't them who called," I repeated. "Ray said it was somebody else!"

And now a darkness passed over his face and I knew he was still capable of rage. And I wondered again where Mrs. Garrett was, what Earl had been doing before I got there. "It *was* them," he insisted. "It *was* them. And even if they didn't make the call today, it was them who got this started. They should have just minded their own fucking business. They should have just never come here!" He spat something out in front of him, chew or gum or the flavor of bitterness. "You too, goddamnit. All of you. You should have just stayed where you belonged."

He reached toward a fallen log to his right and picked up something I should have seen earlier—what looked like a .357 semiautomatic that had been lying within his reach the whole time. He lifted it quickly and almost casually, as if to show me a new item from his store. But when it stopped moving I was staring down its barrel.

"You shouldn't have come," he repeated, and my dog stood up again, alert to the abrupt change in the atmosphere. "You shouldn't be here, and I'm sorry for it. You should have stayed at home."

The owl gave its cry again, louder this time, and I was suddenly gripped with fear. It felt like my whole body had been reduced to my heart, which was beating so violently I thought it might burst; and my lungs, which could not draw breath.

"But Charlie would kill me if something happened to you," Earl continued, "so I'm going to let you go. But you didn't see *anything*, Mike, you understand? That's what you're going to say. You didn't see me. I wasn't even here."

Beside me, my dog gave a low warning growl; he must have felt the tension in the air. I didn't really hear what Earl was saying because my eyes were fixed on the gun. I was staring at its barrel, its sleek long shape, wondering about my chances if I stepped back into the woods and what would happen if he actually shot me. Would I lose consciousness right away, or would I feel the impact of the bullet? I was still looking at the gun when Earl said, "Because if you *do* say something, anything at all, you know what I'll do to you, don't you?"

I was staring at the barrel when I saw it move away, point lower and to my left. And I was staring at it still when the gun went off and my dog dropped down to the ground.

I screamed, "Brett!" and just stood there, frozen. My dog had fallen onto his left side. The bullet had entered through his chest, and blood poured out of the wound, dark red against the white of his fur. He lay still for a moment and I thought he was dead, but then he began to work his legs, trying to lift himself up off the ground. I started toward him and Earl swung the gun back in my direction. "Don't move," he said. "Don't take another step."

My dog struggled to get up, but he couldn't, for something was shattered inside, and now he looked at me and his eyes were hurt and pleading. Every cell in my body told me to go to him, and I thought, I have to save him. I have to stop the bleeding and get him to town so that someone can take out the bullet. He kept trying to stand and then falling, whimpering each time he hit the ground. I stepped forward again, sobbing, and cried out, "Brett!" but Earl moved too and cocked his trigger and said, "Don't make me shoot you, Michelle."

And so I stood helplessly, watching my dog across that impassable distance, which could not have been more than eight or ten feet but which felt like the width of the world. Brett opened his mouth and wailed now, a long, anguished cry that was unlike anything I'd ever heard before or have ever heard since, and that sound entered through my ears and settled into my heart, where I hear its echoes still. I knew there was no saving him. He was panting hard and he couldn't move his front legs anymore, and his back legs began to jerk uselessly. What was coming out of the wound in his chest was darker and thicker. He looked at me with an expression of such confusion and pain that I thought I was going to die of it. "I love you! Goddamn it, Brett, stay with me!" I cried. And then he shuddered violently and his body went slack and my dog, my best friend, lay still.

I cried, "No!" and ran toward him, and now I forgot about Earl or was so upset I didn't care what he did. He did not pull the trigger again. And so I went to my dog and knelt beside him, still crying, "No, no!" I ran my hands over his back and along his sides, feeling the warmth still in him. I lifted his great head in my hands and pressed my face to it, my nose and mouth resting against the length of his snout, my forehead pressed to his forehead, trying to imprint the details of his face and his smell so I'd remember them forever. And that's how we were positioned—me kneeling with Brett's head in my hands, Earl standing with his gun now lowered— when my grandfather burst into the clearing.

I don't know if he had already been in that part of the woods, or if he'd come from the other direction. I don't know whether the distance he'd covered was large or small, but however far he came, he got there fast, and even though I was still in the presence of a dangerous man, I felt safe, or at least less threatened, because my grandfather had come, and I knew he had come for me.

He was out of breath—I'd never seen him out of breath before—but it took him only a second to gather himself. He stepped in from the edge of the woods with a flashlight in one hand and a gun in the other, which he held a little away from him, as if it would burn his leg. Charlie stayed a distance of maybe fifteen feet from Earl, and I was twenty feet away to his left, the three of us forming a lopsided triangle. I watched as Charlie made sense of the scene in front of him—his granddaughter kneeling on the ground, his dog lying dead in her arms, his best friend standing a few feet away and holding a lowered gun. He looked from me to Earl and then back again.

"I heard Mike . . ." he began, and it was only then that I realized Earl's gun hadn't made much sound when it fired; that Earl had used something to silence it. Charlie didn't finish his thought and asked, "What happened here?"

Earl looked him straight in the face. "He started to come after me, Charlie."

Charlie's gaze traveled the distance between Brett's body and Earl's feet. "It doesn't look like he got very far."

Earl leaned forward a bit, as if to put some weight behind his answer. "He's aggressive. Always has been. You know that, Charlie."

My grandfather turned to me now and searched my face—not gently, not lovingly, but in a cold, detached way that made it clear he was seeking information. And he saw from my face that his friend was lying.

But he didn't have time to confront him about it, because just then Uncle Pete stumbled out of the woods, late again for an important occasion. He came to a stop beside Charlie and put his hands on his knees, almost dropping the gun he was carrying. "Sorry, I couldn't keep up with you," he managed between gasps for air. But then he saw Earl's gun, and Brett on the ground, and he pulled himself up straight.

My grandfather hadn't even turned to look at Pete, but he seemed shored up with his brother-in-law beside him. He lifted his gun, a long-barreled revolver, almost imperceptibly. "Where's the woman, Earl?"

Earl looked at him. "The woman? Oh, you mean that nigger nurse?"

"You know what I mean. Where is she?"

Earl shrugged, palms up, gun pointing sideways into the woods. "She's not with me, Charlie. You see anybody with me?"

"That's bullshit. People saw you tonight. People saw you take her."

"She's not with me. Or should I say, she's not *with us*, anymore." He laughed, a sickening, humorless laugh, and I caught sight of his eyes, which were flat and cold.

My grandfather raised his gun a little more. "What did you do to her, Earl?"

Now Earl snapped back to himself. "Do to *her*? Do to her? What about what she did to *me*? I walk into town and I don't know but that people aren't looking at me like a criminal. My son's been taken away, and tonight my wife said she was leaving me. My wife! She's leaving me, Charlie. She's going back up to Wausau. And it's all on account of *this* shit." His voice was shaking and he paused for a moment. But when he spoke again, he'd regained control of it. "Whatever happened to that black bitch she had coming, Charlie, because of what she did to *me*."

And now my grandfather trained his flashlight on the pile of branches that were stacked behind his friend. It was this that Earl had been working on when I first spotted him through the trees. This he'd been adding onto and positioning. The moon was directly over us now, shining through the tops of the trees, and by its light I could just make out what looked like burlap hidden beneath the branches, the wrapped end of something long and substantial. My grandfather must have seen this too, because now he said, "What's that you got on the burn pile?"

Earl looked at him—not with fear or concern, but with the defiant, sheepish, half-pleased look of someone who'd been caught doing something he isn't ashamed of. "Just garbage, Charlie. Just garbage to burn up with the other garbage."

My grandfather seemed to deflate. His shoulders slumped, his gun came to a rest on his thigh, and he lowered his head a little. "Goddamnit, Earl. Goddamnit to hell. Why'd you have to go and do that?"

Earl brought his arms together and covered the barrel of his gun with his hand, as if he was caressing it. "It's only half done," he answered. "Only the female half." And then the awful laugh again. "She had one cooking, though, Charlie. She had one in the oven. She begged me not to kill her for the sake of the baby. So you see, I did pretty good here, don't you think? Two for the price of one." We all stood there in silence, taking in the horror of what he'd just told us. "I still have to find the buck, though," he continued. "You fellows want to help me?"

I yearned to be close to Charlie, to be within reach of his arms, but I had not been able to move because I didn't want to leave my dog. And I realized that something else was holding me back—I didn't really know where Charlie stood. But he looked across the clearing at his friend and shook his head slowly. "It's *all* done, Earl. It's all done. And now you've got to come back to town with us and we've got to go see Ray."

Earl let out what sounded like a half-strangled laugh. "Come on, Charlie. Don't bullshit me here. I've still got to finish this off."

My grandfather looked at him soberly. "I'm not bullshitting you, Earl. We have to go."

Earl cocked his head slightly, genuinely bewildered. "Charlie, what are you talking about? What are you doing?"

My grandfather sighed and his cheeks looked hollow by the light of the moon, and I thought for the second time that he looked old. "There's a body out here, Earl. You *killed* somebody. You think no one's going to figure that out?"

Earl's mouth fell open and he looked from Charlie to Pete and back again. "But I thought you . . ." he said incredulously. "I thought you were with me on this."

"I *was* with you," said Charlie. "You *know* I was with you." He paused, and I could see the struggle in his face. "But you crossed the line, Earl. You shouldn't have done this."

"I had to get them to stop," Earl said. "I had to make them stand to account."

"I know. But you didn't need to do it *this* way, Earl."

Earl stared. "Well, what way did you think I was *gonna* do it, Charlie? Where did you think this was headed?"

My grandfather looked like he'd been punched in the stomach. He was quiet for a moment and then he said, "We could have done it different, is all. We could have figured something out."

"No, we couldn't have, Charlie. They took my son, and I don't know if I'll get him back. And now my wife is leaving, too. Please." He stepped forward and there was a beseeching quality in the way he held his arms. "Let me go, Charlie. All right, I won't go after the buck. You don't have to tell anyone what you saw here. Just let me get a head start out of town."

Charlie shook his head. "I can't, Earl. Come on, now. Don't make this any harder than it already is."

"Please don't take me in." He was pleading now. "I don't want to go back to jail."

Charlie's shoulders were set and he looked resolute, as he often did when he had to complete an unpleasant but necessary task, like telling Ray Davis that one of his men had been caught stealing, or pulling out the finger I'd dislocated the previous summer. "You made some big mistakes here, but you got to face up to them, Earl. You got to meet them now head on."

"I am. I did. Don't do this to me, Charlie."

"You know I have to, Earl."

And then again, colder: "Don't do this, Charlie. I will not go back to jail." As he said this, he raised his gun and leveled it at my grandfather's head. "You're not going to take me in."

And just like that, both Charlie and Pete whipped their guns up and aimed them at Earl. I had never seen either of them move so fast. I remember feeling paralyzed, unable to move, not because I was scared—by this point, my fear had boiled down to numbness—but because time seemed to stop completely and suspend us in that tableau: Earl pointing his gun at my grandfather, Charlie and Pete pointing theirs at him, none of them speaking or moving. But finally Charlie broke the silence with his low command. "You better put that gun down, Earl. The numbers are against you."

Earl shook his head. "You're going to have to let me go."

"I'm not letting you go," my grandfather answered, and both he and Pete dug in their heels.

"Well, I'm not going," Earl said again, and now he turned in my direction. What I remember from his expression was that he didn't seem to see me. I was not a person to him, not a living thing, and I knew that he would kill me with as little concern as he'd shown for Brett and Mrs. Garrett. None of us were real to him. What *was* real to Earl? Was Earl even real to himself?

"Put the gun down, Earl. Don't do this," Charlie said.

"No," Earl said. "No way." Then he turned and aimed his gun at me and tensed his arm to fire, and Charlie and Uncle Pete both pulled their triggers. They fired in quick succession, one bullet catching Earl in the shoulder and spinning him around, the other going in through his side. Earl's gun was thrown by the impact and he hit the ground with a thud. He landed on his side and groped at the dirt with his arms, trying to pull himself to safety. "Charlie, Pete, I can't believe . . ." he gasped. Dark red blood began to pour from his wounds and I thought I saw the heat rise off of it. He tried to plug the holes with his right hand—his left arm was useless—and his breathing was shallow and rapid. Then Charlie stepped toward him, turned him onto his back, and shot him through the heart.

Later, what I'd think of was the silence. After the echoes of gunfire were absorbed into the woods, there was a silence that wasn't just the absence of sound but the presence of a heavy new truth. Nobody moved for several moments. And in that space of time I remember thinking that my life had just changed forever, in ways I couldn't begin to fathom; and that this silence was the interlude between my past and my future, between who I'd been and whoever I was going to be.

I didn't say a word, and neither did Pete. But after a few minutes, Charlie sank to his knees and slowly crossed himself. He touched his friend's forehead like he was taking his temperature, then he gathered him up in his arms. He rocked the body gently and his shoulders began to shake, and I realized with shock that he was crying. "Oh, God, help us," he said, and it was as if he didn't know that Pete and I were there. "Damnit, Earl. Why'd you have to do this?" he cried. "It wasn't worth it. Why'd you ever have to let it get this far? Why'd you give up everything, for *this*?"

Uncle Pete and I both lowered our heads and turned the other way; we knew better than to say anything. But finally my grandfather looked up at us, and though the expression on his face was anguished, his voice held firm. "Pete, take Mikey and go back into town," he said. "Get Ray. Get Alice. Just go and *get* people, damnit, and leave me alone here with Earl."

Pete slipped his gun back into his waistband and

walked over to me. He placed his hand on my shoulder gently and said, "Okay, kiddo. Let's get ourselves to town." When I looked down behind me reluctantly, he sighed and said, "We'll take your dog back, too."

And so Pete crouched down and picked Brett up and carried him back to the car. If I'd been in a clearer state of mind I might have been grateful; I might have appreciated that it isn't easy to carry fifty pounds of dead weight half a mile through the woods in the dark. I might have noticed that he put no barrier between Brett's body and his clothes, so that his jacket and pants got soaked with blood.

When we reached the car, I slid all the way across the backseat and Pete placed Brett in after me. He was careful not to hit Brett's legs on the doorframe even though the dog could no longer feel it. Brett's body was already cool to the touch and the blood was getting sticky and stiff; I shut his eyes, which were now dull and lifeless. I pulled his upper body close so that his head was resting on my lap, just like it had so many times before. And as we drove back to town I buried my face in his fur and felt my heart crack open—for Brett, for Mrs. Garrett, for the lives that awaited the rest of us, lives that we could not yet imagine. And for my grandfather too, for what he had done—to his friend, and to himself.

I wish I could say my sympathy extended to Earl. I wish I could say I felt even a little sadness over his death, or horror at having witnessed it. But I didn't. What I felt was satisfaction. For this man had done awful, inconceivable things, and now he would do them no longer. His son wouldn't have to worry about being beaten anymore. His wife wouldn't have to choose between her husband and her child. Mr. Garrett, whom he'd intended to be his next target, wouldn't have to fear for his life.

But my gladness was more fundamental than that, was about more than his abuse being stopped. Earl had sinned, and I wanted him to suffer. I wanted him to feel intense, unspeakable pain. I wanted him to writhe on the ground even longer before my grandfather put an end to his misery. And I'd enjoyed it, I'd liked his agony, I wanted to see more of it. I didn't wonder what this desire to watch another person suffer might have said about what was happening in me.

EPILOGUE

They came back for Mrs. Garrett the next morning. Ray Davis drove out to the woods with the coroner, and they walked out to where the burn pile was. What they found there was Mrs. Garrett's body wrapped in a burlap bag, which had already been doused with lighter fluid. She'd been shot just once, through the head. There were no other marks on her body, no further signs of violence or struggle. This might have been a relief to some people—Earl might have killed the woman, they said, but at least he didn't do anything else to her—but it did not mean much to me. It seemed to me that a man who went to so much trouble to disguise the harm he'd caused his child would know how to hurt someone without leaving any visible proof. It seemed to me that Earl wasn't the kind of man who would have let her go without making her suffer.

Earl's body was still in the clearing too, and because there was only one coroner in town, both he and Mrs. Garrett were brought there and tended to by the same pair of hands. I can't imagine what old Norm Holden must have thought as he went about his work. And because I knew more now about the town than I cared to, I wondered if it was difficult for him to handle Mrs. Garrett's body, if it was harder than handling the body of the man who'd killed her.

Joe Garrett came back to Deerhorn to collect his wife's body and to meet with the police. But other than Holden and Ray Davis and maybe the people who worked for them, nobody laid eyes on him, including me. I don't blame Mr. Garrett for making a quick escape from the town that had taken his wife and unborn child. But the sudden absence of the people who'd been the focal point of so much attention was noticeable and dramatic. Their house had been a rental, and Mr. Garrett moved out so quickly it was as if they'd never even been there at all—but despite its good location and reasonable rent, the place would stand empty for months. After Christmas, Mrs. Hebig came back from maternity leave, and so her fifth graders finally got the teacher they'd been waiting for. Slowly, children who'd been pulled out of Deerhorn Elementary came trickling back to school, and things returned to some semblance of normal. When Joe Garrett left, nobody ever saw or heard of him again. His departure was as complete and permanent as his wife's.

When I thought about Mrs. Garrett and Earl at the coroner's, I sometimes wondered if their families had met. Of course, Norm Holden would have gone to great lengths to keep them separate. But sometimes I imagined Mr. Garrett and Alice Watson meeting in the waiting room. Would they have spoken? What would they have said to each other? Would they have exchanged accusations and blame? Or would they have been able to put their bitter feelings aside and unite in their common grief?

I don't know what they would have done, but I do know that continuing to live there in Deerhorn was more than Alice Watson could bear. It wasn't that her husband was vilified—in fact, it was just the opposite. Oh, there were a few people, Darius Gordon and Jim Riesling among them, who knew the truth about Earl and so wanted no part in the town's collective revision of his memory. But mostly, people seemed to feel bad for him. He was under a lot of pressure at the gun shop, they said. He was having flashbacks from his war years. He finally got fed up with the accusations, they said, the false accusations about him and his son.

For that was how far they'd go in explaining his actions. It wasn't simply that he had killed someone; it was that it was understandable, even justified, considering what the Garretts had subjected him to. Because Earl Watson, good Earl Watson, war hero and business leader and upstanding citizen, couldn't possibly have burned and beaten his own child. The general facts of the murder had played out so publicly that they could not be covered up or disputed. And so instead people created a digestible reason for them—a justification that allowed them to remember Earl Watson in the most favorable possible light.

But Alice Watson couldn't take part in this fiction, or maybe she just couldn't keep living in a place where people knew so much about her family. Within six months she and Kevin had moved to her parents' place in Wausau, which was only an hour from Deerhorn, but was far enough. Her older son, Jake, didn't join them in the move. He continued to live in Deerhorn with one of his friends' families, and I imagine he lives there to this day.

My grandfather's fate was more complicated. Oh, he

too was given the benefit of the doubt. Yes, he had shot Earl, people said—but only to protect his granddaughter, since Earl was crazy, and my life had been at risk. Because the shooting was seen as self-defense, he and Uncle Pete were not arrested, and there was never any talk of a trial. Charlie LeBeau had done what he had to do, and so he was forgiven.

Except he couldn't forgive himself. He spent hours and hours alone now, sitting on the porch, or working on household projects in the basement. In the immediate aftermath of the killings he'd gone up to the coffee shop as usual, but the constant questions and morbid curiosity and even sympathy had gotten to him, and so he didn't venture up there anymore. He had visitors—Ray Davis, Uncle Pete and Aunt Bertha, and even Jim Riesling, once. But mostly he stayed alone, not talking much to my grandmother, who made his meals and did his laundry and watched over him with a worried eye, but who didn't know how to penetrate his sorrow.

The only person whose presence Charlie seemed to tolerate was mine. And since I was miserable and lonely and missing my dog (my clothes were still covered with his long white hair; we'd left out his bed and water bowl, still filled with water, as if he might return at any moment), I stayed around him as much as I could. One Saturday afternoon in February, Charlie called me out to the porch. He patted the couch and I scrambled up beside him. He threw an arm around my shoulders and took a gulp from his can of Pabst. Several empties stood on the table in front of him.

"In the spring," he said, "I want you to help me plant the vegetable garden. Beans and potatoes, and cabbage and carrots, and maybe some corn and tomatoes. What do you say, Mike? Would you be interested in that?"

"Yes," I said, and I imagined how good that would feel, working outside with my grandfather. But he had started to move more slowly now, even simple things like getting up off the couch were taking more visible effort, and it was hard to imagine him working a shovel or bending over to plant seeds in the earth.

"Or better yet—you're getting old enough to have your own garden. Maybe we'll give you a little patch at one end and you can plant whatever you want."

"When will we do that, Grandpa?" I asked. We were in the heart of winter, and the ground was covered with snow, and it was hard to imagine a time when things flowered and grew instead of withering and dying.

He took another gulp and sighed. "I don't know. When it's warm enough. Hopefully in May. The groundhog went back into his hole, you know, so it looks like we'll have a late spring."

I rearranged myself so I was closer to him. "Don't the Bombers start playing in May?" I asked. "Can we go to see a game?"

"Sure," he said. "Sure. And maybe this summer, you and me can drive down to watch the Brewers."

I sat up straight, excited in spite of my knowledge that Charlie did not like to travel. "Can we really, Grandpa?" I asked. And even though I knew that it would probably never happen, that he was just talking about it to please me, it made me happy anyway; it made me glad that my feelings were important enough for him to attend to.

He squeezed me tight around the shoulders and

laughed. "Sure we can, Mike. Sure, kiddo. We can do whatever you want."

We didn't talk about the killings that day—we never did, actually—but there were things I wondered about even then, and those questions have only deepened with time. Why did Earl aim his gun at me, for instance, when he knew that Charlie would never let anyone hurt me? He must have realized that my grandfather would choose me over him, and maybe that's why he did it. Maybe he wanted to make my grandfather choose and then have to live with his choice.

And I wondered something, too, about my grandfather's actions. His first shot had hit Earl in the shoulder; Pete's had hit him in the side. These did not have to be mortal blows, and they might have saved him if they'd gotten him to a hospital.

But Charlie hadn't stopped with one shot. He'd gone after Earl a second time, and that time he'd shot for the kill.

Why did he do it? Why did he kill his best friend? Was it to save him from the shame that would surely ensue—the shame of Kevin's scars and bruises, yes, but now also the shame of murder? Was it because he felt responsible for what Earl had done and so also felt bound to make up for it? Was it because he truly feared for my life—not only then, but into the future? Or was it because he knew something else, something that my grandmother and Father Pace and other people of faith can't admit to—that there are sins for which there is no redemption?

Charlie didn't make it to spring. He got up to plow the driveway one morning in March, and I was awakened by the familiar sound of the snowblower being started. But when that sound wasn't followed by the usual noise of the machine making its long sweeps down the driveway, I knew that something was wrong. My grandmother and I both rushed out together and found him lying just inside the garage. She cried out, "Charlie!" and fell to her knees. His hands were clasped over his chest and his eyes were half-open. When I touched his face I felt the rough stubble there. The skin on his cheek was still warm.

It would be easy to say his death was of natural causes. It would be easy to say that years of eating fatty foods and drinking beer had hardened his arteries and weakened his heart, and maybe there would have been some truth to that explanation. But I believe that my grandfather died of heartbreak. He had already, for all intents and purposes, lost his only son, and the events of the last eight months had created an unbridgeable divide between him and the people who loved him most. He had sided with Earl Watson, stood by his friend and even stoked his anger—and then watched him die by his own hand. No one would ever know what these choices had cost him. But eventually, they might have cost him his life.

That summer, the summer of '75, I moved out of my grandparents' house. In the wake of Charlie's death, my grandmother's health began to fail; she could barely even take care of herself, let alone an unhappy child. At the end of the school year I was placed in the county group home just outside the town border with half a dozen other leftover children. For months, I hadn't been doing my schoolwork or answering my teacher, and after Charlie died, I stopped speaking altogether. This wasn't because of anything that anyone did—after what happened in the clearing, people left me alone, out of sympathy or because they no longer cared. Or maybe everyone was finally just tired of creating conflict where it didn't need to be.

There was one exception, and that was Jeannie Allen. She left me alone all winter and spring, but one morning in late May, she stepped out on the sidewalk in front of her house and said, "Don't think you're off the hook." I lowered my eyes and tried to walk by, but she took a step sideways to block me. "You don't belong here," she said. "Don't think I forgot you!" I moved forward again, and now she shoved me with both hands. "Go on home! Go back to your country!" she insisted. "Nobody wants you, don't you get it? That's why your parents dumped you here." And I didn't move but Jeannie shoved me again, so hard I almost lost my footing. "I heard your *grandparents* didn't even want you, but they *had* to take you in, 'cos no one else would take care of a half-breed. They—"

She didn't finish, because I was on her. Although I was smaller, the combination of my anger and her surprise made it easy to knock her over. I hit her like a linebacker, both arms around her body, and shoved her down onto the pavement. I straddled her chest and held her hands and punched her twice, three times in the face. Then I wrapped my hands around her throat, digging my thumbs so deeply into her flesh that the nails drew blood. I felt her try to pull my hands away, saw her eyes bulge with pain and fear. I watched all of this calmly, quietly, and I don't know what would have happened if her father hadn't come out and pulled me off.

My encounter with Jeannie led to a conclusion that my silence had not—that something was seriously wrong with me. It was said that I'd endured too much for a child to handle—the deaths of Earl Watson, Mrs. Garrett, my dog, and my grandfather; a gun pointed straight at my head. It was said that my mind was addled because my parents had abandoned me—and since we hadn't heard from my father in seven months now, there was no way to tell him what had happened. It was said that the group home would be good for me; I would have structure and the very best counseling there, which would help me come to terms with all the things that had happened and eventually improve my behavior.

The truth was, my behavior had started to change even before my grandfather died. It could be that the therapists were partially right, that I'd been altered and numbed by all the deaths. But the biggest loss was more complex than that, and harder to define. For weeks after that night in the clearing, something had bothered me, something beyond all the obvious traumas. And after that day on the porch with my grandfather, I finally understood what it was. It was what my grandfather had said as he held Earl's body, the anguished cry that Earl shouldn't have let it get this far, it wasn't worth it, that he'd done it all for nothing. He had shot Earl to keep him from shooting me—I knew that, everybody knew that. But by what he said to Earl's body in his moment of despair, it was clear that the Garretts weren't a part of it. He was not avenging them or defending them or punishing Earl; he didn't think about the Garretts at all.

For Charlie, the equation had been simple—his grand-child or his friend. That the Garretts were involved was incidental.

This, to me, was unbearable. It was unbearable be-cause my grandfather didn't care for a human life, for a woman—and a couple—who had been kind to me. It was unbearable because Mrs. Garrett's death meant as little to him as the deaths of the deer he had hunted. Yes, he'd been willing to turn Earl in, but that had more to do with his innate sense of justice than with the value of the life that was lost.

And this too: he didn't see that people treated the Garretts the same way they'd treated my mother—and me. He didn't see that I had as much in common with them as I did with him and my grandmother. For a while, he'd been able to separate me out—to ignore or disre-gard an entire half of who I was and still hold me close to his heart. But he couldn't recognize that the kind of difference he'd rejected in the Garretts was also what he looked past in me. And in his failure to see, he showed me something that I should have known already—that in America, in 1974 and even today, blood does not run thicker than color.

But I couldn't fully grasp or articulate these thoughts, so I stopped talking altogether. It was more than a year before I opened my mouth again. Then my grandmother, who had moved into a senior facility, would pick me up once a week and take me to the Grimsons' diner, where we'd have halting conversations about my schoolwork (I was being taught at a special school now for emotion-ally disturbed children) and about her plans to sell the house. We'd never had much to talk about, my grandmother and me, and without Charlie there the talk was even harder. At the end of the visits she'd take me back to the group home and give me an awkward hug. I think we were both relieved when they were over.

There is one memory of my grandfather that sifts itself out from all the hours and days that I spent with him. It was from one of the first times we went driving together. I had arrived fairly recently and I was still getting used to the town, and to life without my parents. Charlie had been taking me around—to the coffee shop, to church, to the gun store—and introducing me to his friends. Even with my shyness and still-halting English, I knew that he was showing me off.

But this day was different. This day we went out to the country, just the two of us, with the dog stretched out across the backseat. "Just wait, just wait," he said grinning, when I asked where we were going. Finally he slowed the car down and pulled over to the side of the road. We parked on a patch of gravel and walked into the woods. Charlie was carrying a fishing rod and he made me take one too; I'd already learned that catching fish was mostly an excuse for being out in quiet, beautiful places. We made our way along a leaf-strewn trail through stands of birch and cedar, the dog running back and forth in front of us. After what seemed like an eternity, we came upon a lake—one of those clear, pristine lakes that are like hidden treasures, more valuable because you have to earn them. Above us, the sky was light blue with a few high clouds; around us, birds were calling out their greetings. Two deer stood on the opposite shore, gingerly sipping the water. They lifted their heads and saw us and then lowered them, unconcerned.

My grandfather turned to look at me. "What do you think?"

What did I think? I thought it was the most beautiful place I'd ever seen. The sun was shining at such an angle that the lake was like a mirror, and we could see the reflection of the trees. There was a huge boulder in the middle that I wanted to swim out to. I couldn't understand how such a place could be so secret, so untouched. I looked up at my grandfather and asked, "How did it get here?"

Charlie threw his head back and laughed. He had planted the end of his fishing pole down on the ground and he held it upright with one hand. "Well, it wasn't an accident," he said. "You see how nice it's set out here in these woods where no one but us could find it? It was done on purpose, *all* of this was done on purpose, and it was God that done it, see? God put this here, and when He does work like this, it's up to folks like you and me to come find it."

My grandfather went to church regularly like everyone else in Deerhorn, and said his prayers at night. But I never really knew that he believed in God until that morning in the woods. At home, in church, his words were dutiful and expected. It was only here he spoke with such reverence.

"What's the name of it?" I asked.

"What's the name?" Charlie repeated. He scratched his head. "Why, I don't believe it *has* a proper name. I found it back when I was a boy, and I've never told anybody, not even Jim or Earl, not even your pop or your grandma. No one knows about it except you and me."

And now he put his hand on my shoulder and shook me a bit, grinning ear to ear. "I'll tell you what. Let's call it Lake Mikey. How does that sound? Lake Mikey, as named by Charlie LeBeau."

It sounded great. But what makes that day stand out so vividly wasn't the naming of the lake or even the lake itself. It was the way I felt with Charlie. Out of all the things I had to get used to in Deerhorn, this was the most surprising and wonderful: that this strong, handsome man whose company everyone desired seemed to want nobody's company more than mine. I was not an afterthought or a bother, as I often felt with my parents; I did not have to compete for his attention. In his eyes, I was good enough, complete, and worthy of his love, just as I already was. Even now, no one else has ever made me feel this way. No one else has ever looked at me with such obvious delight.

The hardest thing about suffering a terrible loss is that you usually survive it. The absence of the thing you loved intensifies and grows until it isn't something inside of you, but something that contains you, that you inhabit and can't escape, like a nightmare. And if you are able, through dint of effort and the instinct for survival, to wrestle it down and stuff it back inside, it hardens and scars so brutally that your heart cannot open again.

And if you had something to *do* with that loss, if you had any part in making it happen, then resuming your life is all the more impossible. I'm the one who opened the car door for Brett. I'm the one who let it slip that Mrs. Garrett was alone. I'm the one who drew my grandfather into the clearing, where he made the choice that led to his death. I did these things; I set off these events; I planted the seeds of my own despair. I carry my loss as well as my own culpability, and no matter how much I might want to sometimes, I cannot let go; I can't die of it. So I have to do something much worse—I have to live with it.

When I was emancipated from the group home at age eighteen, I moved out to California. Supposedly I came here to look for my parents, but other than checking the phone listings in all the big cities, I didn't make much of an effort. The truth is, I didn't come here to search for my parents. I came to get away. And after a couple of years of working in Sacramento and saving my money, I went to college and got my degree. I work now in Los Angeles at an alternative high school for troubled kids, and it would be easy to say I'm doing this because of my own life—because of Kevin Watson, and the Garretts, and because I went to special schools myself. But I don't work there out of the goodness of my heart. I work there to try and shove down my anger and bitterness, which, if unmanaged, would eventually consume me.

People sometimes make assumptions because of my job, my race, and the neighborhood I live in. Most people in L.A. have no idea of where I spent my childhood, and those who do see it as a quaint pastoral episode without connection to my current life. A few months ago I was driving in Central California with a woman who was trying to love me. In the foothills just outside of Sequoia National Park, we came across a field trial competition. Even from the road, I could see some of the action: dogs running out to flush planted birds, and then retrieving them when they were shot. I'd never seen a field trial before and I insisted we pull over. When we got out, I talked excitedly to a couple of the spectators about where the dogs had come from and how they'd been trained, what the best guns were for wingshooting now, in 2011. The woman watched my excitement with growing dismay and finally pulled me back to the car. She couldn't believe I was so intrigued by a competition that simulated hunting. This, after she'd already been upset with me the week before for skipping a fundraiser to go to a Dodgers game, and for showing up to a fancy brunch in a wifebeater. She sat seething in the passenger seat of my Pontiac Grand Am—I'd refused to make the trip in her BMW—and rolled her window up to shut out the sound of gunfire. "I always forget," she said, arms crossed and cheeks flushed with anger, "that you're half-Japanese and half-redneck."

And so I live by myself, in the city, with its noises and traffic, its unending procession of people. The asphalt landscape of Los Angeles could not be more different from the open fields of Central Wisconsin. Every day my eyes and ears are assailed by the signs of urban life—the gaudy billboards, blaring car alarms, ringing cell phones; the intensity and rush of the city. And maybe this is what I wanted: to live in a place where there is always so much coming at me that it's impossible to think. But sometimes, on spring nights—it is always on spring nights—I lay awake in my bed with the windows open, and sleep will not find me, and there is something about the quality of the late-night air that takes me back to Deerhorn.

It could be that the warmth of April and May holds the suggestion of the greater heat to come. It could be that the wind stirs the trees in a way that reminds me of the trees in the country. It could be that the birds, which sing here through the night, remind me of what it's like to live in a place where *their* voices, and not the voices of people or cars, are the music of the world.

Whatever the reason, there are nights when I leave my bed at two or three in the morning and step out onto the patio. And then suddenly I am there again, I see it all again—the yard where Charlie and I played catch, the baseball fields in autumn, the trails where Brett and I wandered for miles, his feet silent on the carpet of leaves. I see the cornstalks high and green in the heat of late summer, the geese arcing in jagged V's across the sky, the deer stomping in irritation before they take off in their compact bursts of flight. I see how the landscape reinvented itself with the changing of the seasons—spare brown to lush green to blanketing white. I remember the quiet of Deerhorn, the deliberate slowness of days in which every moment could be felt and appreciated. And I want it back then, I want it all back, the silence and the beauty, that faded world.

But then I remember what happened there and I know I can never return. Deerhorn has changed now, it's a different place, and even if it looks exactly the same, it can never be what it was for me when I was a child, what it was in 1974. It can never be that because of what happened, and because I chose to leave. And when you leave something you love you can never go back, for you have so damaged and altered both that thing and yourself that what you had before can never be recovered.

And the child who lived in Deerhorn and was once a version of me is dead, or must be dead, in order for the grown-up to survive. In order for the grown-up to tolerate the life that her decisions have forever confined her to.

And yet that child isn't dead, not really. For while I will not, cannot return to that town, no city will ever contain me. I walk now in a different place, the Sierra Nevada, with another dog—a young liver-and-white springer spaniel named Netty. Netty and I hike for days between the high alpine lakes, living off the trout that I catch, and it's so quiet up there it almost stills the roaring in my heart.

But no matter how beautiful the Sierra lakes are, I can never forget about Deerhorn. I can never forget that quiet place that has made quiet places so necessary. Still, being up there in the mountains with my sweet, hardworking dog (she, like Brett, flushes grouse I don't shoot) is the only time I feel anything that's even close to peace. The high, pine-scented mountains of California aren't the lush countryside of Wisconsin; Netty's not Brett, and fishing trout by myself is not the same as fishing bluegill with my grandfather. But it's the closest I can get with the way my life is now. It's enough; I have to make it be enough.

My grandfather was buried in the Deerhorn Cemetery on a small rise under a cedar tree. He did not leave much by way of earthly possessions—just the house, which went to my grandmother, who eventually sold it. But he left other things. He left me his love of dogs and of the natural world. He left me his impatience with pretense of any kind, with immodesty or self-importance. He left me with the knowledge of what it is to be loved, to be chosen first among other people. (At his funeral, Uncle Pete came to me with tears in his eyes and said, "*You* were his child, Mike. *You* were.") And he left me with the harder knowledge that love is not enough; that it's those you love the most who are most likely to hurt you, and whom you are most likely to betray.

I still own the gun that killed Earl Watson. I keep it in a box on a shelf in my living room, across from the picture of my grandfather's baseball team. Sometimes I take it out and hold it to feel the weight of its history. I don't really know why I do this, or why I keep it at all—the gun's not loaded and I have no ammunition. But it's important for me to keep it close, close enough to see and touch. Because that gun ended more than the life of a man who deserved his punishment. That gun put an end to my childhood, and broke apart what was left of my family.

About five years after I moved out to California, I got a phone call from my father. It took me several minutes to get over the shock of hearing his voice, and only then could I make sense of his words. He was sorry, he said, for not being in touch for so long. He was in New Orleans now, with a different woman, and he hadn't seen my mother in years. Then his voice got low and awkward and he managed to say that he'd heard about what happened with Charlie.

"He harassed that poor couple and then shot somebody, right? He always was a stubborn old bigot."

My face flushed and I said before I slammed down the phone, "You don't know a fucking thing about him."

Sometimes I dream of Charlie and it is always the same. We are driving in a car on a two-lane highway somewhere in Central Wisconsin. The windows are all open and Brett is in back, holding his head up to catch the wind. My grandfather sits easily with one hand on the wheel, his elbow slung out of the window. He looks at me and grins and says, "Should we push it faster, Mike?" And I say yes, yes, and feel the wind on my face and I know he will be with me forever.

Acknowledgments

I would like to acknowledge the following people for their help with this book:

Jennifer Gilmore and Kyoko Uchida, my wonderful readers, for their thoughtful comments on an early draft. Ron Hicks, who shared his knowledge about hunting and guns. Kate Nintzel, who pushed me at just the right time. Richard Parks, my agent, for his kindness, effort, and unflagging support.

Thank you to Johnny Temple, Johanna Ingalls, Ibrahim Ahmad, Aaron Petrovich, and the entire crew at Akashic Books, who have believed so deeply and worked so hard not just for this book, but for three of them now. It's impossible to overstate how committed and amazing they have been. I'm truly blessed to be a part of the Akashic family.

I'm grateful to my friends and the faculty at Cornell, who brought me to Ithaca for a pivotal season in the life of this story; and to my colleagues at Children's Institute, who continue to provide me with great understanding and flexibility. Thanks also to Elizabeth Bailey and Betsey Binet, for their feedback on the many things I put in front of them.

Love and belly rubs to the English springer spaniels whose spirits run through this book: Maddie Gilmore, the original; Georgia Harris, the explorer; Brett Roy, the majestic; and my own beloved Russell.

And finally, my love and gratitude to Felicia Luna Lemus. It's because of her that I know, in my own life, about falling into grace.

Also available from the Akashic Books

SOUTHLAND
a novel by Nina Revoyr
348 pages, trade paperback original, $15.95
*Winner of Lambda, Ferro-Grumley, and ALA Stonewall awards;
Finalist for Edgar & EMMA awards; *Los Angeles Times* "Best Books of
2003" and *Los Angeles Times* best seller; a Book Sense 76 Pick

"The plot line of *Southland* is the stuff of a James Ellroy or a Walter
Mosley novel . . . But the climax fairly glows with the good-heartedness
that Revoyr displays from the very first page."
—*Los Angeles Times Book Review*

"If Oprah still had her book club, this novel likely would be at the
top of her list . . . With prose that is beautiful, precise, but never
pretentious . . ."
—*Booklist* (starred review)

THE AGE OF DREAMING
a novel by Nina Revoyr
332 pages, trade paperback original, $15.95
*Finalist for a *Los Angeles Times* Book Prize

"Reminiscent of Paul Auster's *The Book of Illusions* in its concoction of
spurious Hollywood history and its star's filmography . . . Ingenious . . .
hums with the excitement of Hollywood's pioneer era."
—*San Francisco Chronicle*

"Fast-moving, riveting, unpredictable, and profound; highly recommended." —*Library Journal*

LOS ANGELES NOIR
edited by Denise Hamilton
300 pages, trade paperback original, $15.95
*Winner of Edgar and Southern California Independent Booksellers
Association awards; a *Los Angeles Times* best seller

Brand-new stories by: Michael Connelly, Janet Fitch, Susan Straight,
Héctor Tobar, Patt Morrison, Emory Holmes II, Robert Ferrigno, Gary
Phillips, Christopher Rice, Naomi Hirahara, Jim Pascoe, and others.

"These seventeen very different stories confirm just how many places
L.A. has become . . . Janet Fitch, as usual, operates at a scary level of
intensity. Her story, 'The Method,' opens with a string of zippy one-
liners that out-Chandler Chandler . . . I wanted to take my eyes off
the page and couldn't." —*Los Angeles Times Book Review*

LIKE SON
a novel by Felicia Luna Lemus
272 pages, trade paperback original, $15.95
*Finalist for a Ferro-Grumley Award

"A writer with an unparalleled literary style and attitude, Felicia Luna Lemus comes charging full force."
—*El Paso Times*

"[A] must read book."
—*Latina Magazine*

SOUTH BY SOUTH BRONX
a novel by Abraham Rodriguez
292 pages, trade paperback original, $15.95

"The novel, Rodriguez's third, takes the Bronx-born writer's longtime concerns about Puerto Rican identity and street-level realism and meshes them with the structure of a classic pulp fiction narrative . . . Rodriguez's South Bronx roots have always been a deeply specific source of inspiration, and in this novel, like in his others, it almost becomes a character of its own."
—*New York Daily News*

SONG FOR NIGHT
a novella by Chris Abani
170 pages, a trade paperback original, $12.95
*Winner of a PEN/Beyond Margins Award

"What makes this book a luminous addition to the burgeoning literature on boy soldiers is the way the Nigerian author both undercuts and reinforces such hopeful sentiments . . . The lyrical intensity of the writing perfectly suits the material."
—*Los Angeles Times Book Review*

"Like the protagonists [of] Flaubert's *Simple Heart* and J. M. Coetzee's *Waiting for the Barbarians*, My Luck is both archetypal and utterly himself. *Song for Night* contains, at once, an extraordinary ferocity and a vulnerable beauty all its own."
—*New York Times Book Review*